RECORD  WEASELS

A novel of addiction

*To Lisa —
Hope you enjoy
this! Richard Blackburn*

RICHARD BLACKBURN

This is a work of fiction. Any resemblance to persons alive or dead is strictly coincidental.

First Edition 2017
Copyright © 2014 by Richard Blackburn
Published by Bopalacious
ISBN: 978-0692907160
Bopalacious.com

For Nomi, Laura, Jackson and Katy
And all my record pals past, present and future

Nympholepsy – n. a violent emotional state brought upon by the pursuit of an unobtainable ideal. Nympholeptic – n. one who suffers from the above.

When waking from a bad dream
Don't you sometimes think it's real
But it's only false emotions that you feel
- Johnnie Ray "Cry" Okeh Records (1952)

CHAPTER ONE

Sweat droplets slid down his sides. He reached underneath his black leather car coat, pinched the soft plaid woolen shirt away from his skin. Beneath a hard blue sky, red and orange foliage surrounded the hotel's parking lot, cars glittering with hyper-realist clarity. It was a late September freak heat day in Northern Connecticut towards the end of the 1990's.

Tense, Kevin Dougherty watched Gil Coates pull a worn red cardboard 45 box from inside his beat up Dodge pickup. Salt and pepper beard, lace up boots, woolen earflap cap - Coates looked like he could've walked off a maple syrup can. Only thing that didn't fit were the delicate gold metal frame glasses. Kevin's stomach felt scraped-out like a Halloween pumpkin. The spoken refrain of Jimmy Patton's 1960 rockabilly classic "Okie's In The Pokie" (on the Sims label from California) stretched out cartoon-like in his head: "He's a baaad boy!"

Gil unfastened the lid and carefully extracted an immaculately double sleeved single. Kevin stared at it, breathing softly. The Blue Jays 1953 "White Cliffs Of Dover" on "webtop" Checker (the silver web design on the famous maroon label's top half was only on issues up to 1957). Reverently, Kevin reached for it, slid it first out of the heavy green sleeve, then out of the plastic lined white sleeve. There was a 39 cent stamp on the label but no writing or stickers. He squinted at it in the sunlight - two small scuffs on the B side and a light scratch on the A side. He ran his fingertip lightly across it, felt nothing. It would be inaudible. He held it out level in front of his face and closed one eye. No warps. A solid Vg++. "How's it play?" No matter how good a record might look to the naked eye, it could have been played with a bad needle or just be a hissy pressing.

Gil nodded towards Kevin's oblong battery-operated Mister Disc player resting on the dirty pickup's hood. The Rolls Royce of portables, manufactured for a brief time in the early 80's before CD's made them obsolete, these machines and a few others like them, had lightweight tone arms, excellent reproduction. As a halogen light illuminated every scuff, scratch, stain, gouge, nick, pressing bubble or hidden hairline crack on a record's surface, so did these, when used with headphones, mercilessly amplify any clicks, pops, heat swishes and damaged groove wall distortion, often inaudible on clunkier portables. Kevin's had been repaired twice. The tone arm's little plastic protuberance was broken off. Underneath, instead of the original removable plastic panel, silver electricians tape held the 3 "C" batteries in place. Still the sonic fidelity was unimpaired. Collectors paid up to four hundred for one new in the box.

Kevin deftly clicked and raised the see-through lid. Halfway down its length the tone arm was anchored in a notched rubber 45 center. He lifted the arm off, fitting the center over the short spindle, placed the record on a turntable so small that 45's as well as LP's extended beyond its edge. He pushed the ON button, flipped the plastic needle guard up and put on the attached headphones. They were plug-ins but, since constantly pulling them out had loosened the connection, giving only one channel or none, he'd had them permanently soldered into the outlet. He moved the arm towards the record's edge. The turntable started to revolve. Gently he set the needle down onto the lead in groove.

For three seconds there was a slight hiss then the Blue Jays were singing into his ears. Kevin's shoulders prickled. The greatest and rarest version ever recorded - ethereal voices interweaving like golden threads, floating like puffs of cloud. The low hiss continued under the music. Not really distracting, normal for an early 50's press. After a moment Gil reached over, lifted up the tone arm. "I don't wanna play this a lot." He removed the record, double sleeved it and returned it to the tote box.

Kevin pulled off the phones, flipped the needle guard up, set the rubber 45 center into its little depression in the middle of the player, fitted the arm back into the center's notches and clicked the lid closed, scrambling rat-like about in his brain, trying to decide on a reasonable counter offer. "Would you take four?" Voice nearly cracking, ruining the studiedly casual tone, sweat now coursing down his sides.

Gil cocked his head squinting through the metal rims, scratched his beard. "Six thousand. Else I go to Henry Krasna. I heard he needs it."

Kevin's heart was thudding. Who didn't need it except for Eddie Winowski and, maybe, Del Ackley? In the demented world of vocal group collectors six thousand wasn't crazy for a piece this good. (45 collectors referred to any disc worth several hundred and up as a piece). Only a handful of copies were known. Krasna had deep pockets. Once Gil picked up the phone the Blue Jays would fly out the window.

Kevin pushed fingers through tumbling brown hair, "How 'bout a few rockabillys from my collection? Ones from your want list?" Kevin was one of a few collectors who not only had ears for all genres but collected them as well. On a bartender's pay it kept him in the financial shithouse.

Through the wiry beard Gil's mouth was a stubborn line. "Nope I need the money." Half a year ago his factory job above Derby had been rendered obsolete. Now all he did was go junking for discs.

Kevin mentally cursed his luck. Too bad the crazy goof hadn't popped the 45 a few years back when he didn't know shit. All of a sudden with the internet and price guides up the yang everybody was an expert. The deal was becoming too intense. He needed time to decompress. "You actually found it in a box of old pop?"

"Yep. Doris Day, Jo Stafford, Eddie Fisher. Fella told me on the phone what they were but it was only an hour away - figured I'd take a chance." He went on about finding the guy's house, going through the junk, spotting the 45, making him a lowball offer on the whole box so as not to arouse suspicion.

"Can you hold it 'til I sell some stuff?" Jesus. Practically begging this inbred hick who didn't know half as much as he did. The more knowledge a record collector/dealer had and the longer they'd been into it the less right they accorded anyone else to charge top dollar.

Gil shook his head. "Roof needs re-shingling. Weather could turn any day."

Kevin was silent. Need to possess blowing up inside him like a crazy helium balloon.

He frowned attempting to convince them both he was still deliberating. "You couldn't do any better?" He didn't want to liquidate his few stock holdings but it'd be better than selling out of his collection or – God forbid - plundering the joint account shared with Marlene.

Gil snorted. "People will probably tell me I undersold it."

"Yeah, sure, guys always say they would've given you more - after it's gone."

"I want six. You wanna take a chance I don't get it it's up to you."

No decision. If you knew the right buyers the rarest records were always the easiest to move. "C'mon Gil, gimme a break here. Think of all the stuff I've bought from you."

"Yeah, most of 'em for more'n what they were really worth."

"Hey! You set the prices."

"Fifty five hundred and that's as low as I'm gonna go. Take it or leave it."

Kevin blinked, pulled the sticky shirt away from his skin. His heart was trying to come up into his mouth. Fuck. Marlene would kill him. But only if she knew! As if under sedation he reached for his wallet. "I'll give you a grand to hold it."

"Well, I dunno."

"C'mon, man." He pulled out the ten hundred dollar bills that had just about gutted his checking account. "Take this now and I'll get you the rest."

"By Friday, else I'm on the phone."

"Friday? How about the end of the month?"

Gil's mouth became even more compressed. He shook his head.

"No selling out here!" A black and white slid up beside

them. The young mustached cop had his head out the window.

Kevin's nerves were already thrumming like high tension wires. His adrenalin began kicking into overdrive. "We're just settling a debt."

"Do it inside."

"It's illegal to hand someone money in a fuckin' parking lot?"

"Sir, I don't appreciate that kind of language. Now, either leave the premises, or go back inside the hotel."

"How'd you know we were there before? Somebody called this in, huh?"

The cop didn't answer. Gil was standing absolutely still. Kevin turned to him. "You believe this Nazi bullshit?"

The cop got out of the car. "Hey! Keep up the attitude, you'll spend the night in jail!"

Kevin's face was hot. His shoulder muscles twitched, wanting to smash the prick cop in the mouth, obliterate the self-righteous arrogance. Behind him Gil opened his driver's door, then closed and locked it. He coughed. "I'm gonna take another look around." He walked away.

For a few more seconds, Kevin stared at the cop, then turned and followed after Gil, feeling the eyes on his back. "This show sucks. There's no early admission so only dealers get first crack. You don't have a table, they won't let you take any records inside to trade or sell. And now they got cops hassling you outside!"

Furiously he pushed through the hotel's side glass doors into the carpeted interior, Gil behind him. The two middle-aged ladies seated behind the ticket table avoided catching his eye. He glared at them, held up his stamped hand for the skinny guy with glasses at the entrance to the conference room. The man nodded, looking past him.

Inside, customers wandered among the rows of draped dealer tables packed with overflowing boxes of 45's, LP's and CD's - the cacophony of voices, punctuated by records being play checked on portable players. Fingers flicked through records - info fragments from the blur of labels registering and disappearing in a nanosecond. Some breathed through open mouths, others hummed or spoke in a constant undertone, most were silent as stone. Like chronic womanizers they noted all those they'd already possessed; sometimes with nostalgic affection for ones which had given great pleasure, but in all cases, alert to make the next big score.

Gil was across the room talking to Jerry Tyler - a twitchy bottom feeder, short and slight with pale freckled skin.. No competition there – guy didn't buy anything over five dollars.

"Hey Captain, check out my stuff." A white-bearded, bug-eyed acid burnout, known only as "The Duke", beckoned Kevin over to his table. Red and purple tie dyed tee shirt, bright lemon yellow sweat pants, hot pink sneakers with mica sparkles. Dress to impress. His wheedling, nasal whine continued. "Got some great new material, Captain. 'Course they're all mixed in now. You gotta check me first thing."

To cool out before renegotiating with the Gill Man, Kevin speed flipped through a box of the Duke's shabby 45's - so focused and fast it became an out of body experience. All surroundings, even time itself, utterly vanished until a Zen-like calm descended upon him and he was one with the search. Suddenly he realized he'd just seen "Stoned" by The Rolling Stones with a $20 sticker. He quickly back flicked. No luck. It was on English Decca. A promo or deejay copy on American London in good shape was worth a grand. If he'd found a stock or store copy he'd have been halfway home with the Blue Jays.

"Hi there Kevin!" A bland middle aged guy in bifocals and a pastel blue Banlon shirt, spoke in a broad Maine accent. "Bring anythin' I'd like?"

Kevin shook his head. "No teeners today."

To his right the intro to "Don't Be Cruel" played continuously under the first three words of "Hound Dog". Elvis singing them over and over while a synth bass dance beat punched it up. "You ain't nothin'! You ain't nothin'! You ain't nothin'!"

An obese light skinned black head banger, shaven head encircled by a intricately patterned white and blue scarf, listened to the 12" single - hooded eyes flat as primer coat while those of the barely-goateed thin white dealer's burned with manic intensity as he went into full blown wigger rap.

"That sucka's really rare now. BMG got in their face for samplin' Elvis. I got lotsa tight jams here. Yo! What crew you roll with down in the city?"

"La'rence," breathed the head banger, lips barely moving in the puffy Pillsbury Dough Boy face.

The dealer's head bobbed enthusiastically. "Yeah, yeah. Lawrence is dope."

On Kevin's left, Tom Dell, a Brian Jones-ish mop topped garage collector, flipped through a handful of 45's. Beneath the dark hair and heavy black framed glasses, he wore a black and tan barrel striped tee shirt, black skinny legged jeans and black high top Keds. He spoke to Kevin without looking up. "Anything?"

"Nope. You?"

"I dunno why I come to this show. Always the same stuff." His voice, a drawling monotone, held zero excitement, sounding as if his nose was stuffed up. "Need a copy of 'Stacy'?

I'm letting a Vg one go cheap." A Connecticut garage disc by The Hangmen of Fairfield County, with heavy drug lyrics, it was always in demand.

"No thanks. Mine's 'bout the same."

"Last week I really lucked out. Found that big Belgian record, the one with the lame-o cocktail piano? Moved it on Ebay for just under a grand."

Belgians were into the weirdest collector genre – the popcorn sound, named after The Popcorn club just over the French border. A record's rpm would be decreased or increased to jibe with whatever the crowd's major chemical intake was that evening. Looking at a want list from one of these guys was always a head scratcher: light soul, cha-chas, pizzicato strings, monster/horror themed stuff. Even if an occasional artist was familiar, the record never was.

Kevin, squelching his envy, nodded. "That's gotta be the most expensive piece of crap ever made."

"Hey, you hear about Sticky?" Opinion was divided whether the nickname of this slim, brooding Jamaican ex-con came from his slickness at boosting records or his weapon of choice. A year ago when Kevin had set up at one of the east coast's biggest shows The Stickman had nailed him for around $1,500.

"What? He die?"

Tom made an amused "hunh" sound from back in his throat. "He lifted some Elvis Suns off of Paul Derrick and over two grand's worth from a new dealer at WFMU." A listener supported FM station in Jersey, WFMU held one big record show a year in Manhattan. "And get this: he was also trying to nick Big Birds."

Yellow and green plastic Sesame Street Big Birds, a

cheesy 70's artifact, were the easiest and cheapest battery operated players to find. Kevin had one himself - the result of an
emergency $35 buy when his Mister Disc had died at a show.
It'd been in a storage closet ever since. Only pink Hello Kitty
or Barbie Doll players looked dumber. It also had a weighty
tone arm made even heavier by a knoblike goggling bird head.
A few owners had customized and lightened their Birds by
decapitation, either slicing or melting so a record's grooves
wouldn't be irreparably fried.

"Hey, believe it or not, Ed Kline caught him with his
player and Sticky said he'd thought it was his. Only of course
he never came into the show with one. No one said shit."

"Guy's a fuckin' plague."

"Maybe he's starting to lose his mind and we'll be rid of
him. Like The Brill's lead guitarist."

"Who're they?"

A lopsided smile. "Jesus, Dougherty, only one of the top
five groups in the country." Dell worked for a small 60s reissue
label, read Billboard and kept up with all the trends.

"So? He have a bad hair day and go catatonic?" Kevin
looked around. Why couldn't he find somebody's mistake?
Something he already had or didn't want - a four figure cash
cow in a dollar box like Tom or Gil. Then he could mostly buy
the Checker 45 with a clear conscience. Might even see a profit. As if. Vinyl junkies were born to live beyond their means.

"Not exactly. They were playing a benefit at the Rock &
Roll Hall Of Fame and he forgot to take his medication.. Halfway through the set he totally flipped. Started smashing all
these glass cases with Duane Eddy's and Jimi Hendrix's original guitars. Guards chased him out of the building into the
street and all the time he's screaming that guitars are living

organisms that shouldn't be locked up."

Kevin shrugged. "Makes sense to me."

Turning out of the hotel lot in his bucket-seated black Trans Am, Kevin rotated his neck trying to get rid of the ache in his shoulders. One of his old radio shows on mini-disc played over the car speakers. The player was connected to a Radio Shack gizmo plugged into the cigarette lighter socket which sent a signal through a chosen bandwidth on the car radio. He tried to identify the jumped up rockabilly cut before the set ended and he heard himself back announce.

This is me right now, he thought, driving my car, listening to my music as I go down this curving road. Here I am living my life. What a trip.

Gil had taken Kevin's grand but had held to the Friday deadline. His promise to keep his mouth shut about the deal didn't mean diddly. Once Lou Andreassi, Jerry Tyler, or any other of the squirmy little pilot fish got wise, they'd make enough waves to attract a Great White. Gil would boost it right back to six K and the record would be gulped down instantly.

Kevin's 45 carrying box - plain varnished wood with side by side compartments - rested on the passenger seat. It was a lot better than a single box - especially those girly 45 totes in pink padded plastic with dancing cartoon teens. He unfastened the lid, took out the Xeroxed multi-paged set sale list that had arrived yesterday. Every 45 was numbered, alphabetized by artist followed by title, label/number, condition, price and (sometimes) remarks. Two 45's were seriously undervalued: a hot rockabilly with the label accidentally misspelled and a great West Coast vocal group hidden under the name of a single artist on the label. Kevin was hoping he

RICHARD BLACKBURN

could beat out the others who'd be hip to them. Each time
he'd called earlier he'd gotten an answering machine. His last
try was just before leaving the record show. Now he hit redial
on his cell phone and plugged the attachment into his ear that
was supposed to prevent brain tumors

"Hello?"

Finally! "Hey Ted, Kevin Dougherty. I've been trying to
reach you since yesterday."

"You an'everybody else. My line was dead. You can't believe what a horseshit phone company we got here."

"Well, look, I just want to check on two items - number
56 and 234." He bit his lower lip.

"Uhh, first one's okay. Somebody got the other. How
bad did I screw up?"

Shit! He could make maybe a bill on the rockabilly but
the vocal group would've brought six or seven.. "I don't know,"
he said brusquely, covering his disappointment. "I never sold
one." Technically true. He found his collection copy cheap.
"Well, send it out to me first class." He still had a chance at
that obscure northern soul 45 ending on Ebay this afternoon.

"You want insurance?"

"Yeah, not that it does any good."

"I hear that. Fifty three dollars and thirty cents."

"Okay. You don't do Waterbury anymore?"

"That where you are?"

"Yeah."

"Find anything?"

"Mmm, not much."

"There's your answer."

At the intersection onto 84 a tan station wagon slowly pulled out of a Dunkin' Donuts on the right, blocking him

from making the light as it went through the yellow. He braked sharply, tires screeching, then honked savagely cursing out the driver. A few faces looked at him out the plate glass window. Jaw clamped, Kevin stared straight ahead. The tread on his tires was almost gone. Naturally he kept putting off buying a new set in favor of more records. Any day now they were going to blow.

"Hey!" Ted's voice came out of the cell. "You okay?"

"Yeah, yeah - just traffic. I'll get it in the mail tomorrow. Can you do the same?"

"Sure. Send a postal money order."

"You got it. 'Bye."

On the interstate, headed up to Boston, he checked his watch. Less than two hours until his show. He took a breath. Time to collect some cash. He dialed his brother in Boston.

"Hi Kevin." Thomas's machine told him who the caller was.

"Hey. How's it goin'? Look man, I want you to cash me in on those stocks tomorrow. If it's a little bit below that's -"

"Kev, there are no more stocks." Thomas ploughed ahead. "They were doing really, really well and you and Marlene were trying to have a kid and –"

"So?" His voice tight, squeezing the cell.

"I bought more on margin. They went down and didn't come up. I had to sell every last one to pay it off."

"Jesus H. CHRIST!"

"You don't want to hear what I lost."

"You're right."

A day trader, Thomas was always bragging about his scores – automotive, feminine and financial. Typical younger brother shit. "Kev, I'm sorry but you can claim it on your income tax."

"What income tax? I'm a fuckin' bartender!"

"Well, it's good for three years. You'll be making more before then."

"Yeah, right. Okay, look, I need to deal with this. Talk to you later." Kevin realized Thomas thought he was upset about not being able to provide for a family. It made him feel like an asshole, fueled his rage and disappointment. Marlene hadn't known about the stocks. He'd bought them before he met her. The Blue Jays was to have been the one last crazy purchase before he eventually became Mr. Responsible Dad. Now he really couldn't afford it.

It'd be a real bitch to sell some of his prized heavies. Some moneyed collectors went after rarities they only mildly liked just for bragging rights. Anything Kevin bought for real dough he definitely loved.

"Jesus," he said aloud, "this is crazy. It's a stupid record. Okay, okay. It's great and rare and won't ever lose its value, might even appreciate. Hey! Smart collectors never go hungry, right? Right."

He could pass on the 45 and get The Blue Jays on 78. But although it'd be a lot cheaper - maybe five to six hundred – the fragility of shellac made Kevin nervous. Each time he'd moved he'd broken some of his 78's. Unfortunately Checker never made "flexis" - vinyl 78's - like Imperial, Columbia, RCA and others. Manufactured for a brief time after the introduction of the 45, they were, in Kevin's opinion, the best recorded format - light, unbreakable and, because of dynamics, the richest sound.

No. He wanted that 45, at the same time knowing, with bittersweet certainty, that obtaining it would exaggerate, not reduce his need to constantly acquire. In a way he saw himself clearly, but being able to confess his addiction only made him sound mature. Marlene had quickly found out he was far from that.

On the other hand he was hip that no matter how many prized 45's he supposedly owned he was just their caretaker. After his death they'd pass on to another vinyl freak. "No one really owns anything" might be a tired hippie concept, but, although he was hardly a retro flower child, the way Marlene had laid it on him - derived from her mom – the concept had clicked inside his skull as solid truth.

Frustrated, he began a running monologue directed at the cars around him."What the fuck is this? Got your signal on but you're not turning? Jesus Christ! Come on, come come on you freakazoid asshole! Get that piece of shit off the road! Oh now you're gonna turn huh? Well ta, ta motherfucker... Hey! How about picking a lane, nitwit!...Oh shit, just what I need - a goddamn bus!"

For years he'd been trying to cool his rage-a-holism. Therapy, meditation, even flotation tanks which at least gave him a nice high. They'd helped some but nothing really took. As he became aware of his endless cursing it wigged him out in another direction. Aloud, he started back pedaling, attempting to argue one part of himself out of beating another part up.

"Just relax, okay? Thomas looked like he could handle this. He did make me some money in the beginning. I agree. I shoulda known he was puffin' himself up but I didn't want to think he was and I lost because of it. Just another fucking life lesson to – JESUS FUCKING GODDAMN ALL THAT MONEY

GONE!!" He beat on the steering wheel with his fist, screamed at the top of his lungs and mashed down on the gas pedal, flying down the highway for half a minute, before he took some deep breaths, de-accelerated and got back a little self-control.

During times like this, his mind, full of buried explosives, any one of which could be triggered by the wrong thought, truly scared him. Desperately trying to mollify the blind anger, he shut off and removed the minidisc player, fished about in the storage compartment until he found a soul jazz cassette he'd compiled a few years back when he was deep into all that Blue Note and Prestige stuff.

He shoved it into the tape deck and heard Big John Patton's bluesy chugging organ on "The Silver Meter". The hypnotic groove, like aural Pepto-Bismol, began transporting him outside himself so that he wasn't choking on rage. Fury almost neutralized, he became merely manic, haranguing drivers with less vehemence and greater imagination. "Let's go you pathetic cockalorians! C'mon you hopeless dragoliacs! Putzos! Move your bellocchis!" These outbursts grew fewer, until they too subsided.

In the car he seldom listened to the radio, preferring compilations of his own or others on cassettes, CD's or minidiscs. Sometimes tokens of male friendships, they were more importantly used to court women – establishing how hip you were and how hip you thought she was, sexual/romantic content musically and lyrically part of the overall seduction.

One unhappily married girlfriend in her late 20's had collected records with an intensity equal to his own. She was a fan of his show, started calling him on the air. They'd exchanged emails, then photos along with cassettes – suggestive lyrics subtly escalating with each comp – which led to some heavy phone sex. On a bright June day they'd finally met and after some hesitancy, enthusiastically consummated their affair on his apartment couch. He remembered her blonde tresses spread over the Elvis throw pillow, arm half shyly covering her beautiful breasts, blue limpid eyes looking up into his own, making him believe he'd at last found his soul mate.

The cassettes, having served their purpose, ended, but they continued their clandestine fucks throughout the summer whenever she could duck out. In time illicit sex lost some of its power. They were confronted with how much alike they were, and became more rivals than lovers, hiding record lists from each other, lying about how much they were willing to bid on auction items - even fighting over dealers' boxes at shows. That fall she made up with her husband. The man's non-involvement in her collecting passion, once a source of estrangement, had become a relief. In her last Christmas card, sent a few years ago, she'd written that she and Mac had a child and another on the way. He thought of her from time to time, usually after a fight with Marlene, wondering if she still listened to his show. In his world it had been a true fairy tale romance. Something few collectors ever experienced. The cassettes she'd made him were put away in a box somewhere. He never played them now.

CHAPTER TWO

While the Trans Am raced up 84 out of Hartford towards the Mass Pike, Marlene Lewis, auburn hair hanging curtain-like on either side of her soft face, was taking a break from her online graphics class. A girlfriend had just forwarded a particularly gruesome item. A global fried chicken franchise, now known only by its initials, had reportedly just been banned from using the word "chicken" because they were frying some blind, beakless, legless, featherless lab hybrid with a reduced bone structure and more meat. Marlene stretched in her dark green sweat shirt and pants shuddering. If it was an urban myth it was a believable one. Not that she and Kevin ate in those places. Funky old diners, classic pizzerias, no frills seafood joints – strictly non-chain – set off by an occasional splurge at a really good upscale restaurant.

First time they'd met, she'd returned his look trying to place him, remembering him from somewhere. Later, when they were talking she flashed on the moment. A full four months ago she was living at home, working part time in her mom's now defunct collectables store up on the Cape. Kevin, tanned, in white tee shirt and shorts, had come in looking for records. He hadn't noticed her. She was trying to lose some weight caused by meds. For a short while they'd helped blot out the hurtful knowledge that an eight year relationship had finally gone teeth to the sky. She never mentioned this to Kevin – one, because she was afraid he wouldn't remember her and two, because she was afraid he might.

Her friends had warned her about getting serious with anyone right after a breakup, especially some omygod slick, pussy magnet bartender who was, well – weird. Marlene had listened politely through several lunches and then moved into Kevin's second floor Providence apartment in a Victorian brownstone. A few months later she was unconsciously humming obscure rock n' roll songs.

Her mom, Joanne, had helped refurnish the messy bachelor digs in Jetson 50's/early 60's modern. Amoeba coffee tables, cluster floor lamps, cocktail cherry wall clock, pointy legged chairs, couch done in nubby dark red weave, etc. Behind the small 1940's bamboo bar with matching high stools was a mini-fridge full of ice and limes. Shelved above it were Marlene's tiki mugs as well as the specific rums and syrups for Kevin's Polynesian drinks from vintage recipes. Finished the place looked like a Shag illustration.

Marlene's old menus, scandal magazines and lurid paperbacks filled wire racks. Rock & roll sheet music and horror/rock n' roll movie posters covered the walls. 1950's cosmetics and beauty ads were in the bathroom. Pop tschatkes everywhere – a real retro museum. Several of their friends had variations of the same. The décor was more her thing, the music more his but it all meshed, a nice balance. The difference was she was less hooked on paper than he was on vinyl.

The only contemporary concession, beside the computer, phones and scanner, was a large screen TV (Joanne couldn't figure how to put a color tube inside a black and white swivel-necked Predicta). Kevin's contribution was a 70's full size double cassette Dictaphone answering machine. Their outgoing messages were recorded over instrumentals from his collection. They always sounded bright and clear – not like the shredded tone from cheap digital biscuits.

Of course records were a big part of their marriage. Following a sedate church ceremony, everyone adjourned to Green's Roller Rink in Warwick. Newly surrounded by a parking lot, the interior hadn't changed since the late 1920's: colorful silent movie actor caricatures painted on the walls above a chipped refreshment stand and ancient rinky dink nickelodeon. Marlene had a postcard of the rink's once gen-teel exterior: green and white striped awnings with matching umbrellas and tables out on a manicured front lawn. She'd used it behind a photo of Kevin and herself for the picture sleeve of the 45 pressed up for wedding souvenirs.

The Stuffies, a whacked-out local rock and roll trio hired to play the reception – chosen over the more pissed-off Flam-ing Doughnuts of Jesus – cut a garage-y version of "Chapel Of Love" by The Dixie Cups and, for the flipside, an instrumental of "Wedding Of The Painted Doll" with overdubbed pie tins and slide whistles. Later, some of Kevin's collector pals joked about how they'd grabbed more than their share of this limit-ed edition to sell next day over the internet.

"You're gonna DIE!" Across from Marlene, as intent on the TV as she was on her computer, blond, eight year old Wiley from downstairs fought Nintendo Pokémon battles, the back of his hockey jersey a snarling tiger head. Francine, his single mom, had given him the name some years back when he used to imitate the Road Runner cartoons. He'd make his round face really sad, wave bye-bye and drop down onto the floor like Wile E. Coyote plunging off a pastel mesa. The tag stuck, partly because Roger, his given name, was also the name of Francine's ex. A man who, she confided to Marlene, had only "gotten his rocks off" by demeaning her.

The phone rang. Marlene picked up. "Hi Mom" She and Joanne always knew when the other was calling. The only time she ever guessed wrong was when one of Joanne's friends rang.

"Hi. Just wanted to see how you're doing."

"Why? You thought something was wrong?" Marlene had picked up a subtle concern.

"No, no. I'm just a little tired. Phil and I did umpteen million yard sales today." She lived with her current P.I. boyfriend in his house outside of Boston.

"Find anything?"

"Odds and ends. Isn't this one of Kevin's record meet days?"

"What weekend isn't? He'll be back after the radio show." They talked for a few minutes, then, as always, the conversation ran down at the same time and they hung up as one.

"ALL RIGHT!" Wiley raised a small clenched fist as blue Snorlax, surrounded by stars, disintegrated in a fire blast from orange Charazad.

Marlene had begun drawing when she was very small. Her first saved picture was a crayon rendering of a rabbit, the thought balloon above its head containing a dog. Because she and her mom were always changing addresses, she taught herself perspective from her bedroom corner in this apartment or that small house, keeping a record of her young life. Soon she was also drawing people recording their hairstyles and clothes. Later she tried photography but missed the satisfaction of physically reproducing the world with her own hand.

Each year Joanne bought her a new black hardcover sketch book. She was never without it except once in the 4th grade when it went missing. Two days later it was returned by the parents of a girl who'd been jealous of the attention Marlene's drawings had received. She'd scrawled over each one with a black crayon. At first devastated, Marlene began to copy her original drawings into the replacement book Joanne bought her, improving them in the process.

By the ninth grade she had her first steady boyfriend. His passionate interest in sci-fi and comic books gradually turned her faithfully copied exteriors and interiors of the real world into fantastical idealizations. Eventually she was zigzagging from the future to the past appropriating and melding what she liked.

Two years later, having fallen under the aesthetic exhibitionism of Andy Warhol's factory, she discovered rock and roll through The Velvet Underground, took to wearing heavy eyeliner and avoiding the sun. For a short while her drawings were either haunted and gothic, or angry and violent, or both.

At Tufts College, she hung with the obligatory art crowd, flirting with drugs, hysteria and deliberate eccentricities. However, her ex-hippie mom had left her very little to rebel against. Hard as she tried she knew she'd never be the risk-taker and loony tune Joanne was so why bother? Nor did she possess any unique Blakeian vision and would never be "the Frida Kahlo of New England" - as a friend from college was tagged during her recent one woman show in Boston. Marlene was less an interpreter than a reproducer. She just liked to draw.

She was, she admitted to herself, an aspiring Bobo, or

Bourgeois Bohemian. Someone who wanted a hipper upscale lifestyle than the mainstream but yearned for rock solid security underneath. Kevin was more like her mom which made that lady understandably nervous about her only daughter's future. Marlene likened her mom and Kevin to how Richard Widmark's character was described in "Night And The City" – "an artist without an art."

The door bell rang. She turned to Wiley. "That's your mom."

Wiley got to his feet, disappointed. "Aren't I going to see Kevin?"

"Maybe later."

Francine entered, torn-at-the-knees Levis, white tee shirt and outsize Levi jacket, She was whippet thin, short dark hair emphasizing a face en route from pretty to pinched. "Hope he wasn't any trouble." She hugged him hard.

"You kidding? He just sat and zapped."

"Mom! I scored one million, twenty-five thousand, three hundred and sixty-six points!"

"Yeah? It's a wonder there're any Pokémon left."

"So how was your seminar?"

"Huh? Oh, okay. Nothing special." Francine thought Marlene was staring at her hands. Her cuticles were picked down to the quick. She balled them into fists, shoved them into the pockets of her jacket. "Come on tough guy."

"I wanna wait for Kevin."

Both women laughed at his stubborn expression. A phone rang downstairs. Francine started. "That's mine. Come on you!" She hurried him towards the door.

"But he said I could feed Herkimer." Kevin's hermit crab.

"If he's here in time," Marlene called after them, "I'll

have him come over and read you a bedtime story."

She turned back to the computer. The course would be finished before Christmas. Hopefully she'd be able to quit managing RISD's bookshop and snag a better paying job before any future pregnancy would show. With luck she could do a lot of work at home.

If only Kevin could be rewired to make more money. So what if he had friends in the music biz? No one was going to hire a guy proud to know nothing past 1970.

They'd talked about starting a CD reissue label, her doing the art work. It was one hell of a risky commitment. Very few relied on it as a single source of income. With quality transferring, mastering, printing and manufacturing it ran about four grand to press a thousand of one title. Until you had at least ten moneymakers in catalog all the net profits for one CD went to finance the next. Distributors didn't pay on delivery, only when they had to reorder or wanted your latest issue.

Doing a compilation legally, at least one aimed at collectors, meant tracking down countless tiny labels and forgotten artists. It wasn't worth the larger labels time to license out one or two tracks for a little indie CD but it was risky to ignore publishing and performance rights. You never knew when one lawsuit could appear out of nowhere and wipe you out. Only time would reveal if such a venture could be self supporting. At the moment they both needed separate jobs.

Kevin swung off the interstate in Cambridge, turned left and looped under the overpass hurtling four and a half blocks down a narrow side street before whipping up a driveway behind a three storied brick building. He jumped out with his record box, sprinted across the parking area, punched in the 4 digit code on the box to the left of the locked steel sheeted doors.

Taking the broad metal stairs two at a time to the second floor, he strode down the torn up carpeted hallway to the WPOP-FM door and pushed it open. A station ID spot played over loudspeakers. He opened the door to studio A, walls covered by a hodgepodge of old folk music posters, current anti-rightwing cartoons and other leftie ephemera.

Behind the board, Stephen, the black reggae jock wore a red, yellow and green woolen cap atop heavy dreads. He looked up and shook his head, smiling cryptically at Kevin's habitual last minute arrival. As he rose, gathering up LP's and CD's, Kevin moved around him, pushing his show's theme - Earl Hooker's "Tanya" - into the minidisc deck. The ID finished. Kevin simultaneously hit the decks play button and turned up the corresponding pot. On the studio speakers, Hooker's slide soared over the infectious beat. Stephen left with a small wave. Kevin raised his chin in response as he snatched out "Twisted" by Peter Preston on CoCo – an obscure r&b rocker out of L.A. - and flipped it onto the right hand turntable. He grabbed up the earphones, cued the record, brought down the instro's volume, flipped on his mike.

"Howdy hi! It's time again for Idiot's Delight – the show that plays the platters that matter, the sounds for real wax hounds - no hits, no done-to-death "oldies" – only the great, the weird and the wonderful from long ago. Yep, AM's back and FM's got it. The Kelvinator is ready to scratch all kindsa boss wax so let's get to it and da-dit-dit-dit-DO IT!" Down went the mike volume as he hit the turntable switch, boosting the corresponding pot to catch the first blatted notes of a gutter tenor sax.

It was just another way not to make money.

He'd been on four years, getting his weekly ego blast by preaching to the converted. No dough but complete freedom to spin whatever he liked. WPOP was now on the internet, roping in listeners from all over the globe who, during the bi-annual pledge drives, were cajoled and guilt-tripped, primarily by the persuasive station manager, for much needed contributions. Staying out of the red for all FM listener supported stations was a never-ending struggle. That's why so many of them, similar to the alternative press, had sold out to demographically-focused corporations. Once that happened, programming was dictated by committee. Any show no matter how long it had been on, no matter how loyal a fan-base, would be instantly axed if listenership started to slip.

Recently the oldest FM radio show playing old doo-wop had gone off the air in New Jersey due to lack of listener support. This hadn't been one of those lame "oldies greatest hits" travesties but one where a single knowledgeable deejay had presented great rarities for over 30 years. Rockabilly and blues attracted some young fans but r&b vocal groups were so generational specific, with no European interest except for jump sides, that harmony ballads might be doomed to extinction. Thankfully Kevin didn't just spin doo-wop. His programming of obscure vintage wax covered almost all genres. Still, that wouldn't help him if WPOP were sold.

The older generation was starting to die off and sell their collections. Kevin knew he was unusually young to be into these records so that his own collection could become, for the most part, valueless before he reached middle age. The only vintage music most people danced to anymore was soul.

Well, fuck it. Not his fault if the whole world was turning terminally square. You saw it everywhere. For the first time in modern history Blacks were dressing worse than Whites who were still copying them. People always got what they deserved, music as well as politics. You thought about it long enough you'd short out. All he could do was keep his head down and play the sounds he loved.

Big, solid and coordinated, Kevin would've been a natural at school sports but had no interest in baseball or hockey and was only effective in football as a lineman. Even there he didn't push himself. Unlike his smaller more outgoing brother, he wasn't a team player, preferring to escape solo into comics, books, movies and of course, rock n' roll. A proven equation: Enthusiasm minus no real talent and/or burning ambition equals fan.

The old man, hauling out his musty boyhood stamp and coin albums, had tried to interest him in those pursuits. Instead it was Thomas who, while concurrently going through a phase of wanting to enter the priesthood, alternately took up both along with model kits, baseball cards and Boy Scouts.

Kevin didn't think of collecting as a "hobby". The very word, which suggested wimpy puttering and cataloging to pass the time, was distasteful. He saw it as a full on manic avocation, a pure aesthetic frenzy hard and true as a speeding bullet to no known target. Its very purposelessness invested it with a mystique outside all base motivation.

He'd given up trying to discover its cause, much as a hopeless pervert might accept never knowing why the smell of women's shoes was arousing. Was it from lack of affection as a child, an attempt to feel in control and powerful? It did give him an identity, made more specific by each acquired 45.

Record geeks, like all hardcore collectors were at least 75% weird, polarized between anal and chaotic but with a fierce individuation. A speech pattern, manner of dress, way of doing business as well as ancillary fixations e.g.: food, sports, religions, conspiracy theories, UFOs, etc. Like snowflakes, no two were exactly alike. Neither were their collections.

Outwardly, the seedlings to Kevin's obsession were planted at age twelve during a family trip to New Orleans. For Kevin everything about the city – the funky accent, spicy cooking, shops selling anything from swords and firearms to old canes - was amazingly exotic. Exploring the French Quarter he'd come upon a place with old records on Iberville. While his brother and parents went off for a tourist lunch at The Court Of Two Sisters, he stayed amongst dust motes in the back playing vintage 78's at the amused owner's indulgence.

"Where you from?" the man had asked hearing Kevin's New England accent.

"Rhode Island" pronouncing it the Providence way: "Row Dyeland".

"Hmpf. I wouldn't live up there - all that cold weather an' ya gotta have a license to buy a gun."

"That's bad?"

"Hell ya, it's bad. I can go right over to Metairie now an' get one in five minutes!"

On the wall was a framed poster. A middle aged man photographed in a chair with a curvaceous half naked woman on each knee. He was smoking a cigar and grinning. Above him were the words "AND THEY CALL ME CRAZY!" and underneath "RE-ELECT GOVERNOR EARL LONG".

The owner pointed first to the brunette "That's Blaze

Starr," then to the blonde. "And that's The Cat Girl. Best strippers Bourbon Street ever had. Carmen Marsella owned both their asses. I know I fucked 'em both." Never having heard an adult use the word literally Kevin stared at him with full attention. The man pointed to Blaze again. "First time with her cost me twenty five dollars at Mary's in Opelousas. Next time out on Chef Highway it'd doubled. Worth every penny though. Beautiful woman."

Kevin stared, thinking he'd found the greatest city on earth. "How much is it?"

"Not for sale an' never will be." The bell rang calling him back to the front of the shop - "Hey man, whatchoo know good?" – leaving Kevin to re-immerse himself in pre-war sounds.

The raw bluesmen and nasal white string bands were a shockingly direct pipeline into a lost world. Old photographs of preserved long ago moments were fascinating but external. Now, eerily, he felt himself inside the head of these, pinch mouthed white crackers and rough toned blacks. He liked everything he heard but had to limit himself to favorites, many of which had sexual metaphors. He blew all his spending money, the precious box containing his well-padded shellac hand-carried on the return flight to Providence, where he amused friends by playing them rasty ditties of lemon squeezing, spoiled hambones and mules kicking in another's stall.

A month later he had his first wet dream: He and Blaze Starr both of them naked and sweaty, she in high heels bumping her ass against his hard on while a blues 78 played: Charley Jordan picking his guitar, singing "Keep It Clean":

Up he jumped; down he fell

Trap flew open like a mussel shell
Roll him over; give him Coca Cola
Lemon soda, chocolate ice cream
Soap and water, for to keep it clean

He awoke, dizzy and confused, feeling the wet spot on the sheet, song playing in his head. Next night he replayed the scene while awake, humping his pillow, this time imagining the sinuous Cat Girl.

Even though, during his mid-teenage years, Kevin liked certain contemporary bands, those played-to-death 78's had inexorably led him to others reissued on LP. He'd be listening to one in his room and drift off into one of many hormone-fuelled daydreams:

"Wabash Blues" being played and sung by The Coon-Sanders Nighthawks on a wind-up phonograph at a 1920's house party. Windows open to the warm summer night. Gleaming Stutz-Bearcats at the curb. Silver hip flasks in back pockets and beaded purses. Kissing the neck of a giggling bare armed flapper, smelling her face powder and whiskey breath.

Or Roy Acuff's "Great Speckled Bird" dominated by Bashful Brother Oswald's ringing dobro coming over a glowing Crosley radio in a Tennessee hills pinewood cabin. Younger brothers and sisters sleeping in the next room. Parents gone by flivver to a tent show. Outside on a horse blanket surrounded by fireflies and chirping crickets, lying on top of the neighbor's oldest girl, tongues connecting. The strong soap smell of her hair. Feeling her plump breasts naked under a dime store print dress, hearing her gasp.

And Charlie Parker blowing his brains out on "KoKo" in a dark, smoky 52nd street club. Everybody transfixed, staring at the stage, catching each spiraling quicksilver note. Beautiful black hipster girl with full red lips smelling of Shalimar perfume. Unzipping his pleated pants, lowering her head in the electric darkness to take him into her mouth. Sucking him to orgasm as Bird himself climaxes.

Although tawny haired Farrah-Fawcett and her contemporaries were also in his intense teenage stroke fantasies, he always felt more possessive about the old timey ones. They weren't being shared by every other kid on the block. His attraction to them was more multi-layered and diffused.

When Kevin was eighteen, the old man took him during Spring Break to a Chrysler Sales convention in Miami. There was a lot of drinking at dinner. On the second night, someone's pretty secretary passed him her room key. Later he realized how lucky he'd been to have had his first fuck from a woman who wasn't a whore or an inexperienced girlfriend. That weekend he'd gotten a crash course in sexual acrobatics with no emotional entanglements. Back home he told Thomas who listened wide eyed, promising to pray for him. Predictably his private sex/music fantasies became less frequent, never again occurring with their original power. A few years later, no longer wanting to be a priest, Thomas himself started dating.

For most of Kevin's early adulthood music was not all important. Even though he casually continued to buy albums, his consuming interest was sex and drugs. The collector bug, like many virulent germs, lay dormant. Then, after his mid 20's, without any warning, it suddenly erupted.

At Emerson College he majored in broadcasting and became a full on pothead, staying ripped through classes. Aimless and bored, after two years, he dropped out and, through a friend of the old man, took a gig in R.I. stripping interiors - ideal for a big guy who didn't want anything disturbing his high. For the next few years he financed a low rent hedonist life style working part time, vaguely wanting something more, not knowing what it was but not terribly upset about it either.

One week he was working in an office building near a used record store. During lunch he'd go in and buy promo reissue LP's - jazz, r&b, gospel, rockabilly, surf, garage - he had ears for it all. Flyers in the store hipped him to a monthly record meet in Northern Mass. He started showing up regularly getting to know other collectors. The old timey seduction of 78's was replaced by the not-so-distant immediacy of 45's, aural flyspecked sepia and black and white turned to Technicolor. For Kevin, single records had become pop culture's ultimate two and a half minute junk food, scarfed down for an instant energy buzz. Growing up in front of the tube with those commercial breaks in between old movies, it just seemed natural.

At Charlie's Sandwich Shoppe Diner, after a Boston meet, a rockabilly collector had pulled out a typewritten, single spaced list from his shirt pocket - the first mail order record auction Kevin had ever seen. He immediately felt a deeply joyous, psychic shock. This, he knew, was but a tiny fraction from the limitless 7" vinyl ocean which people were actually digging up and selling worldwide. Almost immediately he was, buying collectors' magazines, bidding, getting on dealers' mailing lists, his once-desultory brain avidly sponging up names, songs, labels and values.

His knowledge grew in direct proportion to his realization of the depth of his ignorance. Who actually sang on a certain record? Was the artists name on the label made up? Did so-and-so rip so-and-so off? Whose treatment of a song came first? Did this record ever exist? Was it even recorded? How many were there? What was their value? Did all copies have the same numbers in the runoff grooves? If it wasn't a bootleg could it be a second press and how could you tell? Was it reissued on another label? Were some copies pressed on colored as well as black wax? Vinyl or styrene? With or without a picture sleeve? Which was rarer, the short or long version? Such arcane was endless. As the old time collectors told him "Nobody will ever know it all and nobody will ever have it all."

Kevin had once gone backstage to meet Billy Lee Riley, a 1950's pioneer who had cut wild rockabilly for the Memphis Sun label. In his collection, Kevin had a pretty good instrumental 45 from California on the Era label – "Sandstorm" by Sandy and The Sandstorms. The writer credit on the label listed "Billy Riley". Kevin asked him if he'd played on it.

"I sure did hoss" Billy Lee replied, "Every instrument!" There was a solid satisfaction discovering just one other small piece of the great puzzle.

By his late 20's, stripping interiors was getting old. He wanted out. A year and a half went by before he caught a break. One of his Hope High School pals, Denny McCloud, had a cousin set to open a bar in Cranston. Kevin had already been partially schooled by the old man in bibulous formulae. He took a mixology class and after a few months became a bartender - a steady gig which afforded him more girls and records. Soon he was blowing both his dough and his wad way too often.

Once he'd done a double hat trick. Woke up, fucked the girl he'd gone to bed with, made it with a lady vet who lived in his building and that evening picked up another girl and took her home after work. The same day he acquired three monster 45's – one from an auction, one from a set sale, one from a pre-arranged trade in the bar. Stuffing himself with sex and vinyl, snorting and boozing every night, the kicks became muted. "Great fuck," said one of his coked dates the morning after. "Too bad we couldn't feel it."

Group therapy helped slow him down enough to cool the booze n' blow, even put the skids to compulsive woman-izing. To be solidly on the road to mental health he suspected it'd probably be necessary to deep six the all-consuming vinyl jones. He didn't even try.

When Kevin let himself in the apartment Marlene was back on the computer. "How was the meet? Wipe us out?"

"Absolutely.. I bought sealed packets of each Beatles' pubic hair for five hundred grand."

"I hope you got signed documents of authentication?"

"Yeah. By someone called Murray The Z. You think they might be fake?" He put down the Mister Disc player and the side by side 45 carrying case, before going into his floor-to-ceiling shelved record room. "Hear the show?"

"I was working." Back when they were dating she'd lis-ten every time he was on, making a cassette in the process. Now the shows were archived on the station's webpage. "Play any good vocal groups?" She liked them best, then blues, followed by rockabilly, surf and garage.

"Sure." Locating his bootleg copy of the Blue Jays on Checker, he returned to the main room, switched on the old Kenwood amp, put the 45 on his 1970's Dual 1229Q turntable, manually picking up the tone arm with Orfeon cartridge, and placed the stylus on the lead in grooves. In a second the Blue Jays were singing through his one-way Tannoy speakers. The sound was maybe two thirds as good as the original.

Marlene was still locked on the screen, "That one's nice."

"It's better than nice. Too bad it's not real."

"What's an original worth?"

"Oh I don't know," he said vaguely, wondering if she somehow knew of his pending deal, feeling a small leak of fear in his gut. "Depends on who's selling. You had lunch?"

"Yeah, you hungry?"

"I had two hot dogs at that stand up the road from the show. You know, where that teen collector thinks the relish is too hot?" He flicked through his new acquisitions in the side by side box.

Still looking at the monitor Marlene tilted her head towards the speakers. "I don't get why you guys love this music."

"How's that?"

"All this swoony, weepy stuff about 'hear my plea' and 'you're my only love' and 'don't ever leave me'. Most of these meatballs are about as romantic as toilet seats. I doubt if real women even appear on their radar."

"Yeah and they're lots of wispy, sensitive guys who like raging garage records about how fucked chicks are."

"At least they're more honest."

"Bullshit. We're all just a bunch of misogynistic lesbians."

"Hey! What do you think of this for my portfolio?" He went over and looked over her shoulder as she typed: NOW! BY KEEPING YOUR PENIS ROCK HARD 24 HOURS A DAY WITH VIAGRA YOU CAN FUCK THE BANKS INTO GIVING YOU THE LOWEST MORTGAGE RATES EVER!!! She smiled up at him sweetly. "See, two products combined into one spam. People will cut their deleting time in half."

"I would've just made it "FUCK THE BANKS IN THE ASS," but I'm not as refined as you."

"Are you calling me a wimp?"

"No, no, no. I swear you're the world's toughest bitch." He kissed the top of her head."You do the Ripley's?"

Kevin wrote fake record collector themed "Ripley's Believe it Or Not" items. Marlene added drawings and assembled them on the computer. They looked like the real thing. A dealer friend, who put one in each of his catalogs, gave Kevin first crack at any record he wanted. Some previous examples included:

"As a young teenager, Mrs. C. D. Ford of Missoula, Montana left a 45 record of Elvis Presley's "Hound Dog" out in the sun which melted into an outline of an actual dog!"

"Abraham Fowler of Rye, New York owns 620,000,000 record albums - the largest collection in the world – yet he cannot hear one note of music on any of them because he is totally deaf! Instead he looks at the cover art."

"In Falls Church, Virginia, on July 3rd, 1977 it briefly rained Beatles butcher cover LP's that were all still sealed! About 30 copies of this rare collectible valued at $800 apiece fell from the skies and then immediately disappeared!"

Marlene clicked out of her program, went to documents and clicked on their latest collaboration:

"George Mashkin, formerly of Jacksonville, Florida, has ripped off more record collectors than any other dealer on earth! He has sold damaged and non-existent recordings to over 200,000 disappointed customers in every country on the globe, with the exception of Madagascar and Uruguay. He is rumored to use about 60 aliases and operate out of a mobile home. Mr. Mashkin recently won Goldmine magazine's coveted Dealer of The Year award."

She'd used a drawing of some smiling ordinary guy from an actual Ripley's panel with an inset of a prize ribbon. At the bottom a little cartoon figure, sweat drops shooting off his oversize head, stared with popping eyes at a broken record falling out of an addressed mailer. She looked up for his reaction. He smiled broadly, hunched his shoulders. "What can I say? You're a genius." He kissed her again, turned to go into his record room.

"Wait! "Did you hear that?"

"What?"

"My biological clock ticking. Soon as I finish this we can go to bed. This is my most fertile day." The phone rang. "That's probably Chris. He said he'd call back."

Kevin went over to the couch's end table, picked up the wireless handset. "Hello."

"This' Newton. Jus' pulled s'm stuff. Might wanna c'm up n' take a look."

He covered the mouthpiece, looked over at Marlene. "Newton Means." She rolled her eyes, turned away. Newton was a boss weirdo. Runty and mole-like, he believed his knowledge on any subject to be mega superior to anyone else's and talked without opening his mouth like the old Dick Tracy villain Mumbles. A pain in the ass but he served an important function.

Every collector knew of another who was more dishonest, obsessive, cheap, unhygienic, paranoid, childlike, unpleasant, (fill in the blank) so they could say to themselves and to their fellow addicts, wives and girlfriends "Well at least I'm not that bad!" Anybody comparing themselves to Newton usually came out way ahead.

"I'm not going up there to look at bad records."

"These'r sm high tcket items. Might be sm fr yr own cllection."

"That you're actually willing to sell?" Kevin had been down this particular road before.

"Thnk it'd be wrth yr while." Kevin was silent. "Need t'imprv m'csh flow. I'll give y'thrty-five pcent stead of twny-five off. S'gd deal."

Kevin sighed. Thirty-five per cent off an outrageously overpriced record meant zip - still you never knew.

"I gt one o thse Sarg recds . How cn y'tell f'it's orignl?"

"Is it thick?"

"M. Nt rl thck."

"Which one is it?"

"Link D'vs 'Grsshppr Rck'

"Hmm. Okay, run your fingertip over the edge on both sides. Does one edge feel rougher than the other?

"Yp."

"It's a second press. Same labels on both. The owner just used what was left over for the second."

"Whn cn y'cm up?"

"Maybe tomorrow. I'll call to let you know."

"Bttr hrry. Stff's nt gn sit aroun'."

"Okay. See ya." Kevin hung up.

Marlene was still intent on her computer. "Why don't you just stick your head in a rock crusher? It'd be faster."

"Probably," He yawned. "I'm gonna crash for an hour."

"We have to make a baby first. Hold on." She closed out of the program.

Kevin sighed. Fucking as a duty had been steadily robbing him of desire. "Okay but I'm pretty beat." He'd gotten up at 5 am. "You – uh, better get dressed."

He was slightly humiliated. The Teenybopper/Teacher Fuck was a clichéd fantasy. - an embarrassing nerd fixation. He felt he should be turned on by something more exotic like Alien Babes or Lady Wrestlers. Still it worked and the whole point was his ejaculation. No sperm, no baby.

Hearing his request Marlene lost some enthusiasm of her own. Kevin's increasing reliance on such scenarios, blotting her out to get off, wasn't very flattering. But then, she had to admit, lovemaking solely for procreation wasn't very exciting. Perhaps it would return after they had a child. As she dutifully went into the bedroom to change into knee socks, tennis shoes, pleated skirt and high school sweater he called after her. "Can you, put your hair in a ponytail?"

They'd met at a branch of his gym. He'd been to a waste-of-time record show outside Boston and figured to get in a workout before driving home. The place, nicer than the one in Providence, had a health shake and food concession. He'd been on the cardiovascular cross trainer looking through the floor to ceiling soundproof glass at an aerobics class, half-consciously checking out her ass when she and the others suddenly turned and ran right up to the glass, heads to the right side. As if his smile was a signal, she turned and looked right into his eyes.

Fifteen minutes later they were both on the machines in a small workout room. Hands locked behind his neck he raised and lowered his upper body doing stomach crunches on a board. She was flat on her back doing leg presses, straightening and bending her knees across from him. Every time she pushed back he raised looking right up her crotch. The effect was so embarrassingly obscene she started to giggle. He stuck out his tongue, rolled his eyes and she laughed out loud.

Over smoothies at the juice bar she asked him what kind of recorder it was he had been using. He took the mini-disc player out of his shorts pocket. "When I saw you through the glass I was listening to 'The Younger Girl' by the Critters."

"I thought The Lovin' Spoonful did that."

He was delighted. "Yeah, they had the hit and these guys remade it. What were you exercising to?"

"Bjork's 'Hyper-Ballad'"

"I heard her. She's pretty good." He was to say the least vague on anything remotely contemporary but he had heard the singer and liked her. He kept smiling at Marlene nervously but, he hoped, winningly and asked her out.

In a little over a year they were married. The first wave of love/lust had passed – attraction was still there – just not as intense as when they'd call in sick from work to fuck all day. A drama junkie, he'd had his share of obsessive loves and was hip they always burned out. Now as newlyweds they had more than a sexual friendship, less than a mad passion. So, Marlene wondered, did that make it that modern chimera: a mature relationship?

Such a concept was too subtle for the lyrics of records Kevin loved. They were full of murderous jealousy, suicidal sorrows, painful heartbreak, cuttingly comic rejections, ec-static couplings, exhortations to dance and go crazy. There wasn't a balanced feeling anywhere. In the real world hardly anyone loved, grieved or felt as intensely as they did in the grooves of 45's. The best songs memorably distilled emotions, ideas, attitudes in the form of playlets, confessions, psycho-dramas, power fantasies, incantations. One aural injection and presto! You were alive! Even certain bad records were a kick because they blew it big time. Plus there was the security of always knowing what you were getting every play. With a woman the reverse was true. No wonder Marlene saw them as rivals.

Early on she'd tried to wean him away from records by exposing him to vintage postcards - she collected ones of 1950's restaurants and diners. Accompanying her to a big show in a New York hotel, he wandered around, the large interconnecting rooms looking at tables with the cards in long boxes divided into sections like HUMOROUS, ARTISTS, CITIES and more interestingly EROTICA, DISASTERS and BLACK AMERICANA. He stopped at one and the sharp featured dealer asked "What category please?"

As he mumbled a non-committal reply, a plain middle-aged woman walked up "Anything for me Larry?

"Not today, Jean. Sorry."

"Next time," she half admonished half prophesized moving away.

Kevin leaned into the dealer. "What's her category?"

The man raised one eyebrow. "Well, she's got a very specific one." He paused for effect and then half-whispered since she was still close by, "Cows standing in water."

Kevin walked away, totally grooved. He knew of collectors for barbed wire, telephone pole insulators, neon signs and antique light bulbs, but postcards of cows standing in water? That was way beyond hip. Immediately he determined to be part of the postcard scene. For the rest of the show he randomly checked out boxes picking up anything truly weird – a shirt sleeved man pulling a wagon with his eyelids, an alligator eating a praying cartoon "darkie", a goose biting the penis of a little boy pissing through a knothole, a stiff 1920's vaudevillian with a robot ventriloquist dummy. By the shows end he'd blown a chunk of dough. Marlene was happy. They now shared something they could do together. For about a year he'd filled up the postcard album she'd bought him. It was fun but, for him, ultimately too lightweight to be addictive. He never got hooked on the super expensive stuff. Once his album was full he quit. Not long after, so did she.

They'd been hoping to buy a jukebox. She'd wanted a classic gleaming wood, red and green Bakelite Wurlitzer or Rock-Ola, with yellow bubble lights that played 78's. Kevin had eyes for a less visually aesthetic early 60's silvery Seeburg he'd load with bootleg and lesser condition 45s - his rare originals wouldn't survive many spins under a juke's weighty tone arm. Yet as soon as they married all the money, at Marlene's insistence, had been diverted into a savings account for her future pregnancy.

Well, they wouldn't be choosing a baby. It would chose them and their lives would go directly into the Mixmaster. Kevin knew a few friends who'd come out of the experience like shell shocked Vietnam vets. The goddamn relationship itself was becoming like a child - the amount of care and feeding it needed. Not to mention the marriage counseling at fifty a pop for each of them. If only he had something to bitch about in her. But try as he might the only thing he didn't like was her bitching about him:

"I should have known better than to get involved with a 36 year old obsessive-compulsive whose only responsibility is giving a vanilla wafer every month to a goddamn hermit crab!"

"And always making sure he has a bigger shell to move into."

"Right! Unlike your own self who seems to keep requiring a smaller one! If you invested just one tenth of the time in our relationship as you do in those records...seriously there'll come a day you're gonna wake up and find out your whole life's been one giant distraction."

"Life is just a distraction from death anyway."

"Spare me the morbid philosophy."

"Okay. Spare me the self-help psychology."

"Fuck you."

"Fuck you too."

And then they'd make up, make love and for a while, the problems would go underground until she talked to her friends - or her mom. Kevin believed that after married couples fought, the husbands should talk to their wife's friends and the wives should talk to their husband's friends. It probably wouldn't do much good but it'd at least give them both a different point of view.

CHAPTER THREE

Half an hour after the duty fuck Kevin lay in bed naked, still wondering how to get the jack for the Blue Jays. He'd finished reading a story in a Plastic Man reprint and was checking the Sunday Providence Journal TV guide for possible movies. Beside him, Marlene in panties and Tufts sweat shirt spoke about the possibility of intrauterine insemination. He had good motility but a low count. She had some minor blockage.

She hadn't much enjoyed their lovemaking – if that's what it was. First she'd had to go along with all that dumb baby doll stuff about how she'd do anything to get her high school teacher to give her a better grade. When they first started acting out different fantasies she'd gotten off on them too but now his fixation on a few tired scenarios bugged her.

Also, he'd seemed increasingly out of control, scaring her, making her unable to let go and totally inside himself, both of which made her feel at first lonely, later angry. During the final lap he'd driven into her with such force she'd bumped her head against the wall.

He apologized, getting up to make them Mai Tais in the double old fashioned glasses with a 50's gold and turquoise boomerang design while Marlene stared at another of her mother's wedding gifts beside her on the wall. A framed lobby card of "Bride Of The Gorilla", b&w photo insert of Barbara Payton in bridal gown passed out in the arms of a giant ape with the legend "She Would Never Forget Her Wedding Night!"

It didn't seem so funny now.

"I said, 'How would you feel about it?'"

Kevin wrote "T" for "tape" next to "Shakedown" an obscure film noir with Howard Duff. Like his records, once a film was in his possession he hardly ever played it. Abstractedly he took a sip of his drink. Marlene saw that the recent sex, booze and lack of sleep was putting him under. Joanne had once told her with her fondness for pronouncements. "Sex is rarely as bad for a man as it can be for a woman – they come with less fuss." Maybe, she thought, because they had less expectations.

She nudged him with her bare foot. "Well?"

His eyes never left the page. "Whacking off in a bottle? What do you think?"

She slapped his forearm, stifling a giggle. "That's not the constructive way to look at it"

He closed his eyes and lay back on the pillow. "Customer at the bar once told me that when he and his wife were trying to have a kid she got totally obsessed. He had to wear certain underwear, not get his balls near direct heat. They only did it at times when he had the highest sperm count or when she was most receptive or at the end, when the moon was in some phase. Whole thing was about as erotic as making a bank deposit. Finally he got so turned off he couldn't even get it up. Marriage went to hell." He gave her a sidelong look.

"That's an extreme case. Still, ultimately the purpose of sex is children." Since their marriage she had been going to mass occasionally.

"For the Church maybe, not me."

"Mm, we'll talk to Howard about it."

Every week the marriage counselor told Kevin to control his temper, be less of a slob, be more thoughtful. Anytime she couldn't get him to do something she brought it to Howard who usually backed her up in a soothing, rational voice. Having his faults pointed out so often dragged him no matter how justified. He had modified his ways somewhat. At least it was better than going to a priest.

Marlene drained her drink, wincing at the ceiling mobile she'd made in college. Parabolic shapes of well known Rene Magritte images – a reversed mermaid the top half fish, lower half woman, a nighttime suburb underneath a midday sky, a small scale smoking locomotive emerging from a fireplace. Art student jive but Kevin liked it. "Do you want to eat here or at your work?"

"I dunno."

"Well, decide. It's almost seven."

Kevin shot up with a curse, peering at his watch in the semi-dark. "Damn! Ebay auction's ending in six minutes!"

He ran bare ass out to the computer. Marlene fell back, took a breath, reminding herself for the umpteenth she'd accepted his lunacy when she'd moved in. Good thing they hadn't been fucking. She smiled, imagining him frantically pulling out with a wet hard on. Then frowned, realizing he was capable of doing it. Early on in their relationship she'd been initially flattered when a top dealer's auction list was ending and he chose to remain in bed with her. Later she found out there was only one 45 he'd been after for a small upgrade.

"SonofaBITCH!"

"WHAT?" She raised up on one elbow.

"Goddamn thing's taking forever!"

Suddenly she saw Kevin, enraged, throwing their future baby out a window when it failed to burp. "Want me to help?"

"What the fuck can you do?"

"Do you have to swear all the time?" She didn't want him cursing around their child. "Go back to the previous page and try again!" Again she fell back on her pillow.

Scoring records was a constant distraction from the boring business of daily life. Okay. Everyone needed something like this to a degree but Kevin craved it all the time. Once you have a baby you're inundated with the mundane. How would he handle that?

"Shit!" A pause. "It worked!" An $800 - $1000 northern soul 45 on Dore was listed not only incorrectly in the Doo Wop section, but by the wrong side. Kevin had once unwittingly sold one for $15 at a record show. Earlier this morning it still had no bids - a good sign since soul had the largest customer base in the world. Although select 1970's funk and the Motown-ish up-tempo "Northern" stuff brought the highest prices, every soul sub-genre – mod, sweet, group harmony, deep – was collected.

His phone rang. "Damn! Can you get that?" He searched under "Artist". Found the listing and clicked on it. It popped onto the screen with a $15 bid. Three minutes left. The phone rang again. He scrolled down and entered a maximum of $151.77, hit ENTER BID, got the next screen, typed in both his User ID - "quahogman" - and his father's middle name for the embedded password, hit ENTER. The new screen told him he'd been outbid. The phone rang a third time. "Marlene!"

She threw on a Chinese silk robe, a Christmas present from Kevin, walked into the living room and picked up the handset. "Hello?...Oh, hi Chris. He's here but he's doing an eBay auction. You want to know what he picked up today, right?...Hold on. Kevin, Chris wants to know if -"

"Tell him I didn't get anything spectacular. I'll call him back later this week."

A fellow collector, Chris Andrews was now a sound boom operator who'd moved to L.A. He and Kevin kept in touch about what they'd scored at their respective record meets.

As Marlene relayed the information Kevin hit BID AGAIN and typed $207.77. The screen told him he'd been out-bid again by bigsouldaddy, a UK collector. He hit REVIEW. The record had jumped to $400. There were 8 other bids - snipers like himself who had been waiting to dart out of the ether and snag it. One minute to go. His nerves were twanging, hands had a slight tremor. He upped his maximum to $526.77 thinking he could still make some money but when the last screen flashed on with under a minute left it'd reached $700 the high bidder an asshole who'd named himself wins4ever. Jesus! Maybe it was worth more than a grand! Should he push it one more time? No, fuck it; probably just an auction fever bid. He sighed and logged off. It wasn't looking so good for The Blue Jays.

It was late Monday afternoon at The Penalty Box, a strip mall bar in Cranston. Little Christmas lights outlined the picture window. In the dark interior, serious drinkers sat on stools sharing space with guys and their dates waiting for a table. TV always had a game on, usually hockey.

"Whattya think? Red Wings gonna pull it out?" Behind

the bar, Kevin in a dark blue flannel shirt, hair still damp from the shower, shrugged, smiling. He never offered an opinion on sports – ostensibly not to alienate customers, actually because he had none to give.

While taking orders, he thought hard again about selling a few high profile records out of his collection. 45's whose reputations were greater than their musical content. Trophies he'd never play.

Distracted, he fucked up a Cosmopolitan and poured too much Maker's Mark in a double. Lynda, the owner's blonde girlfriend/hostess was quick to chide him. Like always, Kevin thought of the temptress in the Stones' "Spider And The Fly": "Dirty, flirty/She looked about 30". Lynda acted tougher with him than any other employee. He was pretty sure she was attracted to him. He'd only to make a move, put a hand on one of her up thrust tits or squeeze her mandolin butt and they'd be down the rabbit hole. He sometimes got off on the sexual tension but it was a good reason not to seriously lush on the job.

During a lull he used his cell to successfully move the $50 rockabilly for a $100 profit. Ha! Only a measly four thousand, four hundred to go. Hearing the transaction, Lynda came over as he disconnected. "Placing bets?"

"Sold a record."

"Just don't ignore the customers." She looked at him as if making sure he got the point then went back to her post, the points she really wanted him to get pushing out her lavender sweater. As he built his signature concoction - a classy dark rum Mojita - he hoped his boss was due for another ladylove. He didn't keep them much over six months. What Howard the marriage counselor called "serial monogamy".

Next morning Kevin awoke from a vivid "record dream" – a phenomenon familiar to all hardcore collectors. He was driving down an old tree lined street in Providence, the sidewalk split in places by thrusting roots, before stopping at a driveway garage sale. There were no old records but the elderly lady told him her late husband had owned a TV/stereo repair which had been a record shop in the mid 60's. It was closed up and the old records were still there. She'd been meaning to sell them.

In the dream, he followed her car to a boarded-up storefront between a self-service laundry and New York System hot dog joint. She unlocked the padlock and slid back the folding steel security door. He followed her inside. Under an overhead light in the backroom, amidst old black and white TV's, he started going through a wall of wooden shelves crammed with rare dusty 45's – all store stock mint. Gold and silver top green Federals, web top silver and maroon Chess, yellow and brown Suns, orange-red wax grey RCA's, blue and silver script Imperials, star Deccas, yellow Dots as well as early Kings, Fortunes, Mercurys, MGMs, Stardays, Goldbands, Aces - most in flawless factory sleeves.

He pulled obscure rockabilly, blues and vocal groups on labels from Aardel to Zoom, among them Chance, Blue Hen, Blue Lake, Red Robin, Summit, Vortex, Teenage, Parrot, Dootone, Saber, Herald, Dixie and Pink Cloud – all gleaming in his hands, rare gems from Ali Baba's cave.

Dizzy with euphoria, he piled one rarity on top of another, finally pausing to ask how much they were. The woman, who had been standing by, smiled warmly at him. As she was opening her mouth to answer, he woke up.

Home in bed, he shut his eyes. Couldn't he have stayed asleep long enough to hear her price? But then if she'd said only fifty cents apiece before he awoke he would've been seriously bummed. The old blues line popped into his head "Did you ever dream lucky/Wake up cold in hand?"

Marlene had left for her job at RISD. Kevin forced himself up, had a swig of organic apple juice, a bowl of designer granola, pulled on jeans, maroon shirt and black and white pebbly cotton sweater. He took two multi vitamins and went into his record room.

The space itself – a huge closet or maybe small bedroom - was the major reason he'd taken the apartment four years ago. The walls were covered with his framed assortment of signed musician photos, sheet music, posters, picture records and weird LP covers. Even though he'd lined all four sides with shelves from floor to ceiling – LP's on the bottom, 45's on the top and one level of 78's in between – he'd run out of space. Whole genres were now stored in special long 45 boxes bought unassembled at shows. These were stacking up at a steady rate crowding the space. He had agreed - no records stored outside the room. For Marlene his collection was the same as "The Creeping Unknown". Like any other horror flick mutation it had to be contained in the lab. Only their CD's – he had three times as many as she – were shelved together in the living room.

His records were grouped into various musical genres then alphabetized, first by label and then by artist. It was usually easier for him to picture a label logo than remember the name of some unknown singer. Of course sometimes he would forget both and work himself into a fine bate trying to find a particular song.

Whenever possible he put 45's into their company sleeves. Many of these, from smaller labels, were rarer than the records they housed. Several larger labels – Columbia, Decca and RCA – changed their sleeve designs through the years. It was often a judgment call as to what was appropriate for the disc in question. Once one was chosen the sleeved record was put into a second clear plastic sleeve and filed. Record collectors used this word to mean a particular disc was in their collection, as in "I file that."

45's on labels that never had company sleeves were put in old medium to heavy weight sleeves and, if over a hundred dollars in value, blue, yellow or red heavy weight sleeves. The more luxuriant grooming didn't add any real protection – just respect.

One of the duplicate 45's he'd gotten yesterday was "The Last Ride" by The Phantom on Ricky-Tick - a strange intermittent gravel-voiced rant over primitive backing. He needed to compare it against his collection copy and keep the one in better condition. Because the artist might be black he checked the blues/r&b section first. It wasn't there. Next, because he might be white he checked the rock & roll/rockabilly section. Not there. Then because it was nearly an instrumental he checked that section as well. No luck. Since it was such a weird recording he began to search in the novelty/oddball section before remembering that he hadn't played it over the air yet so he'd put it in one of the three long 45 boxes filled with potential sets comprised of three to five singles apiece. Every set had a theme: Cars, Booze, Dances, Rock & Roll, Nonsense Words, Monkeys, Chickens, Murder, Outer Space and many more.

The record was in a hotrod/car song set. He looked at both copies under a desk lamp's halogen bulb. The one in his collection was about a Vg++ with a big black "X" on the label. The other was only a Vg+ but the label was unblemished. Which to keep? He held off on deciding, hoping his 3-step cleaning system might later bring the Vg+ copy up a grade.

Like-minded fanatics could discuss cleaning methods for hours. Some used special vacuum machines, others wore goggles buffing the 45 at wheels after applying esoteric formulae which often included vinyl upholstery cleaner.

Kevin always tried soap and water on a brush whose soft bristles were calibrated to fit inside the grooves. If the record still played with noise he sprayed an alcohol-free glass cleaner on an old towel and rubbed following the grooves. If that didn't work he poured denatured alcohol on the vinyl before again using the brush. And if it was still noisy he coated the grooves with a slow drying liquid that in a half a day could be removed as a thin flim. Any remaining noise not caused by an alien substance came from a bad pressing or damaged grooves and wasn't coming out.

The few latest acquisitions now filed, he started searching for some expensive piece he could force himself to turn over. Rockabilly had been his first kick. Fifteen years ago if a 45 had a slap bass and was affordable he bought it. Now he had records worth top money that did nothing for him. Franklin Stewart's "Long Black Train" on Lu from Tennessee was classic rockabilly but for him, uninspired. Thinking his Vg+ copy might be good for nine hundred to a grand, he emailed Volker Detleff in Hamburg and got a reply right away – no sale. Beginning in the early 1970's, the Krauts had scooped so many rockers out of the U.S. they didn't have to buy from Americans and usually just dealt amongst themselves. After a couple more emails and long distance calls Kevin still hadn't scored a taker. There was nothing else to do but see Newton Means.

The northeast's fave vinyl weirdo lived hermit-like outside Quincy, Mass. in several storage units crammed top to bottom with 45's, LP's, magazines and toys. He'd bought his records over 20 years ago with an insurance settlement after a car had knocked him off his bicycle. For supposedly acting as the night watchman, he got a discounted rate. He had a hot plate, portable TV and cot. He pissed and shat in the surrounding weeds, sometimes washing in public restrooms. The whole scene was like a pen and ink 19th century illustration of drunkards or dope fiends.

Newton hated to sell anything, paranoid about letting records go for less than full value. Collectors, who'd spent freezing or sweltering hours digging through countless boxes and shelves, watched in frustrated rage as he held back nine tenths of their findings. "This' m'only copy. Haveta check 'n ths'n, etc." After which they were usually grossly overcharged on what remained.

Now generally boycotted, he'd been forced to consign to a few local dealers/shops to survive. He'd berated a well known Boston oldies store for not prominently displaying his 45's until the owner finally snapped throwing him bodily onto the sidewalk. Soon as Newton had brought assault charges, the store tipped the Feds that he'd never filed for or paid income tax. The case was pending.

There was a nip in the breeze, temperature changing from warm to cool as grey clouds passed in front of the sun. Kevin swung off the highway onto the dirt drive, curved up a hill along the row of closed corrugated fronts. Newton's was the only one open. The sound of the Trans Am brought him into the sunlight squinting like a blind cavefish. Absently he rubbed a 45 against a filthy tee shirt under an army surplus jacket. He wore his usual frayed Levi cut offs and torn black Keds. "Hmf. Tk y' lng enuf." Newton was never pleased.

"I slept in. Let's have a look."

Inside the dark unit a single workman lamp provided dim illumination, its dangling extension cord looping off a two by four to a hidden socket. Sagging plank shelves jammed with records were supported by cinder blocks, gunmetal filing cabinets tilted and buckled. Sleeveless 45's spilled onto the cement floor out of torn cardboard boxes.

"Thr" Newton gestured to a small record box on a rickety table. Next to it a heater's coils glowed orange.

"I'm taking this into the light."

"Sut yrslf."

Kevin walked out, put the box on his car hood and started flipping through the 45's - most of them common, some obscure crap, anything else hacked up. Half had sleeves that were tattered or stained. Whoa, what was this? Terry Bussy on Jazzmar? It looked like money. He held it up in the light. Seemed to be in good shape - a double plus with a slight warp. He played it on the portable. A white Gulf Coast group. Not bad. His watch read 10:30. Chris Andrews in L.A. knew vocal groups cold. If he wasn't doing a picture he'd be up early. Kevin took out his cell. In a minute he had the value. The gods were smiling - an easy thousand in mint, maybe a little more.

Good not great but stinking rare.

As Newton came out Kevin quickly slid the cell back in his pocket. "Fnd nythng?"

"Yeah, I could use these - depending." He handed over a six record stack – the Jazzmar was in the middle. Newton saw it. "Hm. Might hv t'do sm r'srch 'n ths."

"Well that's the best one. I don't want the others if you won't sell it."

"Wht'll y'gimme f'rt?"

"I dunno. It's rare but it's kinda wimpy. Two fifty?" If he went too low Newton would get suspicious and the record would disappear back into the bowels of the unit.

"Hmpf! I ws thnkin six."

"Can't do it."

"Wht's y'bst offr?"

"Three fifty."

"Fr 'n iz yrs."

There was a pause. "Yeh, okay."

"Y' c'n hv th rst fr nthr fty."

"I might get forty five on these if I'm lucky. Make it twenty five or just sell me the one."

"Thrty."

"Okay okay." He post-dated the check and took off. Luckily for him most wouldn't put up with Newton so every once in a while Kevin scored something good. Heading back on 95 in the Trans Am he started making calls.

By Thursday night the possibilities had dried up. A guy reneged on a $500 Beach Boys promo. A three-way trade fell through and another collector was sending a 45 back due to condition. He'd gotten $800 on the Jazzmar 45 and about

$150 on some other sales. Add that to the $100 from the rock-abilly he'd sold and his profit was about $700 leaving a monumental $3,935 to go.

On Friday he dressed in lucky 1950's colors - pink button down shirt, black Levis - telling Marlene over coffee and poppy seed muffins he was going down to Connecticut to do some "trading". She kissed him and left for the book store. Sunlight streamed through the kitchen window. The Weather Channel warned of light rain towards late afternoon. Outside puffy white clouds were high in a chilly bright blue sky.

Wearing his black leather car coat he gassed up the TransAm. At the local bank branch, standing on the grey carpeting under soft lights, refusing to think about repercussions, he withdrew $3,900 out of their joint account. Gil's number had been busy every time he'd phoned. Trust the inbred hillbilly not to have call waiting. After a last try, he tossed the cell onto the passenger seat and took off. The whole way down opposing voices argued in his brain. He felt like Pluto in an old Disney cartoon - little devil on one shoulder, angel on the other. He didn't have to see their costumes to know who was saying what.

Gil lived outside a small blue collar town at the northern tip of the Connecticut River Valley. Kevin turned off the interstate and rolled down the shabby main street. A dusty junk store, a bad pizza restaurant, a movie theatre with an out of date misspelled double feature on the marquee, a tiny wooden diner called Ed's, a boarded up appliance shop, etc. Brick factories with broken windows lined the opposite banks of the black swiftly flowing river. Outside of town, before the road connected to the highway, was the inevitable mini-cluster of cheerful-looking chains: KFC, McDonalds and a few gas stations.

Kevin redialed, got an answer. Gil's wife saying he'd be right back. A side road led through wooded hills to the small dark brown shingle house. Parked more or less permanently in the driveway was a wheel-less Chevy trailer truck crammed full of records. He braked behind it and waited, not wanting to be trapped in the overheated cramped front room, breathing the wife's constant cigarette smoke. Collectors who'd gotten Gil's records through the mail joked about having to air out the sleeves. They had the acrid stink of an ashtray.

15 to 20 minutes later the Dodge pickup swung inro the driveway parking in back of the Trans Am, rear end almost out in the road. The two got out at the same time, Kevin holding up his hand in greeting, saying he'd come to pick up the record. Gil shook his head, "Too late."

"What the fuck do you mean?"

"Record's already sold. They over-nighted a cashier's check an' I just cashed it."

"SonofaBITCH!!"

"Sorry y'had to come all the way down. Why didn't you call?"

"I did. It was busy every time."

"Oh yeah, that'd be the wife."

"Can't you tell the guy it was a mistake?"

"Doubt if it'd make a difference. Besides he paid more." He dug out his wallet, removed ten hundreds. "Here's your deposit."

Kevin jammed the bills into the front pocket of his jeans. "This fuckin' sucks. You said Friday."

"I said 'by Friday'. Didn't figure you'd be able to get it

anyway."

Kevin took several deep breaths, badly wanting to ram the hick motherfucker into a tree. ""Listen, don't you ever call me on a record again. Whatever you get in I don't wanna know about it. I see you at a meet don't even talk to me." Gil opened his mouth to respond. Kevin cut him off, "Gil? Go fuck yourself, okay?" He yanked open the Trans Am door, jumped in, fired it up, reversed into the pickups front bumper, turned in a semicircle over the leaf-filled yard, across the walkway and out onto the road.

Driving all the way back to his early shift at The Penalty Box he was bombarded with "if onlys". If only he had called Gil Thursday night. If only he hadn't had breakfast with Marlene. If only he'd intercepted Gil by getting directions to the post office from the wife. He could've leaned on the shifty fuck to give the buyer any number of bullshit excuses. The record had a hairline crack. He was selling it for somebody else and the owner found another buyer. He discovered it was a bootleg. He accidentally broke it. Etcetra, et – fucking - cetera The hell with it. Start thinking like that and you really waste your life. He felt righteously aggrieved but way down inside there was a warm spark of relief at not having spent their money.

Overhead the autumn sky had lost its blue, white clouds light gray with dark undersides, Rain was coming just like the Weather Channel had predicted.

Towards the end of his bar shift, he downed a few bottles of Dogfish 60 Minute IPA. When he got in Marlene wasn't home. He went to the bedroom, changed his button-down for a tee shirt with a record label design and pulled off his Nikes, feet cramped from standing all that time pouring drinks.

On the couch he slit open a record package with Marlene's X-acto knife. With his Mister Disc portable player he was checking out the condition of its contents - a cool Telstar-inspired Brit instrumental "Men In Space" by The Vigilantes on Pye - when she strode in green eyes glaring. Astro Boy in flight with clenched fist extended, visible on the white tee shirt under her bulky black cardigan.

"Did you buy that Blue Jays record?" He took off the headphones and stared at her, mouth open. "Chris called on my line to find out when you'd be back. He told me you might be getting an original and that it must be a real good deal 'cause it was so rare. And then because you seemed kind of secretive about where you were going, even though I thought I was probably imagining things, I checked on our savings account for the baby."

"Yeah, okay. I was going to buy it but I didn't."

"What'd he do? Raise the price?"

"He sold it already. Here's the money." He took out his wallet, threw the bills down on the coffee table next to Mr. Disc. "I was only borrowing it. I was –"

"Wait a minute! You mean if he hadn't gotten another hopeless addict you'd have blown how much on that thing?"

"Marlene, it would've been a –"

"HOW MUCH?" She was standing there quivering in rage.

"Uh, fifty five hundred?"

For a few seconds she simply stared at him, nodding imperceptibly. "Well," she finally declared, "I hope you find a copy someday. I'm sure you two will be very happy together. In fact why don't you just get a stack of your precious 45's right now, vaseline the center holes and fuck them because you WON'T BE FUCKING ME!" She scooped up the money and stomped out of the room.

He stayed motionless, unseeing, while the noise of her packing came from the bedroom. Ten minutes later she walked out carrying her red and green striped canvas suitcase. He got up, took a step towards her, "Look, Marlene - "

"Don't you TALK TO ME!" She bitch slapped Mister Disc off the coffee table, strode to the door and walked out.

"Hey! HEY!" He ran into the bedroom, jammed the Nikes back on, ran out, tripped catching himself on the coffee table edge, staggered out the door, turned, verified he still had the keys in his pocket, and slammed it shut. He vaulted down the inside staircase, out into the night. It was sprinkling, Yellowish street lamp halos shone through the chilly mist. Catching a quick flash of her rigid profile inside the pale blue '66 Mustang before it tore down the street, he sprinted to the Trans Am, jumped in, fired it up. The slick tires churned, caught and he was rocketing after her hoping to catch up before she made the interstate. He didn't want a confrontation in front of her mom and that ex-cop boyfriend.

He turned onto India Street, saw her make a left onto Hope. He floored it. The light went red. He ran it, swinging into the turn, swerving sharply to avoid an onrushing van. Losing their grip the worn tires went into a spinning skid. The Trans Am jumped the curb crashing into the iron fence of an apartment complex. Chest and arm crushed against the steering wheel, face gashed and bleeding, he had a flickering of consciousness before blacking out.

CHAPTER FOUR

Some thirty years after their invention recordings were being collected. Musicians and fans traded and sold early classical, opera, hot jazz, country blues and primitive string bands through ever-growing networks. In the early days of the 78 there was no absolute standard of speed or groove width. These recordings then as now needed various width styli and variable speed turntables.

By the mid-1940's collector publications with sale lists appeared. A new generation began acquiring post war 78's of electric blues, bop, r&b, vocal groups and raw honky tonk - many on small independent labels. By the dawn of the 1950's the 45 and LP arrived (courtesy of RCA and Columbia respectively). 78's were eventually phased out. The indie label trickle became a rush and finally an endless flood. One reason for the onslaught is that unlike a book, painting or movie, the majority of single records can be made cheaply in a matter of minutes.

Through most of the 1950's, records, except for those of the mega-famous, were chiefly regarded as promotional gimmicks to bring people into an artist's live show. By contemporary standards few of any one copy were pressed. If something regional started to "break out" it was usually leased to a major with distribution facilities to make it a hit. During the 1960's collectors began getting an inkling of just how many titles on minuscule labels had been, and were being, produced in every genre.

By the early 1970's the U.S. was vinyl rich with bulging warehouses, obscure juke box distributors, untouched radio stations, virgin collections - easy pickings for anyone who tracked them down. At the time American collectors were for the most part focused solely on black vocal groups and blues. Europeans, less affected by the U.S. soft-headed liberal belief that Black Music was not as commercial and so more "real" than White Music, gutted the land for obscure rockabilly. The Japanese looted meets and stores for old jazz albums. The last true Brit invasion on US soil was made by UK dealers specializing in Northern soul - sly pokerfaced teabags picking them up from clueless stateside dealers before hawking them back in Blighty for bokoo sterling.

During the 1980's finds were still being made – just not as many. In New York and surrounding areas, vocal group 45's, once valued in the late 1960's for a mere $5 at Time Square Slim's legendary subway shop, blew up 100%. Price guides and record auction publications began to proliferate. People got hip to the tip and the rush was on. Around the mid 1990's all obvious areas had been strip-mined and others were drying up fast. As a result, collectors and dealers desperate to be first at whatever treasure troves were still extant, became more paranoiac, manipulative and grasping. More often than not old time collectors were heard to moan, "What happened? This useta be fun!"

At the dawn of the 1990's, instrumentals, 60's garage punk, surf, and soul started moving up in value. Approaching

RICHARD BLACKBURN

the 21st century all sorts of categories became saleable to Top 40 freaks, answer record fans, novelty 45 collectors, guys who pursued every version of one song and fez-wearing Exotica/ Lounge LP hipsters grooving to ping-ponging stereo. Jaded pop-culturists got off on the cheerily commercial 1960's and 1970's bubblegum groups. Beatles and Elvis obsessives laid out mucho dinero when a catalog number on the back of a handful of LP sleeves was printed in a darker shade of ink. As long as at least two people wanted it, any record could be called a "collector's item".

Each faction had its own aesthetic. The tattooed, duck-tailed, bowling shirted rockabilly mafia demanded a slapped standup bass instead of an electric. Blues freaks could tell which Walter it was – Little or Big – from the first wailing harp note. Hardcore garage collectors wouldn't buy a record if it had horns but split off between frat, psych & punk, some kicking in an extra $50 if the lead singer screamed before the fuzz break. Surf fans liked plenty of wet reverb on blistering fast guitar instros. Japanese, Northern European and US collectors of the teen sound divided it into Classic, Dreamy, Cutsey and Country Crossover (c&w gone pop). Jamaicans, besides mid tempo teeners, liked sweet soul from the early 1960's featuring lilting deep voiced singers supported by string sections.

The 78 fanatics worshipped big buck pre-war blues, jazz, string bands, even cartoony dance bands - their intensity making vocal group pizza heads appear casual. Devoted to stratospherically-priced shellac their glossy magazine featured articles on collectors rather than musicians.

Some rpm hounds went after only impossible treasures. Others bought anything cheap just to have stacks o' wax. A few bragged about how much they paid, most bragged about how little.

Now with everything but the most recherché sides available on CD, collecting original singles made less sense than ever. Vinyl did sound better with costly tube amp, turntable and speakers, but after a point the more you spent the smaller the improvement in fidelity. Besides how often could you play every record when you owned thousands? The Letters sections of specialist publications had begun voicing these concerns. A few addicts even put on the brakes. But for the majority, well, a rational argument is powerless against an irrational pursuit.

Some held to the responsible-sounding lie of making an investment, the naive actually believing they would retire on their collections. Truthfully most collectors only sell when desperate and, inevitably, take a loss. Even when they do it wisely they never get back all the time and money invested. Sure, the insanely rare items keep going up but old-timers already have the semi-difficult records - the bulk of most large collections. And too, as the generations age, new vinyl collectors step up wanting music of more recent decades.

Over the years many vinyl hounds have become deejays and/or fulltime dealers. Of course like all callings, to be successful at either takes single-minded determination and very specific skills.

Joey "The Weasel" Latella was pissed off. Last night he'd driven all the way up to this backasswards town in New Hampshire almost to the goddamn Canadian border, taken a motel room at two a.m., got up at seven so he'd have all day to check out this supposedly great record collection and it was nothing but worthless swill - a complete waste of time and money. The owner had one of those French names – Baribeaubien or something – and talked that dumb Canuck shit. "Dese here rekkids is from deh fifties, ey?"

The Weasel at five foot four, dark combed back hair, squinted up at the big haystack standing before him. He took a drag off his filter tip, shoulders hunched inside a black camelhair overcoat. "Yeah they're from the fifties, chief but they're worth zip! Don'tcha have anything wasn't a hit didn't get played ta death?" He glanced around the garage.

"You mean bad ones?"

"No, I mean – aww fuhgedaboutit!" Between some tire bolts on a cluttered workbench was an aluminum pie tin. He stubbed out his butt, turned to leave the garage. Lately all the leads he'd gotten weren't worth cat puke.

"Ony ting I got like dat is my brudder's rekkid. But I can't sell it!"

"Oh yeah, how come?" Joey was thinking of the long drive back to Providence. At least the coffee the guy's wife had given him was strong; felt like he'd snorted lines.

"It's my brudder's. Even he don' have one no more."

Walking together across the patchy lawn with the plastic tricycle and other kiddie crap to Joey's leased silver Hummer 2, he could feel the Canuck's sudden admiration. Joey loved this freakin' badass money car, loved how people noticed it, were a little afraid of it, like maybe he was Agent 007 and a machine gun was gonna come up from under the hood and blow 'em away.

The late morning sky, an even milky gray, was swollen with potential rain. He shoved his hands into the fur lined coat pockets. It was a lot colder this far up, away from the shore. "What's it called, your brother's record?"

"Gold Diggin' Papa." The big clown was all puffed up, goofy with pride.

Joey forged ahead wanting to get the hell out of there. Then something tugged at his memory. He stopped, turned back, eyes narrowed. "A rocker?"

"Oh, yeah – rock and roll, ey?" He did a mercifully fast air guitar.

"What's his name?"

"Ernie."

Ernie. Yeah. That was it. The rarest Canuck rockabilly ever made! "Ya know chief, I might be interested in puttin' that out on a CD if it's any good." Joey grinned inside, about to win the pot on a bluff. Dumb fuck was a berry waiting to be picked.

The Weasel did recordings 24 hours a day - sent out lists, sold on the internet, set up at the bigger northeast record shows, flew all over the country checking out private collections, jukebox distributors, radio stations and record warehouses. He'd cop for a dime, gouge for a grand with a mouth and attitude seemingly suicidal in a tiny guy. People said it was a miracle he hadn't been stomped into a grease spot years ago. Everyone dissed him, knew he was crooked and fulla shit. But they still bought from him. Why? He'd say because he was better than those squarejohn dealers or big time money auction houses that sat around on their fat asses waiting for good stuff to come in the door. He was onto it before the competition even got a whiff.

His first cardinal rule was Keep Nothing. Soon as a record got a righteous offer it was goodbye. Of course he'd had to discipline himself. Strangle that sneaky little collector vibe got him into the scene in the first place. His great singles went on the highest grade tape to be played back through a killer system whenever he wanted. None of this CD burner shit. His personal taste was for black vocal groups but he made it his business to know everything, especially northern soul. Last Sunday he'd nabbed a big one off the internet for over seven hundred then turned around, hooked a Brit fish and socked him double. Now that the wimpy teen sound was getting hot, he picked up any and all decent, cheapies with oohing and aahing chicks, hoarding them, waiting until they commanded top dollar and all those doofuses who still dreamed of fucking the high school cheerleader would get charged up the yang.

His second cardinal rule: Do Anything To Score - deny he had quantity on a record when he was sitting on 50 or more copies, press up bootleg reproductions using steel wool to subtly add scuffing and label wear so they didn't look freshly minted, tell a potential buyer a record already had a high offer the guy could match. "It's in X's pile right now chief, but it could be in yours." If someone offered more on an already promised record tell the first customer that it'd been lost or cracked. Play a rockabilly guitar break over the phone, lift the needle, play some of the vocal and then put it back on the same break making the listener think there were two breaks. And finally, polish used records with oil and a buffer, covering up the scuffs and scratches with shine, making it look like it'll play clean. No different than those gypsy horse traders who'd paint over worn patches on a broken down nag's coat, stick pieces of pine between loose teeth and then shove a live eel up its ass to make it frisky.

Buyers'd sometimes come over to the house and pick

out a stack. Joey'd price 'em high, and then when the mark'd only want a few, he'd be told "Unh unh, chief. Those are the prices if you take 'em all." That way he knew which records the guy wanted most so he could bump 'em up more. For all these reasons he was known simply as The Weasel. He never stopped living up to his title.

He was a talented little prick too. A pretty good caricaturist, had always gotten parts in school plays having a decent tenor and facility for mimicry. With a trap like memory he'd coasted through his classes until college when he had to extrapolate and draw conclusions Dropping out junior year, he'd gone to Hollywood to be an actor. L.A. looked like a sleepy Mediterranean paradise, until he realized the endless palm trees, manicured gardens and Spanish style homes covered up rows of relentless jaws. You didn't make the right contacts they'd chew you up, spit you out fast.

He wasn't about to starve, kiss ass to get hired or even study along with the other dim bulbs and neurotics. However, the most important reason he quit thesping was that going inside and touching his own feelings made him anxious. For Joey the deep stuff - mental or emotional – remained terra incognita.

Within the year things had gotten so bad his so-called agent was sending him out as a shill for shopping mall sales. His worst gig had been in July portraying a running shoes trademarked teenage space boy character. Outside on the hot pavement, sweating in the silvery suit with jet packs and bubble helmet, he looked like a giant roll-on deodorant. After being taunted by passersbys he went back inside the store to welcome toddlers - ones that didn't scream at the sight of him – first using a booming voice which reverberated within the helmet nearly deafening him. When he spoke down through the small opening under his chin, the resultant mush mouthed pronunciation made him sound drunk. It got him fired.

A week from the date he'd planned to go back east his luck seemingly turned. He was running lines with Alicia Ann Abbott a blonde former homecoming queen from Ole Miss who smiled at everyone she thought might be able to help her career. There was absolutely nothing real about her. Not the southern belle act, the nose job or tit implants her momma had unwittingly paid for. She had an up-and-coming callback for a TV commercial and Joey'd wanted to fuck her, which didn't happen because her date arrived early at the West Hollywood apartment. Before excusing herself to apply makeup for an hour, she intro'd Joey to the Japanese investor as one of her "oldest and dearest friends".

The Nip smelled like money so Joey ran down several schlock schemes for easy kale. Perhaps because it was the year of the Pet Rock or simply because they were about the same height, Mr. Kenji Yasuda bought his act, setting Joey up in an office at Highland and Fountain. Decorated almost overnight, The Promoter Inc. had as its logo a cartoon octopus, tentacles grasping cards labeled MEDIA, TRANSPORTATION, COMMUNICATIONS, REAL ESTATE, etc.

For a fast hustle, Joey smuggled in a Mexican glass blower, stashed him in a side office and went into full scale production of Smog Balls "A Two And A Half Inch Souvenir Of Los Angeles". Their first meeting was with Uncle Hughie, originator of the glass-sided Ant Farm. "You kiddin' me?" Joey asked Yasuda as they waited in the reception area "He's gotta go for it. Diggit: you haveta bend down to get an ant. Smog you can reach right out and grab!" Unfortunately the sample turned Hughie's fingertips a sulfurous yellow and they were ushered out - a major loss of face for Mr. Yasuda.

Back at The Promoter office, surrounded by cartons of paper wrapped Smog Balls, there was further bad news. Joey hadn't done his homework. Transportation of noxious substances across state lines was a felony. Before The Weasel could implement his second more lethal brainstorm – an aircraft carrier for private planes in the middle of New York Harbor - Yasuda withdrew his cash

No more office or dough. Fuck L.A. Joey silver-birded back to Providence and, while working for his connected uncle, came upon a huge warehouse record stash acquired as payment on a debt. He knew old vinyl was worth dough but wasn't prepared for how much. After consulting a couple of price guides he went to his first record meet and made over five hundred, two hundred of which he kicked back to Uncle Fish telling him he'd sold them for all he could get. He started going to record meets regularly. After clearing twenty grand off a load bought for squat at an estate sale he went full tilt into vintage vinyl never looking back.

Four years ago his folks moved down to Delray Beach leaving him their one story house. The mortgage was nothing - almost paid off. As his profits increased, his behavior got worse, e.g. smiling in the face of other dealers before bad-mouthing them behind their backs as ignorant thieves who paid nothing for what they overpriced to the unwary. Exactly, of course, what he himself did.

Now, inside the Hummer 2, its top of the line system

playing a CD comp of rare vocal groups, he giggled. Scored again thanks to Mister Memory! Only thing less useful than a polite hockey player was a record dealer with Alzheimer's. He'd offered the poor jerk a hundred to re-release the 45, promising he'd send it back after re-mastering it. When the lug saw his portable CD burner in the back of the Hummer, he wanted to know why they both couldn't make a copy of it right there. Joey'd high jived him about having to get rid of all surface noise and still "keep the full range". He really hadn't needed the bit about a "new underwater process to remove ticks" but there was something about dummies that fired his imagination. He had to push them, see how much they'd swallow. "Walkin' On A Cloud" by The Confidential Four finished playing. Great song - he pressed the repeat button.

This Baribeau or Babbineaux or whatever 45 was dead rare - only one other clean copy known to exist. He'd make three, maybe three and a half heavy. Might even treat himself to a nice hotel in Manchester or better yet Boston. It wouldn't cost. He always carried a jar of cockroaches when traveling. Fed 'em on bits of paper. Before checking out he'd call the front desk and complain. When the manager knocked, Joey'd dump roaches on the bed and let him in. They always comped him. Even did it when he pulled the stunt in four star restaurants. It finally got around in record circles. On his radio show Kevin had dedicated "Stompin' Roaches" by Wilmar Walker on Phillips to him. A few days later the Weasel called him.

"What's this with the cockroaches?"

"Thought you'd like the song."

"Oh yeah? Wouldn't be because I'm supposed to use 'em to get outta payin' bills?"

"Really, how do you do that?"

"What're you, taping this?"

"I tape everybody famous."

"Tape this then." And he'd slammed down the receiver thinking that's one I owe you motherfucker.

Of course there were many more who owed Joey one. Every east coast collector and dealer had stories about how they'd been taken. It was in his blood. He'd been taught since he was little. His father, a card sharp, ran a mob bookie joint on the Hill which fronted as a wop bakery. When Joey was five his old man would hold up a dime in one hand, a nickel in the other, ask which one he wanted. Every time he picked the bigger coin he got slapped. After he'd learned, the old man intro'd him to Three-card Monte and the shell game. In a few years getting the better of anyone could practically make the little bastard's dick hard.

Cutting through the bleak New England countryside of rocks and woods, he imagined himself getting lucky in a local bar. Picking up a big blonde he could climb. He knew some good Boston taverns where lonely secretaries dropped in after work. Joey wasn't ugly - didn't have say a big Roman schnozzla – but wasn't handsome either. Nice looking and non-threatening as long as he kept his grating personality in check and didn't come on like a Guido version of Mickey Rooney on the make.

A black curvy arrow on a yellow diamond sign flashed by on his right. He rounded a sharp turn. Only some fifty yards ahead, from a hidden side road, an old pickup with red wood slatted back end turned bumping onto the highway. Joey's reflexes were fast but he was going at least thirty over the limit. He stood on the brakes burning rubber, the driver veering off onto the narrow shoulder as Joey shot past his rear bumper, clipping its left end hard enough to head the pickup over the embankment and halfway into the dark icy river below.

Headed into another winding turn the Hummer's front wheels hit a patch of black ice and started to fishtail. Joey steered into the skid barely able to bring it under control and keep it too from going over the edge. Cautiously he again accelerated wanting to put as much distance between himself and the fucking Yankee dimwit who'd nearly wrecked his baby. The Hummer was built like a tank. Probably all he had was a little ding on the front fender. Take minutes to tap it out, touch it up. That deer he'd hit up here year and a half ago had made a much louder impact and caused only a few scrapes.

Actually he should be thankful the yokel had cut him off. If he was going any faster when he hit that ice it could've been him freezing in the drink. He almost crossed himself then smirked. Might as well kiss a fuckin' St Christopher's medal like all the other stupidos. When it was your time to go you went. Nothing gonna change that.

The adrenaline rush had made him hornier than ever. He thought again of trying to get lucky in Beantown. Naw, screw it. Variety was fun but he had somethin' steady. Didn't have to chase it like a dog. Besides, sooner he got home, sooner he could move this bad boy over the phone. He'd treat himself and his babe to baked lobster dinners in Bristol, drive her back to his place for a real workout. He speed-dialed her on the cell, ready to disguise his voice, pretend it was a wrong number if her Jabba The Hut sugar daddy answered.

Dee Dee Verona was small and dark. She had a sharp foxy face and fucked like a little mink. Joey appreciated that he didn't have to do much to bring her to a boil. The fact that she was living with Fat Danny Silvestriani kept her from getting too possessive. And because the guy only wanted hand jobs and head while wearing diapers, it made her grateful for a normal fuck.

What a time they'd had last month! Fat Danny had taken her to Vegas for the weekend but got an emergency call right after checking in. His crazy mom was running amok in a ritzy Miami rest home and poor pop couldn't cool her out. The fake British accented manager wanted her gone yesterday. Dago panic! Dee Dee's meal ticket had to fly out right away. The suite was paid through Monday. Danny had told her to enjoy herself until he, hopefully got back Sunday. The cab had hardly pulled away from The MGM Grand when she was on a pay phone to Joey telling him what had just gone down,   for a second there she'd thought he'd been faking Danny's father's voice.

He got on the first flight out of Green. Vegas was hot in more ways than one. The only apparent glitch was that Silvestriani had an associate take her around town Saturday afternoon. Joey spent the time checking out used record stores in his rented little T-bird. Guess what? Every one of them sucked - common shit in okay condition and semi-scarce shit in shit condition. Disco albums, 8 tracks, cheezoid repros - guck.

That's when he got the idea to open his own store right in Lost Wages itself. Idiot hordes streaming in every day, aching to throw away their wads, big weekend long oldies shows in the hotels and him with zero competition - at least for now.

Uncle Fish could make it happen but since he thought about as much of Joey as he did a plucked nostril hair something would have to change his mind. And even if Joey had an idea that would change it, which he didn't, he also didn't have much time. Sooner than later another weasel was going to spot that sweet slot in LV and fill it nice and tight.

Fat Danny had a double decker on the East Side. Outside in the Jacuzzi, hot bubbling water up to her neck, Dee Dee nibbled on a diet almond pignolata, sipping a glass of Lacrima Cristi. Two weeks ago Danny had taken her to St. Maartens, the island still recovering from the last hurricane and priced accordingly. Now she picked up the ringing cell phone with a small tanned hand the same color as leaves off the backyard maples. "Yup." Over several generations even Italians had picked up some Yankee speak.

"It's me. I made a nice little score up in Zululand an' I'm maybe two and a half three hours away. You potty trainin' him tonight or what?"

She laughed, pushed the wet fingers of her right hand through her black medium length retro-shag. "We're goin' to some amateur play he's got a relative in."

"I'd rather play with you."

"Tell me." As he complied the tape recorder inside the anonymous tan Camry parked in front of the house picked up every word.

At the same time, inside the blond wood, raspberry upholstered courtroom, Fat Danny Silvestriani in a charcoal three piece, muted striping to reduce his bulk, argued his current client's innocence. A grad of Suffolk University - "Where'd you go to school?" "So fuck you!" - where most of the area's mob lawyers matriculated, he was amongst their most renowned and visible graduates.

"The whole thing Your Honor, was an unfortunate accident. Mr. Giattino had no wish to harm his wife." He gestured to the stringy blonde with a bandaged neck who glared at the big uncomfortable defendant, thinning short brown hair emphasizing the ox like forehead, now puckered in worry.

"He was only trying to fix his stereo. Anybody not a certified electrical engineer knows how frustrating it can be – all those wires an' outlets. So what happens? He loses his temper and throws the screwdriver through the window. He didn't even see she was backin' outta the driveway. Only thing he's guilty of is bein' a fugarazz'."

White haired Judge Connell, practically the last old time Mick left in R.I.'s legal system, frowned, leaning into his mike, "A what?" He'd been thinking about his grandson. At the start of the week the stupid kid had stolen a school bus.

Danny shrugged. "Fugarazz'. You know Your Honor, a guy trying to fix somethin' gets so mad he breaks it more. So okay, even though they had a little domestic spat before she left, he was in no way gunnin' for her. And frankly, Your Honor, if he intended hitting Mrs. Giattino in the neck by throwin' a screwdriver out a window and into a moving car he shouldn't be wasting his time in construction; he oughta be in the Olympics." As he spread his arms widely, signifying completion of the defense, his beeper sounded, forcing him to fumble for it, ruining the gesture's graceful arc.

After Connell dismissed the charges, Danny congratulated his client and went outside to dial the private detective's number. "Mr. Silvestriani?"

"Got something?"

"Yeah, and it won't make you happy."

Big Mike Giattino, in windbreaker, black sweater and jeans, stood in line waiting to get his release papers. He was shot through with nervous relief. No jail time was good. A big lawyer's fee was bad. A divorce was both. When he walked out of the office his wife was facing him across the hall, people moving past her. They stared at each other tears in their eyes. Then began moving closer, making others walk around them and finally in the middle of the polished hallway, wordlessly embraced, she practically disappearing inside his huge arms.

Ensconced in his maroon Range Rover, Fat Danny watched the two of them emerge onto the courthouse steps and kiss under a slate grey sky. Shaking his head at the un-knowable, he pressed the button for the front passenger window, hoisted his bulk halfway across the seat and, sounding his horn, gestured to Big Mike who spoke briefly to his wife and hurried down to the curb. "Mr. Silvestriani, I can't pay you right this minute but –"

Danny held up his hand. "What're you doin' today? I mean now that you're a free man?" Over Mike's shoulder he could just see the wife's head. She looked concerned.

"I gotta pour a foundation in Warwick (pronouncing it "Warrick") and then a buncha us are gonna distribute a truck-load of Thanksgivin' turkeys for charity. We done it three times annually awready."

"You owe me and you're buyin' turkeys for the moolies?"

"Naw, naw we get 'em cheap 'cause they're all disformed. You know, like with only half a wing or somethin'? Anyways they're already bought."

"Okay then. How'd you like to have my bill disappear so you don't pay a penny?"

Hours later, afternoon visibility growing dim, Joey The Weasel pulled up in the drive next to his grey shingled house, He turned on the front door light, hauled in a few 45 boxes from the Hummer before going out to throw the neighbors kid's chewed up soccer ball over the peeling wood fence. Tire marks were on his lawn. He frowned - looked like some juicer had jumped the curb, except that the ruts continued around back. He followed them. There was a dark mass in his basement window. He walked over, reached out his hand. What the fuck? Cement - hard and dry.

Down in the cellar he unlocked his record room door. The opening was solid cement. He picked a crowbar out of a tool chest and raised it over his head. Then he put it down. There wasn't any point. His entire inventory had to be wiped out. That fat fuck must've gotten onto him. A lot of people had a hard on for The Weasel but they were mostly small time mooks or powerless record geeks. It had to be Silvestriani. Joey hadn't the juice to safely retaliate. The fat fuckwad lawyered for too many heavies. He'd have to get compensation from someone else.

CHAPTER FIVE

Marlene awoke with a clanging headache. Last night came crashing through her fragile wall of forgetfulness; the pain pin-wheeled, intensifying.

En route to her mom in Dedham she'd stopped at Twisters, her former Boston area bar. It was like she'd never left. Her high school friends, Kimberly and Jane were at a table nostalgically half sloshed on Rusty Nails, bitching about their husbands. After requisite hugs and assurances on how great they all looked, Marlene said she was visiting her mother on a "family matter". Around nine thirty, an old boyfriend of hers, Buddy Jay, came in to celebrate his divorce. He was buffed, tall, with glossy animal pelt hair. The boyish charm helped not only sell homes but indiscriminately bed women as well. A year ago his wife, had tried to kill him with a pair of scissors.

Buddy slid right into the conversation, admitting that all men, he included, were total pricks. Jane said she appreciated his honesty. Kimberly laughed. Feeling him looking at her Marlene was silent. An hour later when he went to the men's room, the three burst out laughing as they realized each one was admiring his retreating ass.

Half an hour later, Jane and Kim split not about to misbehave with someone in their immediate circle. Besides it was pretty clear Buddy was focused on Marlene, now legitimately whacked. When he slid his hand onto her thigh and told her how she'd always turned him on, her feelings shut down and her body got up and went home with him. In the middle of their second fuck she'd passed out.

She now had blurry action slides of some of their more adventurous positions but no memory of pleasure or satisfaction. It scared her to realize how angry she was with Kevin to do such a thing. Buddy was dead asleep beside her. She slipped naked out from between the covers, wrote THIS NEVER HAPPENED in ballpoint on the back of a used envelope, put it on the pillow.

Suddenly she wasn't sure he'd used a condom. None were in the bedclothes. Bare assed, she searched under the nondescript bed hoping he wouldn't wake up. None there either. She was beginning to panic when she located one in the bathroom's wastebasket lying limp on top of some used tissues. Impressed by his neatness (Kevin would have tossed his on the floor), she gobbled two Advil from the medicine cabinet, downed them with orange juice and slipped out of the small spotless apartment. Driving over to her mother's, she wanted to call Kevin and forgive him. It would be like forgiving herself. For the moment though, she wasn't up to it. In her heart she knew that getting back at someone you love is more self-damaging than anything else. If only it had occurred to her last night.

That same morning Kevin awoke to the feel of starched hospital sheets. He felt himself with his right hand. His head was bandaged, chest and left arm in a hard plastic cast like an insect thorax. One morning Kevin Dougherty woke up and discovered he'd become a cockroach. There was intravenous tubing in front of drawn white curtains on his right side. To his left a window admitted watery sunlight. The throbbing in his head worsened as it all came back. The Trans had to be totaled. His auto insurance was paid but the deductible would more than wipe out the remaining savings account. Good thing he and Marlene were paid up with the health insurance.

A Vietnamese nurse came in dressed in white uniform, flat rubber soled shoes. He smiled at her with some effort. "How am I?"

"You have broken arm, broken ribs, two contusions. You be awrigh'."

"How'd I get here?"

"Ambulance. You ver' lucky."

"Yeah, right."

She nodded. "True. One quarter point more alcohol in blood you go to jail. How you feel?"

"Dizzy. Thirsty."

"Okay I be righ' back."

"Hey! Can I get my cell phone?"

She went to the night table, opened the drawer, took out the cell, "All your stuff here. Wallet. Whatever in pockets."

Marlene's mom handed her daughter the phone. "It's Kevin."

"I don't want –"

"He's in the hospital."

She looked at her mom weirdly, said his name tentatively into the receiver. Joanne went back to making a hooked rug at her loom.

Soon as Marlene hung up she was smacked by twin tsunamis of guilt and sympathy. Her knees went watery and she had to steady herself against the wall. She'd betrayed him with that asshole Buddy while he was seriously wounded.

Joanne glanced over at her daughter, went back to her weaving. "You didn't cause the accident. He did."

"I overreacted. We should've gone to see Howard and talked it out. I mean, I know he's an addictive personality and it is the first time he's ever lied to me."

"Yeah, that you know of. Marlene honey, you had – have – a right to be pissed off. Guy like him, holding onto all that kiddie rock n' roll, it's obvious he doesn't want to grow up."

Every time Marlene heard that line it sounded too simple. Half true. Since her mother had stopped helling around and developed a weary cynicism she considered herself mature. Maybe she was just burnt out.

Still only using a good mind to amass old record info did seem wasteful. Too bad he wasn't as passionate about something more lucrative - or didn't allow himself to be. Joanne was looking at her – reading her – like when Marlene'd come in earlier after leaving Buddy.

"Mom, I didn't give him a chance. Even if he had bought the record he would've sold some stuff from his collection. It wouldn't have been such a big deal."

"Well," declared Joanne pitilessly, "now he'll have to do it anyway." She focused on her work-in-progress, took a drag off her cigarette. "This needs another color but fuck it."

Blitzed on Percodan, Kevin lay on his back half-watching the TV suspended above his bed. TMC was showing "The Dark Corner", a 1940's black and white film noir. Drifting in and out of consciousness, he dreamt his own variation.

EXT. DAY – NAMELESS CITY STREET

Twanging John Barry-type guitar music on the soundtrack. A handsome MAN (Kevin J. Dougherty) runs urgently towards the CAMERA holding a 45 rpm record in one upraised hand. He runs into CLOSE UP breathing hard. A TITLE CARD appears:

RECORD DETECTIVE
A Kevin J. Dougherty Production

Starring, Written & Directed by Kevin J. Dougherty

INT. OFFICE – NIGHT

Flashing neon lights through a slatted venetian blind stripe a wall covered with framed records. Behind a scarred wooden desk KEVIN listens to Carl Perkins' "Boppin' The Blues" on a small portable. He pours himself a beer, raises a slice of pizza from a delivery box to his lips. The phone RINGS.

KEVIN
Record Detective.

INT. RICH LIVING ROOM – NIGHT

A beautiful BLONDE in tight shorts and halter top is on the phone. She stubs out a just lit cigarette in a huge glass ashtray.

As they speak we CUT between them.

                    BLONDE
Thank God! Listen, I need to find a record that starts...
                    (sexy voice)
"You are my baby, you are my dream."

                    KEVIN
You know the artist or label?

                    BLONDE
        No.

                    KEVIN
        Year?

                    BLONDE
        It's – pretty old.

                    KEVIN
Why do you want to find it?

                    BLONDE
That's my business.

                    KEVIN
                    (sighs)
It would be. Okay. I get $400 a day plus
expenses.

>   That includes any records I may have to buy
>   during the course of the investigation.

INT. BASEMENT – NIGHT

A thin HATCHET FACED MAN is tapping into the conversation. He punches a button on a cell phone.

>   BLONDE'S VOICE
>   Is that usual?

>   KEVIN'S VOICE
>   I may have to pass myself off as a record
>   collector.

>   HATCHET FACED MAN
>   You were right. She's hiring him now.

EXTREME CU OF SHADOWY MAN

Wherever he is it is very dark. Only the lower part of his face is visible as he answers in a soft, deep voice

>   SHADOWY MAN
>   Good. We're that much closer to retirement.
>   (sinister chuckle)
>   And, in a sense, so is he...

Kevin opened his eyes. A nurse was shaking his shoulder. He blinked at her. It was time to change the sheets.

Days later Marlene unlocked their apartment. Cradling a bag of groceries she put down her suitcase and turned the wall light on. The windows were black with night. A stack of mail was on the coffee table collected by Francine, the Mister Disc portable player still on the floor. Feeling a small pang, she bent to pick it up and noticed a 45 next to it halfway out of its paper sleeve. Carefully she put them both beside the mail and gave an involuntary shiver. The empty lit up apartment creeped her out. She hadn't yet visited Kevin in the hospital – afraid how he might take her important news, knowing no matter how he reacted her life would be permanently changed.

She checked to see if Herkimer the Hermit Crab was functional, noticed his last vanilla wafer was almost gone and dropped another into his terrarium. As the crab investigated she picked up the remote, turned on the TV, put the groceries away in the kitchen, dumping spoiled vegetables and milk in the trash. Voices from a talk show followed her into the bedroom. She unpacked her suitcase on the unmade king-size, transferring freshly washed folded clothes into the appropriate drawers. Back in the living room she sat on the couch, went through the mail and paid a few bills. She thought of booting up the computer, doing some graphics homework, but instead started channel surfing trying to find a program to distract her from the vague but persistent fear that was tightening her chest.

A few days before his release Kevin got up in the night amidst the breathing and snoring of other patients, Careful not to bump his cast, he walked down the pale green hallway to the brightly lit deserted bathroom and took a one-handed piss. He washed awkwardly, glancing up at his still-battered face in the mirror. It stopped him. He stared intently at the person looking back at him who might speak in a voice he wouldn't recognize. When the silence began buzzing in his head he looked away, afraid that he was splitting off, maybe having some kind of actual breakdown.

Back in bed he remembered the last time he'd seen his parents, before his mother had died. They'd lived in an early 20th century row house on Olney Street up the hill from the poor black section, just far enough into the west side for shabby gentility. He saw himself with his dad under a summer sun at the backyard barbecue, both of them sipping Tullamore Dew and swigging bottles of beer. His mother, dark haired, smiling, came outside, screen door banging behind her, carrying her familiar potato salad with chopped bacon. She was second generation German Catholic. Her immigrant parents, stained glass window makers, had settled in Boston. As they ate she commented on the weather, how well her garden was doing and asked if she'd put too much vinegar in the potatoes.

Now retired from the Chrysler dealership, his father tried to sell himself on the idea of boating up the Amazon or going on safari in Tanganyika. He'd been such a consummate salesman for so long he could unwittingly convince himself of practically anything using the same approaches and arguments that had succeeded with customers. Rarely did anybody, even his family, see the actual man beneath his good humored exterior.

As they ate, Kevin reminded them of that time they'd gone to the Cape where Thomas was spending two weeks at a Catholic camp. Walking along the deserted beach in the early morning, the three of them had happened on the skeleton of a recently burned automobile, his father immediately identifying it as a '68 Firebird.

They spoke comfortably, overlapping each other, absorbing all that was being said. His mother talked of the present, his father planned for the future and he reminisced about the past. It now appeared to him, lying there, looking up at the shadowy ceiling, that since the other two time zones had already been claimed, he'd taken up residence in the third as much as by default as by inclination.

His mother had smoked. His father still smoked and drank. Several times during his boyhood, Kevin had to rouse the old man from semi-unconsciousness in a bar and once in the family car after he'd pulled onto the shoulder and was sleeping it off. Always there were fights with his mother when his father brought Kevin home. Their boozy relationship persisted into Kevin's adult life. They got along best when alcohol dissolved their differences but denied them deeper knowledge of each other. During these bouts and usually at Kevin's request, the old man would be encouraged to reminisce about his childhood in Pittsfield, Mass during the late 1920's.

Even as a boy Kevin's dad was an obsessive car nut who liked visiting his father's auto paint shop. Each job, before lacquer, was done by hand - a long, painstaking process. The old man learned every make and model as well as countless custom automobiles. He had a trick memory and never forgot a license plate.

At that time traveling salesmen often came through small towns leaving free samples on people's porches. One sunny day Kevin's dad and his pal Teddy Finn discovered everybody's porch had a new chocolate candy. They went down the block gorging on what turned out to be flavored Ex-Lax. After the two had made a mess of themselves, Kevin's father's dad rode him into town to see the doctor. It was an early summer evening and they passed a row of the finer homes set atop a hill. Kevin's dad noticed a Kissel parked in front of the McAlister's stone steps. Gunmetal grey, it had been customized so that the headlamps were raised off the front bumper about ¾ of the way up the grill. In the 1920's there were many independent car makers whose product was assembled from individual auto part manufacturers. Their customized output ranged from only a few cars per year to hundreds and even thousands.

Next day, at breakfast, rehydrated from the Ex-Lax disaster, Kevin's dad heard his parents talking about the McAlister's house being robbed. "Oh," he said "I didn't think that Kissel was theirs." He ran down a complete description of the vehicle including plates which his father relayed to the sheriff. The thieves had already left the county, but flushed with success, returned within a month for another snatch job and were nabbed immediately. His father became the neighborhood's Junior G Man.

Kevin loved this story. Muzzy with drink, he always felt close to his father whenever it was told. But such incidents were infrequent. By his mid-20's, Kevin gave up trying to really know his parent, accepting that the outer personality had long hardened over whatever had been underneath. Like a lot of sons he'd promised himself not to become his father but, although he didn't juice as heavily and do the Irish motor mouthed Lee Tracy bit, essentially he figured they were just two Mick salesmen. He pushed booze while the old man had pushed cars.

Dougherty senior was now living in a small apartment on a retirement fund, gradually losing his memory. Outside of holidays, Kevin seldom saw him. It was too depressing. Pretty soon he and Thomas would have to put him in an "assisted living" facility.

Kevin had his father's square face, high coloring and thick curling hair but his mother's blue eyes. Thomas had their father's brown eyes but his mother's oval face, pale complexion and fine straight black hair. As boys, Thomas was as serene as Kevin was troubled. Secure in his faith, he kept his small room immaculate, neatly stacked comics of Marvel superheroes on a bedside table directly underneath a framed picture of Christ.

Across the short hallway Kevin would lay on his cluttered bed, skeptical thoughts of God eroding his already shaky beliefs. Alarmed at their son's apostasy, his parents took him to Father John whom they thought "brilliant." Kevin had expected some subtle Jesuitical thinker who would dazzle him with proof of the Deity's existence. The priest merely tossed an ashtray at him and, when he caught it, claimed it proved he had free will and could decide to believe in God anytime he so chose. His parents nodded, smiling. See how simple it is? Kevin said nothing, resentful at such a cheap bullying trick. Of course it was bullshit. A conditioned reflex like that actually proved the absence of free will. Father John was just another salesman wanting to close a deal. A few months later Kevin left the church.

Now his brother was happily married, one daughter, another on the way and weathering the stock market. Kevin was surviving a near-drunken automobile smashup. Little if anything had changed.

Unable to sleep, he accused himself of following in the footsteps of his friend Artie Webster. The two had met when Kevin started hitting record shows back in the late 1980's. This intense, gangly guy with the short prematurely grey hair was at everyone's table trying to see their records first, his bored kid tugging on his pant leg always wanting to split. Artie, like Kevin, was a vinyl omnivore, but had been into it longer and deeper, possessing legendary rockabilly, blues and group 45's. And he had other interests. When Kevin first visited the small one story house in Pawtucket, Artie was reconnecting with his Jewish roots, heavy into some Hassidic mystical bag.

Nobody had answered the bell. Not surprising since he could hear The Johnny Burnette Trio's frantic rockabilly version of "Lonesome Train" blasting from inside. The door was ajar. Three orthodox Jews in flat black hats and payes sat cross legged on the bare floor listening so intently they didn't notice him. Finding Artie in the kitchen firing up a joint he asked how come the Hassidim were into such extreme goyische redneck shit, Artie winked, took a hit, held in the smoke and said in a choked voice,"Man, they dig the contrast."

The two began bombing around together, trading with other collectors, hitting thrift stores and meets outside their immediate area. In the meantime Artie picked up, in rapid succession, a chiropractor's license, a night gig playing rhythm guitar for a house band and a runaway heroin habit. Kevin, who had driven him into some of the worst areas around Providence and Boston, to score dope, became curious about the rush. Artie finally agreed to shoot him up. Then, at the last minute, H cooked, ready to be slammed, Kevin looked from his bulging arm vein to the hypo and passed. Artie took the hit instead and zonked, asked Kevin what changed his mind.

"I guess I don't dig needles." Flippant but true. Compared to say, smoking opium, shooting was raw. The biggest reason, however, was his addictive personality. At that eleventh hour he had became scared he would like it too much.

To finance his snowballing habit Artie got involved in an insurance swindle, inventing chiropractic patients who supposedly suffered injuries riding the city's bus line. When the heat came down, his partner, an MTA claims adjuster, rolled on him. After his indictment, his wife divorced him and was granted custody of their son and baby daughter. The court forced him, pre-trial, to go to a Methadone Clinic.

Out after a month, he quickly sold his 45 collection (a lot of it to Kevin) to afford an attorney and gigged as a bouncer in a Providence strip club above the 95 interstate. One of the girls, a black Latina named Tawni, moved in with him and got pregnant. While his court case dragged on for several years they had twin boys and lots of screaming fights. One night she stabbed him with a kitchen knife and drove the kids back to her parents in Philly.

Artie, finally convicted, did a few years inside. Kevin ran into him just after he'd been released. He looked like fuckin' Papillon, head almost bald, a dozen rings in each ear, a bunch of pins in his tongue, speaking in a hoarse rasp about his guru who could fly into trees. Kevin hadn't seen him since.

Yeah, Artie was taking the express train to hell but maybe Kevin had boarded the local. Lying in the hospital, he got a chill across his shoulders. Silently, he apologized to his friend for making him into the bogeyman – he knew Artie was more than that – but if it scared his compulsive ass away from self-destruction so be it.

In group therapy, Kevin had been told that because people created what happened to them they were responsible. They also needed to forgive themselves for the bad, reward themselves for the good. But, he now thought, if he was so self-punishing, so full of poisonous guilt that he'd nearly killed himself, would forgiving make a difference? What new ways would his subconscious devise to destroy him? Only after doing enough penance nightly, torturing himself with thoughts of possible alcoholism, drug addiction, suicide and insanity, was he able to sleep.

Nervous and excited, Marlene sat in the hospital lounge, twisting about in an orange plastic chair every time a patient entered. How would she react if Kevin were subtly disfigured? When he finally shuffled in, self-conscious in the dopey striped robe, face only slightly lumpy and discolored from the accident, she got up and, vastly relieved, kissed him on the mouth.

Seated under the florescent lighting, amidst the constant susurration of other patients and visitors, punctuated at times by a sharp word or querulous yelp, they were awkward with each other. She asked how he was. He was okay. He asked how she was. She told him the same, privately steeling herself to give him the news, thanking God they were able to tell when it had happened. Imagine worrying the whole time if the baby was going to look like Buddy Jay.

"I'm pregnant."

He was silent for a long time. Sweat popped out on her upper lip. Finally he spoke. "Would you be here if you weren't?"

"Kevin, I didn't leave you."

"Coulda fooled me."

"It was like being with John but instead of women, with you it's records. I needed to get away."

"So we're back together?"

"Kevin, we're going to have a baby, not a divorce!" She shook her head. "Jesus God!"

Kevin flashed on all those sad little houses he'd driven by with the scattered kid's toys out front. Eventually he'd be in one too, unable to take off record hunting when he wanted. Life was taking measurements of his ankle before fitting him with the old ball and chain.

"Hello?"

He raised his head and took a breath – a baby. He was scared shitless. "Look, uh, I'm gonna straighten up. No more crazy buys. I'll even go through my collection and sell off, you know, whatever I can live without."

Marlene rolled her eyes, craned her head around. "Medic!"

Kevin laughed, looked at her green eyes, full lipsticked mouth. "I miss you."

"Me too."

"I mean I make these records so important. They're just records."

"Not to you."

"Yeah, I know. They're uh, compensation for something I think I don't have'."

She stared at him. "You've lost weight."

"So would you. Food they serve here."

"I brought you a survival package."

"Good."

"There's a whole bunch of record lists came in the mail."

"Toss 'em," he said gloomily. "I get outta here I gotta be sellin' not buyin'."

"The insurance for the Trans Am came in."

"How much?"

"Little under a thousand. It's enough for a down payment on a five year old Jeep Grand Cherokee." Kevin opened his mouth to protest. "Hold on! I know an SUV doesn't exactly jibe with your bad boy life style but we're gonna need a safe car for the baby. You can drive the Mustang."

Kevin sighed. Robin's egg blue with a wussy 206 engine but it was better than looking like a total squareass in a suburban shmuckmobile. Besides a cassette player it had new disc brakes so he wouldn't have to drive a zillion yards behind anyone on the interstate. "Guess I'm lucky just to have a car."

"You are." He could tell she was pleased at what looked like the beginning of a late-blooming maturity.

The morning Kevin was to be released they removed the chest cast leaving the one on his left arm. Marlene picked him up in the '97 Jeep – a forest green V6 with tan interior. In spite of himself, Kevin was impressed by the comfortable seats, sun roof and a system that played both cassettes and CD's. He named it The Sexy Mom Car, reached over and started squeezing her thigh tops with his right hand; Marlene giggling, slapping him away as she drove.

They went straight home to change before going out to eat but didn't even get to the bedroom. Kevin, stiff, out of shape, hampered by the arm cast was still ready to rock while Marlene, desiring him as before, because of the pregnancy wanted to cement their relationship anew. They came together as if magnetized, he undressing with one hand, she helping him, getting her own clothes off as they hungrily kissed. Devouring each other on the couch in a breathless, gasping flurry, she used her right hand to support his left shoulder as he entered her, trying to take it slow, not making it, thrusting faster and faster until it was over only minutes after it had begun.

Winded, happy, reassured at the familiarity of each other's bodies, they were preparing for another more leisurely session when he noticed the lone 45 next to his portable player – The Jamies "Summertime, Summertime" on Epic. He kissed her bare shoulder. "I thought you didn't like those guys."

"Mmm. I don't."

"Then why would –"

The doorbell rang. At first they tried shushing each other, pretending they weren't there and spoiled it by giggling. Marlene yelled out for whoever it was to wait. They scampered about, struggling into cast off clothes, suppressing their laughter, Kevin leaving his shirt out to hide his hard on.

"Shall we come back?" Francine called from the hallway right before Marlene opened the door.

Wiley ran in wearing a Batman mask and cape, "Hey, Kevin! Look at me!"

Francine was apologetic. "He was dying to show him." She nodded at Kevin's cast. "When does that come off?"

Kevin in stocking feet ran fingers through his disheveled hair. "Next week." He looked at Wiley. "It's Halloween already?"

"Thursday!" Wiley examined Kevin's cast. "Does that hurt? Can I touch it?"

Francine had gotten a whiff of the room's heavy sex. She began apologizing, this time in earnest, trying to pull her son away. Wiley broke free and handed Kevin a sheet of computer printed paper. Kevin read it, Marlene resting her chin on his good shoulder.

The Record King
by Wiley Rogers

Once upon a time there lived a Record King. He liked records so much his house was full of records. So he sold some records. But they gave them back because they were bad . So he gave them his good records. So he only had bad records. Then he gave bad records to the people who liked them so they gave him good records and he lived happily ever after.

Kevin laughed out loud, told him it was perfect. Marlene said it was a good fairy tale. Kevin said he was going to put it on a tee shirt, sell it to all the record collectors and split the profits with him. Wiley beamed, eyes shining and asked if they would get rich. Kevin said absolutely not. As Francine was pushing him out the door, Wiley asked Kevin if they could go to the new Batman movie tomorrow. Kevin said he'd try.

It was dark when Marlene took him to dinner at Al Forno. Driving down Wickendon Street in Fox Point, Kevin automatically glanced out the passenger window at the used record/CD shop. It was still open, a warm yellow glow in the window. Even though his vinyl-starved synapses were bucking with need – he hadn't scored a 45 since that fateful Sunday – he forced himself not to ask her to stop. Marlene saw the mini-struggle, rewarded his decision with a smile. He shrugged. "Aw, they never have anything good anyway."

They parked, walked through the brisk air into the restaurant early enough to be seated at a candlelit table for two in the long glassed-in room that looked out on the moonlit sparkle of the Providence River. Marlene had dolled up in that slightly 1940's retro look Kevin liked – auburn hair in a snood, rich silk print dress with padded shoulders, deep red lipstick. He wore a white bulky cable knit. It'd taken them a while to get the left sleeve over his cast.

He ordered a bottle of Pinot Grigio. Marlene had a saffron seafood bisque and warm lobster salad. Kevin had curried corn crabcakes before an entrée of linguica with littlenecks and hot scotch bonnet peppers surrounding garlic mashed potatoes. She helped him get the clams out of their shells. Over coffee and a cinnamon gelato Marlene told him a dealer had called. He was sorry to have heard about the accident but was Kevin going to be selling anything from his collection?

He laughed. "Musta been Joey the Weasel. Remember I told you about when I lived in that apartment building on Broyard? One of the tenants overloaded the wiring and started a fire? Gutted half the building but I was on the other side so it just knocked out my hot water and electricity. People were standing around front with clothes and stuff, fire trucks all over. Five minutes after it was on the morning news the Weasel calls me up wanting to know if the Elvis Suns survived!"

"So are you gonna sell anything?"

"Well considering we're gonna be parents." Choking on the word, coughing to cover it up.

"I hope you meant it when you said you'd take Wiley to the movies tomorrow. It'd mean a lot to him."

"Yeah? Okay."

"So what'll you sell?"

"Well, I can't do any show 'til the cast comes off but I'll comb through stuff in the morning." She looked at him with a cocked eyebrow. Solemnly he crossed his heart.

Like most men, Kevin held with the Aristotelian view of the world and not the Platonic. You were what you did. He might be able to minimize his habit but not go a full terminado. Collecting gave him an outline, a character. Without it he felt his edges would blur, his image dissolve. If he were some comic book superhero he'd implode in deep space, particles spinning off into black, howling chaos.

The wine made them needful and affectionate. Soon as she drove them home they went right up to the bedroom and slowly made warm love, a streetlamp's lambent shine falling across their languid movements on the crumpled sheets.

Later they lay entwined; her head against the right side of his chest, breaths and heartbeats blending together, sweat sheens evaporating. Muscles deeply relaxed, pubic hair damp in the sheltering darkness, lulled into happiness and absolutely content, their minds temporarily at peace.

Like all lovers such fleeting jewel-like moments felt like the true reality and all else distraction. Yet when they had returned to mundane consciousness, this would seem only an intense pleasure and later yet when they inevitably had a fight, it would be recollected as a biological trick to propagate the race, keeping them from realizing how miserable they could make each other. But for now, they fell asleep wrapped in each other, seeking comfort and warmth - two small animals in a deep dark wood.

Next morning, a Sunday, Kevin awoke sated and happy

hearing Marlene on the phone. She came into the bedroom, hair brushed, fresh makeup, dressed in her left bank existentialist drag - Capri's, flats and a black and white striped jersey. "That was Francine. Can you take him to the movies this afternoon? I'll drive you both."

Kevin nodded and sat up, running his fingers through his hair, yawning. Inside the cast he felt only a slight healing itch on his left arm. She kissed him warmly and went back to the phone. He flopped back onto the pillow thinking that without her he'd probably be just a lonely fantasy-ridden bachelor.

Later, showered, wearing his white terrycloth robe he sat with her at the chrome and Formica boomerang-patterned table with matching cherry red plastic seated chairs. They ate a typical Rhode Island breakfast: coffee, chorizo and onions in scrambled eggs with Portuguese sweet rolls. Kevin was a native. He put celery salt on his hot dogs, vinegar on his french fries, ordered cabinets not milk shakes and never gave a direction that didn't have at least one doughnut shop as a landmark, On the other hand, he was no great fan of johnnycakes, even less so of Indian Pudding. Coffee milk had been forced on him when he was quite small and he hated it.

In keeping with the rest of the décor, the kitchen's walls were hung with old menus and food posters, a mammy memo pad holder and framed pizza box top from Pepe's in New Haven. The vintage yellow Chambers gas stove had pride of place but was only used half as much as the microwave. Magnets and snapshots were scattered over the refrigerator's front. On top was a Mr. Peanut plastic peanut butter maker. Nuts were fed into a hole in the figure's top hat; you turned the handle and peanut butter squeezed out from the side of his head, dropping onto a plate fused to his shoulder. Neither of them had ever tried it.

He was watching her do the cleanup when she laid a new concept on him. "I didn't want to get into this earlier but the only place we can make into a nursery is your record room." She tensed her shoulders.

Kevin bristled, willed himself to relax. "I thought the baby was gonna stay in our room."

"Only for the first month."

"So where do they go? It'd be a real hassle to put 'em in storage."

She sighed. "The living room I guess. Up high. We should start baby proofing as soon as possible so we're not pressured to do it later. The more records you can part with now the better." She checked the black and white Kitty Kat wall clock replica with shifting eyes and tail. "You can start going through them anytime. I told Francine two o'clock."

He nodded, seeing his immediate future crowded with constant projects from alien worlds. It was like they had become a little coastal town threatened by a huge hurricane forming out in the Atlantic, forced to wait until it came howling onto shore and blew them right out of their socks. He got up, leaned in and kissed her on the cheek.

Still wrapped in his robe, he opened the door to the record room and padded inside. For seconds he just stood there stupidly. The 45 shelves around all four walls were empty. So were those that had held 78's. Below them the larger LP spaces were only half full of reissues. The blood pounded in his face. Maybe it was a joke – a little extra zinger to punish him for almost blowing the four grand. As soon as he questioned her and saw her genuinely puzzled expression he knew he'd been hit.

Instantly he was plummeting down into a dark elevator shaft, flailing blindly before crashing to the bottom. He moved on leaden legs into the living room and collapsed onto the couch. Marlene was saying something but the words didn't reach him. Everything was muffled and unreal.

From time to time he had wondered if, one day, he might wake up and no longer care about records, just as others had spontaneously put down the bottle. Could the blinkered obsession suddenly vanish, a newly washed expanded vision trained on some greater reality? But if his eyes had indeed been covered all these years, the bandages had been ripped away too quickly. His sight was blurred by loss and defeat. In an instant the depressing feeling that he had no real identity without his possessions turned him into The Invisible Man.

Frightened, Marlene watched him leave her, sinking farther and farther out of her reach, she standing there powerless to help. Once before she'd experienced this black mood when he'd missed a major record collection because of one wrong digit in a phone number. It turned out to be one of the biggest New England scores worth over a hundred thousand dollars. The owner was intending to take it to a dumpsite. Before Kevin could get back to the person who'd tipped him, some dealer had heard about it, driven up and hauled it away. Even though that had put him under for a week at least he had talked to her albeit negatively.

Now he was dead silent, spooky as a zombie. To stifle the unsettling fear that she might be forced to have the baby with no emotional support, she buried herself in studying the computer graphics course and reading her preparatory childbirth books.

In the bedroom, covered up, he'd gone to sleep in a fetal curl, a lost cause. Marlene took Wylie to "Batman And Robin" herself. She told him Kevin was "sick" thinking her supposed lie was actually the truth. Neither enjoyed the movie that much. Wylie was disappointed not to be with Kevin, Marlene just couldn't concentrate. Her stomach was in a knot wondering how he'd be when she got home.

As she'd feared there was no change. He ate some of the dinner she'd prepared, then went straight back to bed. When she came in that night he was lying there staring up at the ceiling. She wanted to scream at him only mastering her frustration by reminding herself that the blow he'd suffered was, for him, enormous. Wanting to communicate with him but not knowing how, she said his name.

"What?" His dead tone put her teeth on edge.

"Don't take this the wrong way," she began hesitantly, navigating through imaginary landmines, "but this could be a sign."

A bitter smile twisted his face. "You mean from God? Punishment for all sins past and future?"

"No, not punishment but something telling you to get out of collecting for your own good. I mean disasters can be instruments of positive change." There was a long pause. "What do you think?"

"I think that's superstitious bullshit. Next you'll be asking your mom to throw the I-Ch'ing."

"Well it couldn't hurt. You just have to be open to –"

"That shit's just Rorschach tests. Everybody interprets it the way they want. It's too scary for people to think there may be absolutely no reason for anything."

"Well, but –"

"I don't want to talk about it anymore." He'd already accused himself of somehow causing the theft same as he'd done with the accident. But the first had only caused physical harm, this was annihilating his identity. The idea that self-destructive impulses had helped bring it about was too painful to entertain.

He got up, went into the living room and turned on the TV. Marlene knew he'd sit numbing himself with old movies until dawn. It was over an hour before she was finally able to fall asleep.

Sometime next day he was back in bed wearing shapeless clothes, trying to drug himself with more sleep when the phone rang. He answered without thinking, "Yeah?"

"Kevin? Joey Latella. You were in the hospital, right?"

"Yeah."

"You don't sound so good. I wake you?"

"No."

"Oh. Okay. Listen, reason I'm calling, don't think I'm some fuckin' hyena or anythin' but after what you've been through I thought you might need to sell a few biggies outta your collection."

"Why?"

"Well you know, word is you got a kid comin' and no job. Not tryna pressure ya y'understand, just bein' realistic."

"Yeah."

"All I'm askin' if you do decide to unload any goodies gimme a shot." Kevin was silent. "That's all man. Sorry to disturb ya. Good luck." Kevin heard the click on the other end. He replaced the receiver in slo-mo as if it contained nitroglycerine. Then he sat down on the couch staring off into space with the hollow feeling of a stuffed animal without any stuffing.

CHAPTER SIX

After a few days of enforced silence, Kevin began to emerge from the dank recesses of his mind and make plans. He had scratched a little symbol in the dead wax of most of his records. This proof of ownership was done to prevent switches in case he traded or sold something that the recipient later complained about. He could then be sure the copy in question was really his. Most civilians would think his paranoia needle permanently stuck in the red. For a record collector it was simple survival.

He considered putting the word out by phone, then 86'd it. He might unknowingly call the thief who could obliterate his ID. Whoever had done this, unless they'd sold everything overseas or across the country or simply added it to their own collection, had probably moved some locally. If he went to all the shows, meets and flea markets chances were he'd eventually find one of his 45s. Also he'd be driving Marlene's twirly girly Mustang. No one would see him coming.

He pushed back the worst of his depression, plotting and planning, counting days until the removal of his cast. As the week wore on, Marlene adopted a noncommittal pleasant attitude towards him. They exchanged practical information but little else. However, she sensed that his emotional freeze had partially thawed and so bided her time until he once again could give of himself.

Friday morning she drove him to the hospital on her way to work. The cast was removed. No problems. His bones had knit beautifully. The doctor gave him a ball to squeeze. Told him using light weights would build his strength even faster. Kevin thanked him, went home in a cab and drove off in the Mustang.

The closest old record store was a few blocks north of I-195 on Wickenden. Same one they'd passed on the way to Al Forno. A weathered brick front with used CD's, videos, 45's and LP's. Kevin pushed through the door into the small interior. The prematurely grey owner, listening to one of his pals spout off, nodded at him. The shorter man, in tan cap and windbreaker, glanced over once, still talking. Left hand squeezing the rubber ball inside his car coat pocket, Kevin absently flicked through the common title 45's in wire racks.

"What I'm sayin' here is that these kids oughta be made to work inna mills like they did before the labor laws – that'd stop 'em from destroyin' private property an' takin' drugs an' everthin'."

"Jesus! Whyn't you just put 'em onna chain gang?"

"C'mon. Workin' conditions are a helluva lot better now than inna 19th Century."

"How'd you know seein's you never left it?"

"Just wait till one of 'em fuck's with ya. Then see how liberal you feel. I gotta go."

"Hold on. I'm gonna grab a smoke."

Kevin followed them out the door. The short guy crossed the street to a white late 80's Chrysler sedan covered in rust spots.

The owner lit up and leaned back against the side of the entranceway. "Hey Jack! How much you pay for all those polka dots?" Over his shoulder, Jack flipped him the bird, and opened the door. It squeaked. He got in slamming it shut. The owner watched him drive away, "Too bad. I was hopin' it would fall off." He turned to Kevin. "Haven't seen you in a while."

"Yeah. Reason I came by, a friend of mine got his entire collection ripped off an' I told him I'd ask around, see if anybody local got offered anything."

"What kinda stuff?"

"Mostly 45's - 50's and 60's. Rare stuff. All kinds."

"Nobody's come to me with anything decent for freakin' months."

Kevin gave him his number on a folded piece of paper. "Well if they do gimme a call. My friend will definitely make it worth your while."

A Brown University student type, scraggy goatee, jeans and grey hooded sweat shirt with one of Coop's naked fat devil girl designs, walked up the sidewalk, stopped before them. "Got any Tom Waits?"

The owner took a drag, not looking at him, "Maybe." As the young guy went inside, he wearily flicked his butt over a parked car and followed, turning back to Kevin and rolling his eyes. Look at the wannabes I gotta deal with.

Next stop was Denny Arcaud in Woonsocket. Lead guitar for the neo-rockabilly band Denny and The Demolitions, he had the highest pompadour in the Northeast keeping its artful construction a secret. Barber to many local musicians, he always knew the latest gossip.

Denny lived in a garage apartment in back of a twelve unit building. He finally answered Kevin's knocks on the weathered door at the top of the wooden stairs. Stooped and noodle thin in a red and black reindeer sweater from either a Goodwill or garage sale, he started groaning, "Oh no! I meant to tell you to wash your hair before you came over. There's no hot water. Pipes're screwed up."

Denny was perpetually broke. So were his appliances - tape deck, TV, refrigerator, you name it. Last haircut, he'd just done a major salvage job on his yellow rusted-out '60 Caddy Eldorado. And if he wasn't bitching about his ride or getting fired from some hair salon it was not getting booked in a good club. Two years ago the Demolitions were supposed to have played New York – some big rockabilly festival at Coney Island. The standup bass player came down with projectile vomiting and they had to, excuse the expression, blow it off. Denny never stopped bitching about missing his big chance, begging Kevin to talk up his group to Norton, a label that did a lot of reissue and retro stuff. Kevin didn't really know the owners. He'd leant them a 45 for one of their New England rockabilly comps years ago. Probably wouldn't even remember him without checking the "Thanks To" section in their liner notes.

Denny's space was like a cramped low rent version of his own. Ugly anonymous 1950's prints, a busted up checked convertible couch, some scarred Swedish Modern chairs. He was madly in love with the blonde blue-eyed actress Anne Francis. Pictures of her from "Blackboard Jungle", "Forbidden Planet" and "Honey West" were tacked up on the walls. His red Fender Jaguar was in the corner propped against a black Peavey amp - surprisingly out of hock.

Kevin, having shampooed and rinsed off holding his head under the sink's cold water spigot, was seated under the tiny kitchen's bare bulb, covered in a wrinkled black plastic smock. While Denny snipped away he repeated the story of his "friend's" ripoff.

"I know t'is guy?" Denny had a slight Canuck accent.

"No. He keeps a low profile; doesn't want people knowing his name. But if you hear anything he'll take care of anybody leads him to who did it."

"Wish I knew. I'm hurtin' here. T'is guy was supposed to give me a job at his new salon. I been waitin' to hear from him two weeks. Always busy, won't take my calls. 'He'll get back to ya.' You know what I'm sayin'."

"So – nobody come to mind as a possible?"

"Well, only guy I can t'ink of is what's his name. Real tough? Shaved head. Earrings. Tattoos everywhere. Did time for robbery. Anyway no way he could've done it!"

"Who're you talkin' about?"

"You know, ey! He used to play rhythm for Brain Fever 'fore they moved up to Boston."

"Artie Webster?"

"T'at's him."

"It wasn't robbery. It was insurance fraud."

"Yeah, sure. The firs' time."

"Naw, he wouldn't rip someone off. What do you mean he couldn't?"

"You mean you didn't hear?" Denny crossed himself. "I t'ought everyone knew what happen'."

"Tell me."

"Okay. After he come out and sold his collection he goes out on Christmas Eve to rob a Cumberlan' Farms, screwed it up and got arrested. And while he was inside waitin' trial, he'd call up Don Mackey, you know, the band's lead singer, tell him he wasn't goin' back to prison 'cause t'is was his third offense. Anyway, right before trial he fell off his bunk – maybe on purpose - fractured his arm. T'ey put him in the prison hospital. So when he heal up a couple of weeks ago t'ey ready to take him back to jail but he grabs t'is cop's gun, shoots him in the stomach, jumps in the police car and takes off up 95 chased by all the other cops. They corner him jus' south of the state line so he takes the gun, sticks it in his mouth – an' blows his head off!"

Kevin had frozen in his seat. "What? Artie Webster is dead?"

"Oh yeah. Oh yeah. Sure t'ing. And here's the weird part." Denny chattered on. It was just a story to him. "The band was playin' that night at Barrington's right offa the interstate, ey? T'ey were on a break an' heard the sirens an' saw the lights go by an' wondered what was happenin'. Move a little to the right for me. That's fine. Anyway I t'ink they should've known the guy was, you know, suicidal."

"Why? Just 'cause he sold his collection?"

"Well, yeah. I mean t'ink about it. What else did he have? Hey, sorry if I upset you. I jus' t'ot you knew."

Kevin sat close to shivering in the unheated Mustang, Artie's death making him cold inside as well. There was an older sister but he'd never met the family. Artie'd told him both parents had tattoos on their arms from being in the death camps. They owned a few apartment buildings. Kevin could call up and say "Hi. Artie was a good friend of mine." But what comfort would that be? They'd always thought their son was crazy. Probably think Kevin was too. Even if Artie's young son remembered him, he'd be one of those guys he'd associate with record shows he'd had to endure. Probably best to do nothing.

Not long after Artie's divorce and before he'd been sentenced, Kevin had taken Marlene over to the little apartment Artie rented from his parents. Kevin'd been there many times. Uncovered floors, beat up couch, two chairs, a record player and stacks and stacks of teetering 45's all in stiff green sleeves with Artie in their midst, either straight or doped up, digging them on an old Caliphone player.

That July night, when he'd opened the door, two hard-looking skinny Vietnamese guys were standing behind him, see-through short sleeve shirts over scoop neck tees, gray baggy pants. Soon as they split, Artie thanked Kevin and Marlene for saving his life - same as someone might thank you for returning a wallet. He went into the bathroom to fix, came out smooth and serene, charming and smart. Marlene had liked him. She'd also made Kevin promise never to bring him to their apartment.

Sitting there in the Mustang's chilly interior, Kevin wanted a cigarette for the first time in years. Before quitting, he used to bum Artie's. Shit. Half his collection was Artie's. The fuck who'd ripped him off robbed them both. Maybe Kevin had hastened Artie's end by buying his 45's. Well, someone would've. At least he'd been a friend. What the hell was all this? Record Collector Ethics 101? Shit had happened and the guy was dead. No more hassles for Artie Webster. He squeezed his eyes shut, wiped away a tear from each.

Even though he'd been a self-destructive maniac Artie had burned with honest enthusiasm. Not like those soulless robot collectors who need to own every Beatles variation, or some slick trophy hunter bragging about how much coin he'd blown on the framed pre-war Robert Johnson blues 78 hanging in his glassed in corporate office. Fuck them. For Artie records weren't dilettantish artifacts. They were hits of life energy short-wired into his system which, had for a while, successfully balanced the death current of smack.

Two weeks passed. After making the Boston show and the one out in Chelmsford, Kevin hit the Taunton, Mass flea market, a depressing jumble held in a defunct movie drive-in. The days had gotten bone cold. Sellers in knitted caps displayed their junk on blankets and rickety card tables. Buyers huddled in groups on the tarmac holding Styrofoam cups of bad coffee. After next month the place would shut down until spring. Two summers past it had gotten briefly famous. A diminutive sniper, hidden in a van's rooftop cargo carrier, managed to shoot three people with a scope rifle before some of the less oblivious collectors realized that the whining past their ears wasn't being caused by mosquitoes. The shooter, a dealer in WWII memorabilia, had purposely only wounded his targets. In custody he said he'd wanted to awaken people so they'd stop wasting time on useless material things and seek salvation. After reading that quote in the papers the diehard buyers only shrugged. Most figured copping a rare item for cheap was as close to heaven as they were going to get.

Kevin walked down the rows of cast off items, squatted down only once to go through a messy stack of sleeveless 45's. These flea markets were for bottom feeders not high rollers. Even an average score got more unlikely with each passing year. He'd come only to see one specific dealer.

Taffy, a dyed blonde with a stiff face like an Indian Head nickel, no hips, okay tits, and slitted, bruised-looking eyes was one of the few sellers to knowingly bring out valuable records. Today she/he pulled up in the familiar 1960 two tone Dodge La Femme, sliding out of the swivel seat wearing white running shoes, black lycra stretch pants and a heavy Pepto-Bismal pink knit sweater. Taffy's sex was in constant debate - a swishy guy or a dyke acting fem?

Billy Borchak, a round little gnome with a bad wig who collected r&b girl groups, swore he'd seen him/her at NYC's 57th Street show in the early 90's asking a dealer to hold a copy of The Primettes on Lupine - the Supremes first 45 – and promising to come back in an hour to buy it. Billy went to take a leak, found Taffy blowing some john against the men's room wall. After three tricks she had enough to buy the 45 for $150 - a good NYC story but, considering the source, possibly apocryphal. If it was true Taffy had scored big. These days an original in mint brought up to $800.

Transsexuals in record collectordom, known ones anyway, were a definite rarity. Even the legendary Reg Smythe, a London guy who blasted Howlin' Wolf 78's while rigged out in ball gown, earrings and makeup was only a weekend cross dresser.

Taffy was talking to Wayne Barrett – a tall balding collector in glasses who knew everything about vinyl as opposed to music. He flattened warps, removed skips and corrected sticking.

"Capitol used a reground plastic as opposed to virgin," Wayne's monotone held a ripple of excitement. "But they used a very superior grade of reground so this came out pretty well.

You'll hear a slight "Huhhh" at the beginning – not quite a heat swish – and then it goes away." He handed Taffy a sleeved 45 he'd de-warped over a candle flame.

Taffy pulled it out, examining the record, "Great. How much?"

Wayne held up a long finger, "One dollar." All he ever charged.

Taffy's 45's were all inside fresh white paper sleeves which in turn were inside clear protective plastic sleeves and genre separated by stiff white cards. Kevin went through BLUES, VOCAL GROUPS and ROCKABILLY . Three quarters through GARAGE he came upon The Pilgrims' "Plymouth Rock" on The Note – a local Massachusetts label. He pulled it out, checked the dead wax and saw his mark. Like many collectors, he had a weakness for records from his own area.

He replaced it, went a couple of aisles over until he found a worn Louisville Slugger lying among beat up appliances and doll heads. He paid two dollars to the old man in a yellow and black check woolen jacket and returned to Taffy's table, confused about the ethics of laying waste to a woman even if she had once been a guy. Instead he held the bat over her table and picked up his 45. "Did you rip me off? Lie to me and swear to God I'll bust up every one of these fuckin' records."

As he raised the bat Taffy's hand shot out and seized his wrist - hard. Surprised at his/her strength, Kevin wavered then pushed against it. For several minutes they stood straining. Kevin smelled something familiar, a perfume favored by an old girlfriend. "Are you wearing Opium?" Taffy nodded. "Where'd you get this?" He flipped the 45 up, now unaccountably sure he/she was innocent of the theft.

"Put it down." Taffy spoke in a slow husky voice, made

even lower from exertion. Kevin looked into his/her eyes. They were hazel. He'd never been this close to Taffy before and could see the pitted skin under the makeup. He relaxed his arm. She/he released his wrist. The bat clattered onto the tarmac. "I got it from Jambasian's list."

Kevin frowned. Pete Jambasian, one of the biggest dealers on the eastern seaboard, was an eccentric recluse but didn't have a thief jacket.

"How do you know it's yours?" Kevin pointed out his mark in the dead wax. "You think he stole it?"

"I'd rather not say 'til I'm sure. You get anything else from him?"

"At his prices? Honey, you have got to be joking. Far as I could tell this was his only bargain."

$150 was written on the sleeve. "What's the best you can do?"

"Sell you back your own record?"

"It's not your fault you bought it."

"Well, I wanted to make something, but seeing as how - I've got at least ninety into it. Make it ninety-five so I'm not out postage."

"Thanks." He took out the bills from his wallet, handed them over. "Do me a favor. Only you, me and whoever took this knows about it. Keep it that way, okay?" Taffy nodded. "Good." Thinking only a few of his records had been stolen it was less likely she/he would blab. He rubbed his wrist. "You work out?"

Another nod, "I've been beat up in the past. I don't really care for it." Taffy fished out a Kool, torched it with an old Checkered Demon Ronson, took a drag, blew out a smoke plume and grinned. "You looked like a cop breaking up a speakeasy in those old Prohibition photographs."

That evening Kevin and Marlene returned from their LeMans class and heard an excited phone message from Chris Andrews. He'd found one of Kevin's records at the Pasadena City College Record Meet. The seller had forgotten he already had a copy after buying it off Jambasian's latest list and was looking to unload it.

Kevin, too preoccupied to continue their conversation, fell into silent thought. Marlene asked him if he wanted a drink, got no answer. She sighed, went to the bamboo bar and made them Navy Grogs, crushing the ice with a spiked plunger fitted over a tall blue glass. Kevin put on one of his remaining reissue LP's to hear Boyd Raeburn's band deconstruct "Over The Rainbow". Marlene brought over the drinks and raised hers, "Only one more month and then no more of this for me."

Surrounded in shifting orchestral colors, lost in imagining how an encounter with Jambasian would go, he didn't reply. "I SAID I WON'T BE ABLE TO DRINK AFTER ANOTHER MONTH!" Kevin looked up at her blankly. "That's right! I'm upset! You've been catatonic for a whole week! You go to the classes with me but you don't really want to! You never really listen whenever I bring up anything about my pregnancy. You grunt once in a while but you don't really care do you? I'm in this goddamn thing alone! You can't really feel for another human being! Sometimes you do me a big favor and try to pretend. And even then it's a piss poor imitation. You just love your stupid overpriced fucking records because they don't ask anything of you! Well how the fuck could they? They're just things!" She tossed her Navy Grog into his face, burst into tears and ran into the bedroom.

Kevin looked through his dripping eyelashes at where Marlene had been standing. He blinked stupidly. Was this just her or one of those "mood swings" pregnant women were supposed to get? Something warned him she wouldn't want him to come in and try to make it all right. He sighed. Soon as he got back what remained of his collection he promised himself to be more attentive.

Pete Jambasian was a 60 year old, 300 pound plus ex-dope fiend turned Jehovah Witness who lived with his ancient mother, rarely going outside their house in Riverdale, New York. Some believed she kept him fat so he couldn't leave home even if he'd wanted to. Others figured he just didn't dig a world that had gone so far past the 1950's. Whatever the reason, he wallowed in his basement rec room absorbing vinyl much as that other New Yorker, Nero Wolfe, used to inhale orchids in a penthouse apartment. He even had his own Archie Goodwin – Billy Lanear, a fast talking legman, sent out to check possible loads while Pete networked on the phone and scoured record lists searching for underpriced sleepers. Nowadays however, when Billy called in asking what to offer a seller for some vocal group 45, rare or not, Pete no longer felt the old excitement. He had sold just about all of them anyway. What really gassed him was laying out bread for a new piece of equipment bringing the sound that much nearer to absolute true fidelity.

Today he was washing down a hot cherry pepper laced hero with a plastic quart bottle of Dr. Brown's Cel-Ray as he listened to The Orioles sing "Till Then". The mint minus red wax 45 played on a belt-driven Technics three speed 103 turn table fitted with a Shure V15 type 5 cartridge and hyper elliptical stylus. The signal traveled through both a Wellburn Lab Moondog preamp and vacuum tube amp and thence by way of specially coated gold wiring into a pair of English Lowfer one way speakers encased in custom made cherry wood cabinets. Besides the $900 recording the whole audio rig cost around $10,000.

The squawk of a buzzer shattered his aural cocoon. Like a prehistoric cave bear or Lovecraft's Cthulu monster he bestirred himself to lift the arm with one pudgy finger as he hit the intercom with another. "Records," he said tiredly. Having dealt with gibbering nuts and pain-in-the-ass collectors for so long the mere contemplation of any unknown interaction was enough to sap his psyche.

"I'm Dennis," said the voice through the tinny speaker, "the guy with the vocal group stuff?"

"What vocal group stuff?" Pete spoke guardedly with subtle scorn, black eyes suspicious under heavy brows, balding under a swirl of salt and pepper hair.

"Jerry G sent me. I gotta move my family an' he said you'd give me half of book. I got a couple of boxes here."

"Jerry sent you?"

"Yeah, he gave me a couplea names. You wanna take a look or what?"

Pete shrugged. Jerry wouldn't do him any real favors. He'd probably creamed the guy's stuff. Still, Jerry didn't know soul groups too well. Why not? Pete pulled a string of capacolla out of his teeth and hit the buzzer. Kevin strode into the room wearing his black leather car coat over a navy blue sweater, gripping the baseball bat. He spied Pete through the maze of wall to ceiling record shelves, turntables, speakers, amps, tape decks, computer monitors, printers and crisscrossing wires.

"Remember me?" He ducked under two liana-like cables, walked over to Pete, imagined grabbing him by his tent like sweatshirt, hearing the seams rip. The effort to control his anger made his voice low and without inflection. "Where're my records, thief?"

Pete goggled up at him. He raised a fat white finger, "Careful, man. I got a bad heart."

"Then gimme an answer! Where are they?" Kevin was almost shaking with an effort not to lash out with his fists.

"How should I know?"

"'Cause you sold one of 'em!"

"What? What'd I sell? And who are you?" Kevin told him. "Oh yeah, I recognize the name. You're a customer."

Holding the bat, ready to lay waste, Kevin squatted, unzipped his duffel bag with one hand and came out with "Plymouth Rock". He shoved it in Pete's fleshy quivering face. "Okay. I've had that a few times! How's it yours?"

Kevin pointed out his mark. "Now where're the others? Or do I start smashing up the room?"

From upstairs came a voice like ripping cloth. "Peter! Who's down there?"

"A customer!" Pete yelled back not taking his eyes off Kevin. If he told her the truth the old lady might have a seizure. Also he didn't want the law around. Not with all the undeclared income.

"Well hold it down for Chrissakes!"

"Ma! Don't swear!" He turned to Kevin. "See what you're doin'? Be nice. Besides I didn't steal your records."

"So how'd you get this?" Kevin put both hands against the chair and leaned in close enough to see the greasy sweat on Pete's forehead

"Lemme get over to the computer!"

Kevin stood staring at the wide white face, pissed that he couldn't have just beat the shit out of this whale. He straightened up. "Do it."

Pete grabbed his chest, breathing hard. "I could have you arrested entering a place of business under false -"

"And I could have you arrested for receiving stolen goods. Go on!"

Pete moved himself crablike in the wheeled chair over to the monitor. Neither spoke while the computer booted up. The screen came on and downloaded the programs. Pete double clicked on a 45 icon. A box appeared. He typed in the group's name, song, label and number, hit ENTER. The record appeared three times on the screen.

"Okay. Last copy had a small tear on the label's B side –"

"Yeah, mine – see? Where'd you get it?"

"Hey! You know how many records I get in a month? It coulda come from anywhere. At a meet, through the mail, in a trade." His shoulders raised slightly. "Who knows?"

"You make any big buys recently? "

"Last week at the Allentown show I got a guy's whole table for half price - mostly groups. This record wouldn't have been in that load."

"Before that?"

"Oh yeah. A whole collection."

"Whose?"

"I don't know. Very weird. Guy wouldn't give his name. Had this kid front for him. He was goin' through a divorce an' wanted to sell so's his wife wouldn't get her hands on it. Same problem Marty Schulenberg had."

"Yeah, under the condition he could buy it back after the settlement."

"Not this time. Guy wanted to dump it. Cash only. Soon's the kid came down with everything in a panel truck the guy called me and we worked it out. Great stuff. I didn't get it free either."

"Anything big?"

"Plenty."

"Like?"

"Lemme think...uh... Pauline Rogers on Pink Clouds. First issue."

"I had that. You sell it?"

"Like a shot. Two grand."

"Fuck."

"Yeah. Most of the biggies are gone. And don't swear."

"How about the truck?"

"Light colored, maybe white but beat up. Young kid driving had a baseball cap turned around, pants halfway down his ass, wearing one of those shiny zip up jackets with a name on the back."

"What name?"

Pete shrugged. "Ball club I think - maybe the Sox. Van had Massachusetts plates."

Kevin smashed his fist down on a desktop. Pete looked at him, waiting for more. Kevin raised his hands placating. "Okay, okay. I'm a little – lemme see if you got any more."

A half hour later they'd found five with his mark that were waiting for payment which Jambasian sold back to Kevin for less than half. Some rare ones remembered from his collection weren't logged in the computer and must've been sold earlier. Jambasian gave him a printout. Said he'd call if the guy should contact him again. Pretty unlikely. Whoever it was had to be someone Kevin knew or knew of. Someone whose voice he'd recognize. Most of the northeast collector/dealers had heard about his accident which meant the rest of the country knew it so the heist could have been masterminded by a Professor Moriarity type from just about anywhere at all.

"Hey," said Pete, as Kevin was leaving. "You come in here threatnin' to bust me up and my place of business, callin' me a thief with no real proof, upsettin' my mother. Okay, okay. I understand the pain you're in but even with all that, and in view of what has happened here, not to mention my willingness to assist you with your loss, I believe you owe me one thing."

"What?"

"An apology."

"I'm sorry."

"Even before I accepted God, no matter how messed up my head was, I never stole anybody's records."

Soon as Kevin left, Pete popped a Stress Tab, washed it down with a fresh Cel-Ray Tonic from the mini-fridge. He was shaken, hadn't gone through any of this Wild West craziness since the old days. Put him in mind of that hassle back when he'd been using. In a drugged haze, he'd sold a rare group piece to Del Ackley after first promising it to Ritchie De Marco. Ritchie had come over same as this Kevin nut, hauled Pete's ass onto a Greyhound all the way to Philly. They waited four solid freezing hours on Del's front lawn in the dark so Ritchie could make him give up the record. The first Magic Notes on King - the hard one.

Pete belonged to the first generation of East Coast vocal group fanatics – a mix of junkies, hoods, preppies and average Joes who had come of age in the late 1960's at Time Square Slim's shop in NYC. Group harmony was their world. With only taste and rudimentary guesswork as to value, they swapped more than sold, making new discoveries daily, wild dope and booze parties often ending in threats and punch outs over vinyl.

Collecting then was fiercely regional. National lines of communication did not exist. Small labels from other parts of the country were largely unknown. In the early 1970's the Lucchesi Brothers from Northern California drove a station wagon overflowing with West Coast 45's to New York. Pete and others still got jazzed recalling the resulting feeding frenzy.

"It was like Columbus discoverin' America!"

"Our own personal Gold Rush!"

"They came outta the car an' records were falling onta the street – Rhythm, Aries, Christy, Lucky – we'd never even heard of these labels!"

By the mid 1970's Pete, only slightly overweight, kicked the needle and started overeating, traveling everywhere making legendary scores from jukebox distributors, radio stations and warehouses. A mail order business begun with his duplicates was mushrooming, cleaning up. Had he held onto only half of the better things he picked up back then he'd now be living off them. Even today, with all the new competition, he did steady business. He had the rep, vinyl came unbidden to his door and Billy, his legman, occasionally sniffed out a hidden stash.

He knew his days were numbered. Already half a dinosaur, he refused to go whole hog into the exploding soul/funk market. For him it was too big, too changeable, too – foreign. When his old customers stopped buying, he'd stop selling. Eventually all the big money records would be in collections. Dealers would have to line up after a collector died. When there was no more sense of discovery or excitement left he'd pull the plug.

Now, entombed in solitude, he played a 78 of The Five Crowns on Rainbow, concentrating on the voices weaving through the melody, miraculously holding it all together. He was back where he'd always been happiest – at one with the music.

Kevin drove south on the Henry Hudson past the George Washington Bridge. The broad river on his right had an ice crust near the banks. Sun was bright in the sky, buildings standing out crisp and clear on the Jersey side. He navigated through downtown Manhattan pot holes banging over manhole covers, boxed in by a snarl of taxis, produce trucks and town cars, then rumbled over the Brooklyn Bridge and shot down Flatbush to Avenue L.

Out of the Mustang he hunched his shoulders against the slicing wind. A modest red brick collector shop, one of the most popular in the three boroughs, had "Dusty Discs" in chipped gold lettering on the display window. Whitened by countless summer suns, doo wop LP covers were taped against it from the inside.

The front door bell jingled as he stepped into steamy warmth. Several guys in winter wear filled the small space. Jerry G., skinny, grey frizzy hair, wearing his usual white shirt - a pack of Marlboros beside him on the counter - nodded as if he'd last seen Kevin a week ago instead of several years.

"I" by the Chantels was on the turntable.

"Hey, uh, Jerry," piped up a squinty, rabbity looking guy, "th-this's rare, right? An' uh it's a g-good one too - r-real good."

"Yeah, book's way off on that one." Jerry spoke in a back of the throat whisper.

A short stocky crew cut collector in a worn brown leather bomber jacket snorted as he looked through a small stack of 45's on the counter. "On that and practically every other girl group." Amongst fans of the genre "The Kreiter Price Guide to Vocal Groups" was always referred to, positively or negatively, as "The Book".

A nondescript blond guy, round face, pale blue eyes, stopped jingling his pocket change. "Comes with another name on a different label that's even harder you want it mint."

Without looking up at him Crew Cut asked, "So Del, how many you ever have mint?"

"Maybe four. Couplea weeks back I traded a weak Vg to Garza."

"For what?"

"Infascinations."

"On styrene?"

"He thought it was styrene."

"Clean?"

Del shrugged, "A solid double." Meaning Vg++ the grade right under Mint.

"Jesus! Guy needs to change his prescription."

"Forget it," a big gravel-voiced, black-haired character growled. "His glasses were any thicker he couldn't lift his fuckin' head."

When The Chantels finished singing Kevin raised his

voice. "Hey! I'm Kevin Dougherty from Providence. Somebody stole my collection. I got "KD" scratched in the dead wax so you can tell 'em if they turn up around here." He turned to Jerry. "Okay if I leave my number with you?"

"Yeah, sure. You know who did it?"

"Not yet, but you get any in I'd appreciate a call. I'm gonna be sending out a list of some of the better groups that were stolen."

"Hey!" said the black-haired guy. "I know you. We did a few trades onna phone. I'm Bobby Ciccone."

"Yeah, I thought I recognized your voice."

Jerry laughed,"Who could forget it?"

Ciccone tilted his chin at Kevin. "So what'd you have?"

"Some heavies on the big labels and a lotta super rare one-offs,"

"F'rinstance?"

"Uh...Marvelettes on How-Fum, Montclairs on Sonic." Someone whistled. "They were my two rarest."

"What else?"

"Little Sonny Day And The Clouds on Tandem." Kevin's tone was bitter. It had been a top favorite.

"Seriously fucked up," said Ciccone, "but great."

"What's it worth?" someone asked.

"Mint, I dunno." He turned to the crew cut guy. "Gary, whatya think, eight? Maybe nine to the right guy?" "The Right Guy" always meant that hoped-for buyer who'd pay top dollar for a record that didn't appeal to all tastes.

Gary snorted. "Nine? Yeah, with a gun."

Jerry G. nodded. "He's right. I moved a double plus last year for five to a guy had it on his want list."

Ciccone turned back to Kevin, "So, what else?"

"Uh …Billy Stafford on Jab, Terry Evans on Kayo."

"Those're groups?" asked someone.

"Fuckin' right they are," said Ciccone, "both L.A. So's the Sonny Day who by the way is actually Donnie Brooks singin' on nitrous oxide or some shit. You from L.A. originally?"

Kevin shook his head. "I trade with a guy out there."

"Whatta the other two sound like?"

Kevin made a "go ahead" gesture to Ciccone.

"Ahh, the Jab's rare but too bluesy for me. Kayo's great. Bass never quits. I tried doin' what he does an' turned blue. Fuckin' nigger musta been on intravenous. Jerry, you remember when I brought that record in here maybe two, three years ago an' we're playin' it an' De Marco comes in? I didn't know him then. He wants my record. Says if I don't sell it to him he's gonna pull a gun on me. I tell him 'You little pussy-faced fuck I was in the Tet Offensive. Pull a piece on me I'll shove it up your skinny ass!' " He laughed a rasping laugh that ended in a smoker's cough. "Now we're pals. Eh, happens like that sometimes. Guys're gonna kill each other one minute, next minute they're best friends."

"You gotta be the only friend that psycho's got!"

"Hey talkin' about rip-offs," said Del. "Any o' you hear about Krasna?" Henry Krasna was a big vocal group collector with a nice job, pretty wife and kids. Nobody answered . "You guys are too fuckin' provincial. It was in all the Philly papers. He got caught embezzlin', just missed goin' to jail."

"No shit? What'd they do? Let him resign?"

"Yep."

"He's gonna have to make restitution, right?"

"Oh, yeah."

"Y'know, I was wonderin' why I ain't heard from him."

"So he might haveta go inta his collection to make good?"

"Doesn't he owe all the dealers big time?"

"Twenty six hundred to me from all that stuff I got in Austin," said Gary. "No, twenty four. Month back he sent me a whoppin' two hundred."

"Too bad," rasped Ciccone. "What you make sellin' onna phone, if you were legit you could claim a loss."

The next day Kevin wrote out fifty rare records that had been in his collection and weren't on Jambasian's printout. He emailed, faxed and sent it by mail to top of the line collectors and dealers with a rep for absolute honesty – not a long list. The cover letter asked if any of the fifty were bought in the last three months.

His former place of employ, The Penalty Box, was close to a post office. After dumping off the letters, Kevin headed over, parking as usual in the strip mall's lot. The low clouds looked like cotton full of dirty water, a cold wind rising. Inside, behind the bar, the owner, Larry, stood close to a thin big titted brunette. Two male customers sat on barstools at either end nursing drinks. The blonde hostess/girlfriend wasn't there - probably history. Eminem rapped over the speakers.

Tall and rangy, Larry had thinning pale hair and a slab like face scarred from a few years of pro hockey with the Bruins. He intro'd the sharp nosed woman as Monica. She flashed Kevin a quick smile, then turned intense dark eyes back on Larry like she was figuring out the fastest way to eat him. Over a couple of drafts, Kevin asked if there were any shifts open. Larry shook his head, the small grey blue eyes pained under colorless brows. A late spot might be available at the end of the month for three nights a week. He shrugged, apologetic. Kevin forced a smile, said he'd take it if and when. Both were relieved to stop talking about it. After a few more minutes of forgettable conversation he split, mumbling a "nice meeting you" to Monica. She barely nodded.

Outside the cold wind had grown teeth, moisture points needling his face. Seated inside the car rubbing his hands, Kevin realized that although he needed it, he didn't much want his old job back. He hoped he hadn't made it too obvious.

CHAPTER SEVEN

The days dragged on with no response to the mailings. His depression returned, drowning him in a miasma of defeat. Jobless, aimless, sick inside, he couldn't rally his spirit to break free. If this was a test of character he was flunking badly.

When he was able to look out in brief flashes from his unhappiness he could see how tired Marlene had become trying to keep up a brave cheerful front. Knowing he should be giving her support instead of letting his poisonous mood sap her energy made him curse and devalue himself further.

All that week he couch potatoed in front of daytime TV, only rousing himself to interview for two other bartender gigs - neither of which he got or wanted. All enthusiasm shot, he no longer picked up The Providence Phoenix, the city's free weekly, to check the latest films, books, recordings and club dates. Marlene was right. Instead of just serving boozehounds, amassing little round pieces of vinyl and distracting himself with frivolous entertainment he should be doing something better. Yet every time he concentrated on finding a way out his mind hit a blank wall. It was impossible. Might as well try swimming to Block Island in an iron lung.

Years ago he'd asked Artie Webster what he, Artie,

eventually wanted to do. "Well, I can't be an artist, got no real talent. Business is boring. I'd be a lousy manager or agent. I'm too impatient to teach. Nobody pays you for likin' cool stuff unless you're a critic and I'm no writer." He thought a while longer and shrugged. "Basically, I just want to listen to music. Guess I'm fucked."

Kevin had gone still when he'd heard that scary self-analysis. He privately suspected he might be close to being the same thing

Colorless days blurred by without will or purpose. Every set sale list or auction in the mail was a jab reminding him of what he'd lost. Marlene began tossing them soon as they came in. Phone calls from collector friends piled up on the answering machine, emails on the computer. His books, discographies and price guides went unused along with his minutiae-rich memory. Like HAL in "2001" he had SHUT DOWN.

Then in a few days, late on a Friday afternoon everything changed. He was alone in the apartment immersed in "Angel Face" on TCM, watching Robert Mitchum's obsession with Jean Simmons suck the guy down deeper and deeper in spite of his knowing she was unhinged or more perversely because of it. When the phone rang, Kevin let the machine pick it up. Ron Delgado, a New York vocal group collector, apologized for not getting back to him sooner. He'd been on location in Louisiana working as the stand-in for the star of a new cable series. Kevin grabbed the phone.

"Ron, it's me. You got one of my records?"

"Yes I do. It's right in front of me." His calm even tone was like the voice of reason. "The Madison Brothers on Sure.

I bought it down in Austin. There were some others on your list there too." Kevin asked him to look in the runoff grooves. Does it have "KD"?

"Hold on. Let me get it under the light...Yes, I can see it - scratched in very lightly. When I bought it I didn't check the dead wax since it'd never been booted."

Delgado told him the seller was someone no one knew. He called himself "Tom Ryder", was in his late twenties, had arrived like many others before the weekend of the actual show, selling pricey records in the hotel where most of the dealers and buyers stayed. He claimed they belonged to his father who was too busy to attend. They conferred by cell phone over price negotiations. No checks accepted. Some of the rarer pieces went on hold with a deposit. The balance, cash only, was sent to a private mail box. Ron had heard no complaints from other buyers. Being an actor he, remembered Ryder had an East Coast accent, more New England than New York, dark hair and wore a turned-around baseball cap. He had not set up at the show.

The mailing address was in Fall River, little under a half hour east of Providence. Kevin thanked him and hung up. He went into the bathroom, took a hot shower, shampooing twice to get rid of dandruff caused by the weeks of worry, tension and bad diet. Newly shaved, he dressed in jeans, running shoes, sweater and the black leather car coat. He checked to see he still had the old P.I. license Joanne's boyfriend had given him on impulse when they'd all first met for dinner.

He drove the baby blue Mustang along 195 under an ominous grey sky. While the needle kept to a steady 80 mph, a cold Atlantic wind whistled between unseen cracks in the car's body. Over the Bragga Bridge Kevin took the off ramp into Fall River. A once rich 19th century mill town, its high society, composed of a handful of families, had been more exclusive than that of Boston. Wealthy residences up on "The Hill" overlooked the busy harbor. Lizzie Borden, after being acquitted of murdering her parents, bought a mansion up here with her inheritance. During the textile crash of late 1920's, many of these Victorians were sold, families choosing to live year round in their elaborate Newport homes. Boom over, Fall River's economy began a steady downward slide.. These days its glory was a lost memory.

Kevin drove past a large redbrick mill boarded up and gutted, wind blowing refuse about its graffiti'd walls. Some years back it had been made into a shopping center but that too had failed.

The mail box building was on a side street off Bedford next door to a small Portuguese bakery. A skinny unshaven guy, do-rag covering blond frizzy hair lounged behind the solid blue counter at the rear wall. He wore an unreadable tee shirt and a gold earring. A radio on the counter played hip-hop. Kevin strode in holding a $50 bill, flipping his wallet flap up and down quickly to flash the outdated P.I. license. "I need some information."

"Sure." Do-rag reached for the fifty.

Kevin pulled it back, shook his head, "Questions first. Mind turning that off? Good. When did the current owner of Box 1677 start renting?"

The guy blinked narrowing nearly crossed, light colored eyes, went to a computer monitor and punched in some numbers, "Few weeks ago."

"Got an address and phone number on the previous holder?"

Do-Rag stepped back, raised his hands. "Unh unh, no way, that's totally confidential."

Kevin looked about, leaned in. "I'm afraid you don't understand. This is a mail fraud investigation. I've been hired by one of the victims. If I don't get cooperation it'll go to a federal agent."

"Hey, whatever. I'm not losing this job."

"Look, you write it down, you get the fifty and I've never seen you. You make me do it official, you get nothing, this place gets closed and you're back at a drive through flipping burgers. Nothing personal, it's your call."

Do-Rag looked at him, sucking his teeth, weighing the odds. He shrugged acceptance and consulted a worn loose-leaf notebook, pages in cloudy plastic holders, tore off a piece of scratch paper, scribbled on it. Kevin handed him the $50 bill. He held up the paper. Scrawled in ballpoint was "Lino Tierra 36 Ryder Street". Someone calling himself "Tom Ryder" had sold Kevin's 45's in Austin. Dom-da-dom-dom.

Ryder was on the other side of downtown, past an area of small factories and warehouses. Swinging in the wind, a peeling Narragansett Beer sign hung from a corner clapboard bar. The narrow tree lined road had no sidewalk. One story wooden houses, some with metal awnings, were fronted by small patches of lawn. He spotted the Jambasian-described off white panel truck before finding the house number, then parked two houses away and walked to the back of the banged up truck. It took under a minute to un-kink the twisted, rusty coat hanger holding the doors closed. Pieces of rotted grey carpeting partially covered the corrugated steel floor. Along the left side were some paint cans, brushes and crumpled up overalls. Probably what he and his "father" wore to fool any curious neighbor when they ripped him off. "Are you movers?" "No lady, painters. We got to clear this stuff out before we start."

Kevin swung himself inside the truck reaching around to reinsert the bent hanger into the handles. At last he got the doors pretty well shut. He took out his cell, ran through the spiel he'd worked out on the way over and, squinting in the half light from the dirty back windows, called the number. A woman answered.

"Is Lino there?" He tried to make his voice like Do-Rag's – thin and sulky.

"Who is this?"

"Jason at MailBoxes Inc."

"We don't have a mail box there anymore."

"I know, but Mister Tierra didn't get the advertised discount on the old one so my boss says we owe him a refund. And um, because it was my, our fault the first two weeks of any other box rental are free."

"Well, I'm his mother. Can you give this refund to me?"

"Only to the person whose name is on the account. Mister Tierra has to come in and sign for it."

"How much is it?"

"Just a second...One hundred, twenty-seven dollars and twenty-eight cents."

"Fine. He'll be down tomorrow mornin'."

"Well, if it's at all possible it would be better if he came now. We um, think one of the other employees has been stealin' and my shift is about up. My boss could put it in the safe but um, after tonight he's goin' to this new trainin' session and won't be back 'til Thursday."

"Oh, all right. I'll send him now."

"Thanks and about the stealin' um, we'll take care of it but we'd prefer you didn't mention it to anyone."

"Sure, g'bye."

He sat back pleased with himself. That last part he had improvised on the spot. Some five minutes a house door opened and closed. Kevin took a peek, saw a medium tall figure with turned around baseball cap coming down the steps. He ducked down. The truck's door opened on the driver's side, a weight settled into the front seat. Kevin shot up, grabbing Lino's head in a hammerlock, making him cry out, hands grabbing at the forearm around his neck, head pushing back against the front of Kevin's leather coat. Kevin tightened his hold cutting off the kid's air. Lino finally stopped struggling, hands still clutching Kevin's forearm. Kevin loosened his hold by a fraction.

"This is Kevin Dougherty, Lino. I know you stole my records. Gimme any shit I'll hurt you." Part of him split off listening to the tough guy act. It sounded okay. Keeping his right arm locked in place, Kevin surreptitiously fished out his minidisc player with plug in mike and hit the RECORD button. "What's your full name?"

"Lino – Tierra."

He punched up the player's recording level. "Louder!"

"Lino Tierra!"

"Okay. You sold my collection in New York and Austin using the name Tom Ryder, right?" A pause. Kevin retightened his hold, jerking Lino's head back, "Right?" Lino tried to nod. "Answer me!"

"Yes."

"Louder!"

"Yes!"

"How'd you know to rip me off?"

"I didn't know anythin'. It was Joey!"

Kevin tightened up, "Joey who?"

"Joey Latella - my uncle. He found out you were in the hospital."

"So you two dressed up as painters and stole my records?"

"He said you cheated him on a deal."

"I'll bet he did. Hope you got a nice cut." Lino was silent. "How much?"

"Couplea grand."

Kevin made a sound that wasn't quite a laugh. One handed he shut off the minidisc player, slipped it back in his car coat. "Okay, we're going to Providence. My car. You drive." Forearm still pressed against Lino's windpipe, he maneuvered himself over the top into the passenger seat, opened the door and, holding tight onto the back of Lino's Red Sox jacket, hauled him out. He then force marched him across the street and over to the passenger side of the Mustang.

Off in the gathering dark came the sound of thunder. "Get in." Lino worked himself over the steering hump into the driver's seat. His baseball cap had fallen off. Eyes averted, he tentatively massaged his throat. Kevin got in, shut the passenger door and gave him the keys. "Drive." Lino started the car, swung it around in a U turn. Fat rain drops began to splatter the windshield. "Turn on the wipers. Your mom Joey's sister?"

"Yeah."

"Tierra, huh? What'd she do? Marry a goose?"

Lino looked straight ahead, clenched jaw visible in the

oncoming lights. "Yeah."

"It's nice we're all Catholics." He took out his cell. "Uncle Joey owe you any money? You owe him?" Lino shook his head.

The Mustang swung up onto I95 west. For a split second a lightning flash whitened the interstate. A clap of thunder sounded nearby and rain began to pelt down on the roof. Kevin took out his address book, turned on the overhead light. He dialed Joey's number. "Okay. You just found a record back in the truck underneath the carpeting - Jim Foley on Lucky. It's got a red label. Warn him and I'll seriously fuck you up." He reached behind him, hauled up the Louisville Slugger and held it up briefly before hitting SEND. The phone rang. He was about to hand it over when Joey's answering machine kicked in.

"Hey Tara, it's almost six. I'll see you at the festival. Better bring an umbrella. If this is anybody else just leave your name and number."

Kevin smiled tightly. "Pull over."

"But we're on the bridge."

"Pull the fuck over!" Lino obeyed. The rain was now torrential, pelting the car's roof like gunshots. Kevin turned off the ignition, pulled out the keys. He opened the door and getting soaked, ran around to the driver's side from the front. A car swerved around him, honking. He pulled Lino out, the kid's face white and scared. Kevin jumped in, slammed the door. He wiped the water off his face, fired it up, checked the left hand lane and took off. The wipers swept back and forth battling a permanent liquid curtain. Red taillights swam in front of him, pairs of glaring headlights rushing past on his left. Five minutes after passing the blue and white Rhode Island Welcomes You sign, the rain stopped. Overhead, the clouds remained massed, hiding a half moon.

At quarter to seven the San Gennaro Festival on Federal Hill was nearly at overload, crowd partying full tilt before the heavens decided to reopen. Kevin parked on the other side of I-95, got out shoving the baseball bat down his right pants leg, taking off in a stiff legged walk. An overpass led onto Atwells Avenue – the area's main drag. Splintered refractions from multicolored paper lanterns danced on rain slick streets. Above him on a pole, Dean Martin's voice, amplified by a loudspeaker, caressed "Come Back To Sorrento". A small line stood outside Camille's Roman Gardens – the capo di tutti capi of the area's old line restaurants. Red white and green everywhere - from storefronts to crackly plastic hats. Garlicky cottechino sausages with peppers and onions hissed and spit on street grills.

Amongst the food stalls, on the side of a long white trailer a crudely painted goggle-eyed junky was about to fix - "$2.00 to see the DOPE FIEND!!" Posturing Guidos pointed, laughing, yelling an occasional insult. A muscled guy in a puffy jacket open to a white tee shirt and St Christopher medal walked heavily down the metal exit steps at the far end. He whipped out a comb, ran it through his dark pompadour. An olive skinned brunette, eyes like black olives ran over and asked what it was like. He shrugged spreading out his hands. "Whattya think? Stoopid!"

Feeling like a bog dancer in Goombalandia, Kevin searched among the milling throngs of celebrants for Joey's face, swiveling his head to take in both sides of the street. Above came a faint rumbling of thunder. A few blocks down by the fountain a platform stage had been erected draped in the tricolors. At the mic, a Rayban'd singer covered in gold chains and rings, wearing a dark three piece suit, shirt open, fired off a rap song full of guinea slang in the Hill's slightly mush mouthed accent:

> "I tosh a bone to the dumb cafone.
> Whatta shtrunard! He playsh the wrong card.
> Dealer bumpsh the pot. The play'sh gettin' hot.
> Sanbuc' all around then we really get down."

The crowd was smiling, calling out to the performer, digging it. Near the stage an upturned Dom Perignon bottle was lowered uncovering Joey the Weasel, one arm hugging some hefty pouty-faced blonde that cleared him by an inch. Joey laughed, took another swig. Kevin's face burned in the cold air. He withdrew the Louisville Slugger from his pants leg, squeezed through the mob, all faces intent on the finger snapping rapper. Joey spoke into the blonde's hair, ducked as she slapped at him and locked eyes with Kevin, who, bat raised, was plowing towards him. For a second The Weasel froze, then slung the champagne bottle at Kevin's head, and turned squirming his way through the mass of bodies. There was a crack of thunder. A voice yelled "Here it comes!" Seconds later heavy sheets of rain drenched everyone.

Kevin pushed past the jostling crowd, sprinted around the periphery. Joey emerged from the left side of the stage, glanced over his shoulder, took off towards the park. Kevin vaulted the low iron fence, saw Joey leap over it at the far end and did the same slipping on sodden grass, recovering to pursue him, splashing down Atwells in the downpour. They side stepped and twisted through an oncoming group of people who - sight partially hidden by poncho hoods, newspapers and umbrellas - were hopping over streaming puddles.

In front of Kevin, a large party from Angelo's Restaurant spilled onto the sidewalk, men and women getting soaked, yelling to each other as they ran to their cars. He slowed to get past them then raced down the block. Two streets ahead, just before Atwells continued over I-95, the traffic light changed to yellow. As a gelato truck sped up trying to clear the intersection, Joey took off from the curb. The truck's brakes screeched sending it into a skid, front bumper slamming into Joey, knocking him flat. It fishtailed around 60 degrees, before coming to a stop in the continuing deluge, barely audible chimes still repeating the same fourteen note melody..

Kevin took a few halting steps, paused to thrust the bat down his pants, moved forward again. Joey was sprawled on his back, one leg bent, whitened face pelted by raindrops. Over the crouching driver's shoulder, he stared up at Kevin who, lightheaded, took out his cell, dialed 911 and reported the accident. He pocketed the phone, leaned down and whispered "Now it's my turn." Joey's eyes followed him as he splashed off across the street.

Back inside the Mustang, Kevin sluiced through hammering rain to Joey's house. Around back he smashed the cellar window with the bat, knocked out the glass fragments, lowered himself inside onto a dark leather couch. There was a subtle odor of cinder blocks. A table lamp sat on an end table to his left. He turned it on. A multitude of little charcoal grey bits dotted the walls and ceiling. He rubbed his fingertip against one. It was rough and hard. Cement.

A brand new computer and printer were on a white desk board supported by double white filing cabinets. The monitor showed a record list. Boxes of 45's, sleeved and priced, lined up on the carpeting against the wall. Another tabletop supported a motorized buffer. Next to a few cans of lightweight machine oil, several lesser condition records were in a box ready to be polished.

Kevin crawled back out into the torrent. He backed the car up to the window, hoisted out every record box from the basement, jamming them into the trunk and interior before making his way back to the apartment. Marlene's Grand Cherokee wasn't at the curb.

When the last of the wet boxes were inside the living room, he hung the black leather coat's sodden weight on the doorknob where it dripped puddles on the floor. He wiped it down with paper towels, dried off his face and hair and sopped up the spills noticing with amusement how well Marlene had trained him.

Where was she? The computer and printer were missing from her workstation. There was a handwritten note on the bare white desk top.

Dear Kev,

I'm going to stay with Joanne until you're able to adjust to your loss. I've got no more to give you. Your depression is strangling the energy and good spirits I need for our baby. I no longer think your record mania is eccentric or charmingly neurotic. It's become dangerous. I don't want to preach but you really need to get a job and start at least acting like an adult. Please don't call for a few days. I'm wiped out. I still love you.

M

P.S. I needed the computer.

P.P.S. If you want us to see Howard together let me know.

He set the note down, got the mail from downstairs, returned, locked the front door and tossed a fistful of envelopes onto the boomerang-shaped coffee table – the one they'd found at the giant Brinfield Mass. antique fair. He started over to the bamboo bar and realized he didn't have the heart to make just one drink. A chill went up his spine. The fault was in him. No marriage counselor was going to fix it. He thought of playing a record but there was nothing he wanted to hear.

Inside the shadowy bedroom, he stripped off his clothes and got under the covers. The bed felt vast without her. Surrounded by the rain's incessant tattoo, his hand found his limp cock. He tried to stimulate himself - sex partners morphing into each other – first a blonde movie actress, then Larry's former girlfriend, then, inevitably, Marlene. Neither mind nor body was interested. The images dissolved. Arms at his sides, he just lay there in the still darkness, feeling himself grow older.

Next morning the Journal had the story half way down page three: SAN GENNARO ATTENDEE HIT BY TRUCK. The Weasel was recuperating in Providence General with a broken leg, sprained arm and a few cracked ribs. Kevin figured they both had been lucky. If it had gone differently he could've killed the little prick. He was sure that the premeditated taking of another's life would damn him irretrievably - his spirit form, lost and isolated, suspended forever in nothingness. Like many people, his belief in hell was a lot more real than his belief in heaven.

The relief at not being a murderer didn't cheer him up. Marlene had left. Joey's records, sorted and spread out into piles, seemed, under his unenthusiastic gaze, dead and alien. He had no bond with them. No matter how he justified it, they were stolen. He felt his whole life was wrong, that he was going off the track, unable to stop himself.

His expression creased in pain. Tears sprang to his eyes. He put his hand over his face. All at once he was sobbing bitterly, broad shoulders heaving. Twice he stopped wiping his eyes and twice, after a few seconds, was crying again. When he emerged from his sorrow, taking a few deep breaths, he felt clearer.

He picked up a stack of Joey's 45's and thumbed through it. Two blue wax Little Esthers on gold top Federal - one Vg++ the other almost as good. The Rockin' Continentals best release on Casino in M-. There was even Walter and Jimmy's titanic harp classic "Easy" on Sun. Only Vg but so what? For twenty years it was among his top wants. If he'd gotten any of these through the usual channels it would've been like Christmas. Now everything was tainted. Maybe he should just sell 'em off and quit collecting. Maybe Marlene was right. Maybe God or whatever was giving him a chance.

Acutely lonely, he still wasn't going to visit the old man. Wanting fatherly advice was just an excuse to get blotto. Been there, done that. These days they always met at The Colony, a cave-like, phlegmy old bar with the stamped tin ceiling and cigarette smoke. Rummies wolfing down hot oil pizzas – some bizarro Cheese Whiz concoction – laying a foundation before the endless whiskey shots chased by Bud's on draft. Place wasn't Italian. Not even Irish. Maybe Polish or something.

How at his age the old man could still put it away was a

mystery. Oh well, let him drink himself into the next world. Being only half Irish probably helped Kevin stay away from full tilt dipsomania. He was still young, had things to live for - Marlene, for one and of course, their baby.

"Whoa, whoa, I'm not saying you're not justified," Joanne amended. "I'm just asking what you'd do if I wasn't around." More disinterested than welcoming, common law Phil had told her Marlene could stay as long as she wanted. She'd moved into the small back bedroom with the chintz curtains and Maplewood twin.

"He was like a puppet with his strings cut." Having just jabbed herself helping to make a vegetarian pasta, Marlene put a Band-Aid around her fingertip..

"Men can be sexy when they're moody but not when they're depressed." Joanne turned over the eggplant slices sautéing in garlic and oil. "Even a total asshole is more attractive providing he's got some confidence – unfounded though it may be. Talking of that you should've married Marvin Sager. If you had you'd be nearly rich."

"Out of the question."

Marvin Sager, a short, obnoxious, ponytailed health freak, was always trying "to get his head together". He ate more as a vegetarian than any ten carnivores, hand rolled his own cigarettes of no-additives tobacco, and hadn't the slightest idea what to do with his inherited trucking millions. Obese and bedridden he'd nearly died of heart failure in the spring and wasn't expected to live through next year.

"Well I admit hindsight is no sight. He looked like he was going to live forever." Joanne herself seldom thought of past boyfriends she had rejected. They all had been devoted to her so she had seen them as merely average.

Marlene was still analyzing Kevin. "Maybe all Peter Pan type guys are manic-depressive. Maybe he should be put on medication."

Her mother sighed. "What is this attraction to fuckups? Are we all cursed? Your grandmother married an alcoholic and wasted her entire life trying to save him. And then I do her one better!"

"You and Phil are okay though."

"Just barely. And now you're about to have a baby with a depressed record addict."

"Well at least he hasn't tried to rob any banks."

"Give him a chance. He's still young." Joanne transferred the eggplant slices to a platter she had warming in the oven. "Basically all men are a pain in the ass. But you better believe I'd go round the bend if all I could talk to was women."

In 1970 Joanne was doing summer stock, working in the chorus of "Damn Yankees" at the Warwick Musical Tent Theatre where she met the cast's drug connection, a 26 year old prop man complete with a dazzling smile, shoulder length corn silk hair and killer weed. He moved into her apartment and for a few months they were a couple. Then, to make them both rich, he sunk all his coin into a major drug deal. It came off beautifully only his double-crossing partners vanished leaving him flat busted needing enough to buy into another stash.

He spent that August night inside his bronze Road Runner in the empty parking lot of a Shawmut Bank. Awaking early to fogged windows and a pattering muggy drizzle, he sucked down smoke from the last of his Panamanian Red and waited for the doors to open. Then, totally ripped, sheathed in a ski mask, carrying a cocked shotgun under a shorty raincoat he'd stumbled inside, demanded all their money and shot himself in the leg tearing hell out of his calf. He pulled a dime up in Spofford. Eight months later his daughter was born. He came to see Marlene only once after his release. She remembered the back of his embroidered Levi jacket and his gift - a picture book of colorful exotic butterflies.

Working in the small kitchen, Marlene wondered if she'd cut herself on purpose, either to relieve tension or, maybe, in some weird primitive attempt to open herself up and flush out the embryo. She was terrified of having a baby with Kevin. Maybe if it was born with a 45 for a head he'd be interested.

Joanne checked the water. It was near boiling. "You never know for sure what another person is capable of or how they'll react."

Even though Marlene felt this was true she half resented it as she did all of her mother's definitive pronouncements. "Well, I knew Kevin'd be depressed once he got ripped off."

"Feelings aren't hard to predict, it's actions. Men and women don't understand themselves, let alone each other."

One of her mom's favorite sayings. Marlene had heard it many times. "Phil coming home for dinner?"

"Nope, he had to go to Albany on some case. Anyway, wait and see if Kevin stabilizes on his own. Don't try and guilt trip him into growing up. Doesn't work. Men are either addicts or not. So you get to choose between passionate/interesting/self-destructive or predictable/boring/well-adjusted."

"Why do you have to be such an absolutist? Some guys

are both interesting and mentally healthy."

"I'm sure. But like most top collectibles they're not easy to find." She glanced over. "You can put the spaghetti in."

Marlene said "Oh!" She whipped off the lid to keep the now furiously boiling water from spilling over.

Joanne watched her daughter's neat graceful movements. The love she felt helped balance her gnawing sense of having missed out in life. Ferocious realist that she had become, Joanne of late was visited by memories of being in her 20's. The romantic feelings and sense of infinite possibility were all so fresh in that forever lost time that to recall them was to feel a thin knife blade twisting slowly within her heart.

She clenched her teeth to shut down the threat of tears and began to set the table. Marlene was looking at her as if about to speak but did not. Grateful, Joanne let out a breath, vowing silently to have only one glass of wine with dinner. Well okay, no more than two.

CHAPTER EIGHT

One cold bright morning a few weeks after Marlene's departure, Kevin, in green plaid Pendleton, black tee shirt and Levis, was removing the shelving from his record room, turning it into a nursery. As he worked alone, chattering away in a free-associative monologue, he paid no attention to what he was saying. Carrying on like his own radio program while doing mindless tasks was a habit he'd had since childhood.

The entire load copped from The Weasel had been sold to Pete Jambasian for ten grand. All past bills were now paid, including credit cards, rent and his and Marlene's latest inflated insurance premium. The weird thing was that after recording a few 45's, he hadn't kept a single one, not even those he might never see again. It made him realize his collection had been like a dead star. The bigger it grew the more records it pulled into itself but once the gravitational force had been cut so had his rampant desire to collect. Unfocused and weightless, it now bobbed slowly about inside him, a toy balloon in a closed room. But would it stay that way?

If so his best shot was to become a seller. He had a sponge memory for titles and values as well as a rep for knowledge and honesty. He'd communicated regularly with enough big time dealers and collectors to create a strong mailing list.

Ads in the collector magazines and trading addresses with others would help the business grow. Combined with luck and whatever Marlene earned they might get by. What he lacked was product. A huge quality load, ten times the size of Joey's stash, and he'd be solid. Right. Like that was ever going to happen. Until it did, and to get Marlene back, he needed a job starting yesterday.

The phone. Kevin hastily put down a shelf section. Maybe someone's shift had opened up at the bar. "Hi, it's Francine am I disturbing you?...Oh good. Listen, Wylie's cub scout troop is scheduled for a father and son sleepover December 14th, that's a Saturday. It's on a battleship docked at Fall River..."

Listening, Kevin flopped down on the couch, bit into a partially eaten crumb cake, washing it down with lukewarm coffee. "Oh yeah, I remember doing that with my dad."

"No kidding? Well would you be his father this once? He really wants to go. I'll pay for it. Do you think you might be able to? It should be fun, maybe nostalgic too."

"Yeah, okay. I guess so."

"Great. He will be so thrilled. They want you there anytime between noon and one thirty."

"No problem." A bell rang. "Someone's at the door. We can talk later, okay?"

He opened up to two men in dark overcoats. The taller one with the heavy eyebrows wore a yellow scarf, the other's was Burberry plaid. He had a cigarette in his gloved hand and was losing his hair in front. His companion said "Mr. Bonnano wants to see you."

"What Mr. Bonnano?" In his sinking gut he already

knew.

"Mr. Vincent Bonnano. Put your shoes on. We'll take you to him."

Kevin rode numbly in the back of a heated black Lexus with black leather interior. While the two in front argued college hockey, he imagined the police trying to determine from the staleness of the half-eaten crumb cake when he'd been abducted. He looked out the window at sidewalks, wooden frame houses and leafless trees. They appeared both familiar and alien. The idea of promising God to attend St. Malachy's more often occurred to him. He sighed. It was really pathetic the way no one could escape their past.

The car continued into the Edgewood area. Many of the gracious old waterside homes here had been summer residences for early 20th century merchants, their regular houses, twenty degrees hotter, but a few miles inland – a far more modest version of the lavish Newport mansions.

The Lexus turned off the street, stopping in front of white iron gates. The window slid down. The driver pressed a speaker button on a pole. "Sally and Joe - we're back."

The gates creaked, opened inwards admitting them up a short curving drive to a three story, wedding cake Edwardian Villa. At the side was a four car garage, three of the spaces filled. Flanked by the two overcoats, Kevin walked along the flagstone pathway to the porch.

The taller of the two men rang the bell. They waited, breath streaming in the bright cold air. The front door opened, vestibule filled by a bald giant with pale jellyfish blue eyes behind heavy black frame glasses. He wore a dark blue and green plaid sport shirt, solid green sport jacket and tie. The magnified eyes slid from Kevin to the two overcoats. He motioned them into the vestibule with a small jerk of his head.

They passed through a second glass door into the house's warmth. The bald man left them to wait under a many-tiered chandelier surrounded by gold and pink patterned wallpaper. Through an entranceway on the left a mechanized little seat was fitted on tracks following the curve of the staircase up to the second floor.

On the right through an open doorway Kevin saw a room out of the early 1920's – ottoman sofa , small fireplace, oriental rugs and a red tulip-horned, windup gramophone Small gold framed photo portraits dotted the tan and dark green striped wallpaper.

The bald man returned. "You guys go back to the office." Watery blue eyes regarded Kevin, "This way." Kevin followed him along a short hallway to a bright, glassed in sun room. Outside, the land ran some fifty yards down to the inlet's cold sparkling water. Hereabouts, close to shore, the anchored British warship Gaspee was burned by American colonists as a protest to unfair taxation – a source of pride for Little Rhody. Before Ma Bell went all numerals in 1963, GAspee had been one of the city's premier telephone exchanges.

A man with combed back iron grey hair sat atop summery floral print cushions on a white rattan couch. Large sunglasses covered his bony face, the tip of a white scar just visible above his right eyebrow, his cheekbones like subcutaneous walnuts. About 5' 10", slightly thick around the middle, white open necked dress shirt under a double breasted navy blazer.

To his left, Joey the Weasel was in a wheel chair, right leg thrust out in a single plastic cast. He stared balefully at Kevin, who, much as he disliked him, felt an unexpected kinship. His cast had come off only a month ago. Of course Joey was a lot more responsible for Kevin's accident than Kevin was for his. Not that the little psychopath would see it that way.

A golden retriever padded over, sniffing at Kevin's pant leg. Kevin patted him on the head. Satisfied, the dog went back to the sliding glass door lying down on the carpeting. He looked wistfully out at a pair of squirrels rushing about over dead leaves. The tall bald man gestured to the man on the couch. "Mister Bonnano."

Bonnano gave a small nod. "Have a seat." Kevin lowered himself onto the cushion of a white rattan chair. Bonnano popped two Rainbow Lite Multi-Vitamin pills and washed them down with a glass of green algae-looking water. As the muscles worked in his throat, the sunlit room was silent. He drained the glass, shuddered, set it down next to a bottle of San Pellegrino and a jar of Metamucil. The bald man lifted the tray off the glass topped table, disappeared into what looked like a pantry and returned immediately.

Bonnano looked at Kevin. "You smoke?"

"Quit twelve years ago."

"I ought to hire someone who smokes. At least I could smell it once in a while."

"That's secondary," said the bald man neutrally. "Almost as bad."

"I smoke," said Joey. He scowled at Kevin. "Can't do it now 'cause of possible infection."

Bonnano took out a stick of sugarless gum from a pack on the table, unwrapped it and put it in his mouth. He looked at Kevin. "You are here because this little fuck is my nephew. People saw you chase him out in front of a truck. You did that?"

"Yes."

"Because you believe he stole some old phonograph records?"

"My collection."

"Why makes you think he was the one stole it?"

"Lino Tierra told me."

Joey couldn't keep silent any longer, "After you almost strangled him to death! Coercion, right Uncle Fish?"

Bonnano ignored him. "What did Lino say?" Kevin told him. "You got any proof of this?"

While in his bedroom putting on his shoes Kevin had thought to bring along the minidisc player. Now he pulled it out of his pocket and depressed PLAY. Lino's brief lo-fi confession began. Bonnano cut off Joey's protest with a look. When it ended the side of his mouth turned up in a half grin. "Any cops in your family?"

"Not anymore."

Bonnano nodded. "Traditions are dying all around us."

"Tell me about it," Joey blurted. "Those gook nurses they got now hardly speak English."

Bonnano pursed his thin lips. "Experientially, I believe you. Back in '71 I started Joey off with a job in real estate. He wasn't altogether honest with me."

"Uncle Fish, this mother –"

"Shut-the-fuck-up-and-don't-call-me-that-anymore." Bonnano enunciated each word without looking at Joey or raising his voice. The family had dubbed him "Fish" when he was a kid working on boats out of New Bedford. Grateful not to be known by some dumb mob-conferred nickname, he certainly wasn't going to let his pissant nephew tag him now.

In the absolute silence which followed he continued focusing on Kevin. "You got balls but you're too hot tempered -

running around with a bat in the middle of Federal Hill during San Gennaro with half the world looking." He shook his head. "Then you break into his house, take his records."

"Bought from what he made off mine."

Bonnano removed the gum from his mouth with a paper napkin. "These things last about ten seconds." He put the wadded napkin onto the glass-topped coffee table. "See Kevin, what you did, threatening a member of my family right in the middle of my own neighborhood, I cannot ignore it no matter how much he deserved it. So here's what's gonna happen. You're gonna wash dishes at Villa Tuscano for a couple of months. Ever been there?"

Kevin nodded. His stomach began to relax. "Good food."

"Yeah," Bonnano sighed regretfully, "Six to eleven thirty, six days a week with Mondays off, fifteen an hour plus dinner."

"I get paid?"

"Naturally. Every Tuesday. Otherwise it wouldn't be legal. And you," he turned to Joey, "for disgracing the family and putting me through all this – when does that come off?"

"Next Thursday."

"Good, 'cause then you're gonna be doing the same thing right next to him." He looked over at the tall bald man. "We're done here. Have Joe Low and Sally Lipstick drive 'em home."

As Bonnano's gofers, followed by Kevin, wheeled Joey out to the Lexus, Fat Danny Silvestriani drove through the gate in his maroon Range Rover. He parked and descended, swaddled in a charcoal grey cashmere overcoat. He glided over smiling at Joey, a Cuban Hupmann in his mouth. "Looks like it's not gonna be too difficult to keep it in your pants for a while."

"At least I can find it," Joey shot back over Joe Low's shoulder as he was inserted diagonally into the back seat. "Hey!" he yelled from inside the Lexus. "I smell poo poo. Whyn't you change your diapers?"

Kevin got in next to Joey. The Lexus turned onto the street and drove away. Danny watched it go. Even in the cold his face felt hot. No more credit cards for Dee Dee – the little shtrunard bitch.

A buzzer sounded. Bonnano rose, mounted the stairs to the entrance of his wife's room. Laura was sitting up against a large stuffed backrest. Bright sunlight shone on her bowed head. Only a few glittering strands of silver were visible in her black hair. A large folding tray held a bottle of Elmer's Glue, newspapers, homemaking magazines and a scrapbook. A huge spray of red, orange and white fall flowers were in a milky green vase on a corner table.

"You want to come down for lunch later?"

"Charles can bring it up. Did you make an appointment for the you-know-what?" Using large silver scissors she trimmed the edges off a cut out recipe for Chicken Tetrazzini with Sicilian olives from Martha Stewart Living.

"Yeah, he'll get back to me."

"Well don't wait for him! You should've done it years ago." She squeezed some white glue on the back of the clipping before carefully centering it on the page. "Just because you've never had any real complaints doesn't mean you shouldn't take care of yourself."

"I'll call and remind him."

Bonnano walked back downstairs. He knew Laura

wanted him to be well so he could look after her. Who could blame her? If he was her he'd act the same. And how could he expect her to love him? He hadn't loved her for years if he ever had. They simply had their roles to play for each other. Neither one wanted them changed.

Kevin and Joey sat silently, Joey's plastic leg cast extended in between the front seats. The dark browed driver glanced out the window at a neighborhood Portuguese market with a giant white chicken statue out front. "Huh! It ain't even Thanksgiving an' Pollito's got Christmas lights on his bird."

His companion with the receding hairline grunted. "So maybe he's a Jew goose." He took out a cigarette, pushed in the lighter.

"He don't hafta be anythin'. T'day ever'one's tryna make a fast buck." The lighter popped out. The driver put his hand on the other's arm as he reached for it. "Whattya doin'? You know he doesn't want anyone smokin' in here."

"Hey" said Kevin, "Which one of you's Sally Lipstick?" The men up front said nothing. "I mean I know you guys got some weird nicknames an' all but 'Sally Lipstick'? What's the deal on that?"

"Listen pal," said the driver, "you're just a fuckin' package. I pick you up, I drop you off - doesn't mean we gotta converse."

The other turned towards the back seat and shrugged. "He's in a bad mood."

"So'd you be your kid blew his scholarship."

Joey said, "I know."

"Know what?" said the man in the front passenger seat.

"Why he's called Sally Lipstick. You guys were in high

school –"

"Naw, we'd graduated awready."

The driver hit the steering wheel. "Will you kindly shut the fuck up?"

"Hey Sally. This story's gonna be told it oughta be told right." Sally shook his head in disgust but didn't protest. "Anyways the 1984 graduatin' class was havin' its senior dance out at Rocky Point with the full shore dinner."

"Those rides were great, huh?" said Joey. "Easiest way to tell if what the girl had was real."

"Anyway," said Joe Low, "it was dark. Sally and his date and me and mine were sittin' at one of those wooden benches lookin' at the lights on the water. Talkin' about how we're gonna miss the school. What we wanna do with our lives."

"What everybody does," said Kevin.

"An' that summer was a real bad one for mosquitoes – even at the shore."

Sally winced, the memory too uncomfortable for him to remain silent. "They wouldn't let up. I got this stick of insect repellant outta the girl's purse. G-12 or somethin'. They don't make it anymore. Put' it all over my hands an' face. Didn't do jack shit."

"Alla time he's bitchin' 'bout how he's bein' eaten alive. So we all get up to dance. They had these bug zappers 'round the whaddyacallit."

"The pavilion," said Sally.

"So, soon as we get under the lanterns his date gives out with this giant scream. Coulda heard her all the way to Greenwich. Reason was he'd grabbed her lipstick 'stead of the repellant. Looked like he'd taken a header through a windshield. After that we always called him Sally Lipstick."

Kevin frowned. "Didn't some people think he was gay?"

Joe Low laughed. "Sure – at first."

"I straightened out a few."

"Plus it fascinated women. Anytime we met two of 'em, he'd get first crack and I hadda good shot with the other."

Joey shifted in his cast. "Maybe I'll get a slight limp outta this. Kinda like John Wayne. Tell women it's a war wound."

Kevin leaned back against the seat. "Or hopefully you'll lose the whole leg and have your pick of amputee groupies."

Down by the water's edge, Vincenzo Bonnano, now encased in a forest green polar fleece jogging suit, pedaled on a stationary bike. Fat Danny stood beside him. A moist wind from off the water blew their hair.

Twenty yards away, up towards the house, the bald man, Charles "Charley Tuna" Fortunato, threw breadcrumbs from a glassine bag to red and grey squirrels, watching them zig zag down trees, make short sprints across the dead leaves. When the bag was empty he opened the sliding glass door. The Golden Retriever shot out barking, at the scattering squirrels which, making ninety degree turns, scrabbled halfway up tree trunks.

The dog had come from Little Compton - a small seaside village south of Tiverton settled by swamp Yankees, later enjoyed by rich preppies. Not Bonnano's style but very scenic - low stone walls, lush green fields and shade trees, private and public beaches - all with very strict zoning laws. Only clapboard shingle houses and Cape Cod cottages. No chain stores or chain restaurants allowed.

In the 1970's Bonnano, representing R.I.'s mob boss Patriarca, was taken to lunch at the Sakonnet Golf Club. A pink faced guy wanted to buy back some family heirloom his son had used to make payment on a gambling debt. Kid had been too much of a Brown hockey fan for his own good. Vincenzo had dressed in conservative sports clothes, no wop flash whatsoever but instead of blending in amongst the magenta and lime floral pants, madras jackets and goofy hats he'd stuck out like Joe Friday at a love-in.

Q: "Why do white guys play golf?" went the outdated racist joke.

A: "It's their only chance to dress like niggers."

Two and a half years ago he'd been down there again. Young couple had bought a vineyard and needed help getting stores to carry their product. Nice people. Wine was pretty good too. They were also dog breeders. Had two young male and female purebred Goldens left from a recent litter. Housebroken and obedience trained. They told him to take one if he wanted. Bonnano figured a pet might be nice, make the house a little less lonely with Laura basically confined to her room. He couldn't see calling a dog Cognac so instead he took Brandy, the boy.

The retriever liked Vincenzo but because Charley Tuna fed him, spent more time with him, he regarded him as his master.

Charley had been Bonnano's bodyguard, cook and handyman for almost twenty years – a long relationship by mob standards. It wasn't that Vincenzo had done him any great favor to win his fealty – hadn't saved his life, his parent's investments or his sister's reputation (actually he had no sister). Charley just had no greater ambition. Four years ago his mother passed away in her sleep. As one of her old friends seeing the obit had said in Rhode Islandese: "Ooh, look who

took themselves a haht attack and died in the newspapeh!"
He had no other living relative. Vincenzo and Laura were now
his only family.

He had tried staying in the small house without his
mother but it made him uneasy and he sold it. He lived comfortably above Bonnano's garage, stretched out when he wasn't
needed, on a white iron frame bed either watching TV or reading mysteries. These paperbacks were neatly displayed, three
shelves high, all around the low ceilinged room. Charley had
never married nor had a steady girlfriend. Once a month he
drove his black Lincoln sedan to a residence hotel and had sex
with a thirty two year old prostitute named Sharon Darrow.
The whole thing, from the time he left the garage apartment
until he returned, took a little over three quarters of an hour.

Down by the water Silvestriani lit up another Hupmann, shielding the flame with his black gloved hands. He
nodded back towards the house. "They bug you again?"

Vincenzo took precautions. He had a cleaning lady once
a week, never the same service or person consecutively. Even
so the Feds might sneak in an agent. All incriminating papers
were kept in a hidden safe. The radio was cranked up when it
had to be. He used a cell for anything sensitive.

Bonnano grimaced. "Guys gotta justify their job. The
mayor's been popped so I'm what's left. Idiots don't want this
city to run well. They'd rather have all their chickenshit laws
obeyed and cripple the small businessman."

"You talkin' about the porno?"

"And the sports betting and the juice. We're not con-
trolling much else since losing those construction contracts."

Fat Danny gave a small shrug. "Where you gonna go -

New Orleans?"

"Only a matter of time anywhere. What I should do is become a stock broker or investment counselor. Move up to some CEO position and rob fuckin' everybody. You run into Joey out front?"

"Yeah."

"He never bitched to me about the cement."

Fat Danny smiled. "Had no proof. Maybe he figured he wasn't as important as the guy who did it."

"That'd give him half a brain anyway. Meanwhile I'm settling nitwit disputes over phonograph records. How's the bridal shop?"

"You'll have papers on Monday." Bonnano's older brother and wife had retired, to Phoenix leaving their lady manager in charge. Vincenzo was now co-owner, splitting the modest profits 40-60 his favor.

"And Lou?"

"One more week he should be a hundred percent clean."

"Soon's he walks out I want him back working for me. Same salary but he kicks back half."

"How's he gonna live on that?"

"Econo-fuckin-mize. Put the kids in public school. It's not my problem. Je-sus Mary and Joseph. Anybody else's accountant did that they'd gut him on principle."

Fat Danny shrugged imperceptibly in his heavy coat. "Then they don't get paid."

For a while Bonnano pedaled in silence. "Y'know, I useta think my parents were real squares. How could they be happy when they had zip? Now I don't know. I can't eat or drink anything good, gave up smoking, supposed to lose weight all the time. They never had to go through that."

"People weren't expected to live long back then. Sixty was way fuckin' old. Nowadays ya gotta give stuff up to keep goin'."

"Yeah, but what's the point?"

Danny took the Hupmann out of his mouth, regarded it. "Peep and them're 250 K short on the construction."

"So? Those three jokers wouldn't get one more dime even if I had it to give."

"Another fire?"

Bonnano shrugged, "Why not? It's a different company."

The Ballona brothers had kept their Seekonk restaurant going since the 60's. Whenever one was in prison the other two would take over. The place was in their sister Desiree's name, so when the IRS did periodic audits they couldn't attach it. Vincenzo had a 25% interest since its opening.

For a while now it'd been losing to more modern joints leaving a few steady customers, some of them priests. Peep Ballona, so heavy he made Fat Danny look trim, straddled two counter stools and would tear up any check brought to the register by a turned around collar. Once in the 1970's, Joey the Weasel had donned vestments to get a free shore dinner. Only his uncle had kept him from serious injury.. A few months back, Bonnano and the brothers had agreed to torch the place, collect and rebuild.

The job went off smoothly but all three brothers had dipped liberally into the insurance money to respectively pay off an alimony, a second mortgage and some back taxes. The workmen, tired of constant promises, had finally walked off the site.

Bonnano grimaced. "Gimme some good news."

"The Indian'll meet."

"Good. Tell the printer to be ready."

"This comes off, Boston'll get a hard on."

"Yeah, 'till they need to pass the buck again." Still pedaling, Bonnano snorted. "Making deals with the Pequots! Just like Roger friggin' Williams. I oughta become a Protestant."

Vincenzo was Calabrese. In 1911 his future father, Carmine Bonnano, and mother, Maria Volpe had emigrated with their parents to Boston. Six other Calabrian families, two from their old village, lived in the same small rooming house on the North End. Sixteen year old Carmine took the train down to Providence and began working for his Uncle Don Nido – an importer and seller of Borsalino hats. He worked hard, learned the business and wrote to Maria every week. At eighteen he was drafted and sent to Ypres to fight the Bosch. He survived, returning with a slight limp, the result of a bullet-shattered hip bone set hurriedly in a field hospital.

He proposed to Maria in 1921. They were married in Providence. Next year a son, Eduardo was born. Due to complications during the pregnancy Maria never wholly recovered her full strength. Seven years later she succumbed to diphtheria. Uncle Nido turned his business over to Carmine who remarried in 1933 to Maria's cousin, Lisa Gambino. Ten years his junior, she was also part of one of New England's burgeoning crime families. In 1935 a second son Vincenzo, was born. Two years later they had a daughter Lucia.

The older son, Eduardo, worked with his father in the shop. Like Carmine he was quiet and industrious. He married Rosa Fratenelli in 1950. The store was his inheritance but by the late 1950's hat sales were declining. When Carmine died in 1962 Eduardo and Rosa turned it into a bridal shop, an idea Carmine had vetoed years ago. Profits slowly picked up.

From birth the younger son, Vincenzo, was restless and independent. As a teenager, working on a Portuguese fishing boat, he fell onto a gaffing hook. The resultant 3/4" white scar above his right eyebrow would help his rep as a tough guy. After a stint in the merchant marine, and still in his early 20's, he worked for his mother's family. Four years later, after being sworn into La Cosa Nostra, he was put in charge of the Seaboard Vending Machine Company in Providence only four blocks away from his brother's shop. He came up slowly through the ranks under first, Patriarca Sr. then Jr. By the time he was made an underboss, both Patriacas were in prison and the seat of power in New England had shifted to Boston.

LCN hung on, what there was of it. Throughout the 1990's RICCO had leeched its power away in case after case. All the big guys were dead or doing heavy time. Drug trafficking busts resulted in stiffer sentences which meant more motivation to break the code and rat out associates. It didn't seem like the good old days were ever coming back. Plenty of made guys were looking to take out second mortgages and could no longer get credit.

Vincenzo's wife Laura was a distant cousin of the Gambino family. They married in the mid-1960's and tried to start a family for half a decade before going to a specialist. All reproductive organs checked out but she had kidney cancer. The necessary dialysis left her too weak to cope with an adopted child. He believed this was the reason he hadn't been permitted to move higher up. Knowing it wasn't her fault, he tried not to blame her but it estranged them. He had a succession of mistresses until a few years ago when they became more a chore than a pleasure. At risk for heart failure, his cholesterol intake was severely limited. With food and sex gone his only remaining pleasure was making enough money to hope his lack of heirs wouldn't be held against him. As time went by it didn't seem to make much of a difference either way.

Computer graphics course completed in late November, Marlene had immediately begun interviewing at ad agencies, graphic design firms - even an animation studio. She'd snagged a gig at a Boston greeting card company, translating artist's ideas into pixels and altering designs to cover different occasions. The okay pay would be enough to qualify for unemployment when she really started to show and would probably be let go.

She sat now in front of the monitor altering the background of a card featuring two deer in a snowy nighttime forest looking up at the Christmas star. The message read "Peace on earth". Now she lightened the sky to early morning, removed snow from pine branches, replacing it on the ground with grass and wildflowers. The shimmering, silver star became a warm yellow sun. The message now read "Wishing you a speedy recovery".

As she experimented with oranges and red streaks on the horizon she imagined using the cutesy deer for other holidays: a witch on a broomstick crashing into their antlers, Washington's falling cherry tree flattening them, a pilgrim blasting away at a wild turkey and taking off one of their heads. Kevin would like that one.

The impulse to create for him was there before she could slam it down. Fuckin' asshole. Okay, she missed him She still wasn't gonna bring up a little kid in the same house as a depressed lump. Mommy, daddy's staring out the window again! Well, not unless he could halfway control himself, which she seriously doubted. It could be worse but so what? She wasn't about to fall for some crack addict or woman beater.

CHAPTER NINE

The Villa Tuscano, in North Providence, served Italian Italian as opposed to New England Italian - no scungilli salad. Tricky to find, basically tourist-proof, it attracted young to middle-aged locals. The large polished wood and brass dining room had a big fireplace, Sinatra crooning over the speakers. The family made periodic trips to Italy to discover new dishes. Fredo, the chef, spoke only broken English but his seasonings and sauces which enhanced the natural flavors never covering them, were understood by all. An annual raise kept him from jumping ship.

Kevin was into the kitchen's swing by the second day. The constant hosing, soaking, rinsing and drying mercifully turned off his brain. Sheathed in headphones, head full of constant music from minidisc compilations, he simply zoned out.

The old guy, Nonno something, worked efficiently and silently alongside him. The food was a bonus. Even though the better entrees were often gone by the end of the night, nothing was less than fine. He kept the gig secret from Marlene. If she knew he'd pissed off the New England Mafia she might freak permanently.

Each day he did his time, being friendly to the rest of the

staff when their dinners coincided. Fredo and his two smiling
assistants spoke Italian amongst themselves while Umberto
who made all the cold dishes was mostly silent. Three wait-
ers covered the dining room, one was a law student, another
somebody's cousin and the last a high school science teacher
who was working two jobs to support his family. Carlo, the
30's something maitre d' with dark spaniel eyes, was affable
unless he was bitching about liberals. Giorgio Famiglietti, one
of the owners and acting manager, was average height, light
brown hair, blue eyes. He wore square black rimmed glasses
with yellow tinted lenses, worked most of the time in his office, coming out on occasion to welcome old customers.

There was restaurant seating in the bar next to the
main room, five tables covering a black and white tiled floor.
One of the two bartenders, a smooth cocky paisan', seemed to
be buddies with half the young male clientele. The other was
a black woman.

Philippa Roberts, tall in her late 20's, was lushly gor-
geous - black curly hair, smooth coppery skin, green slanted
eyes, cheekbones like flying buttresses on a Gothic cathedral.
When she tried de-emphasizing her just-this-side-of-over-
ripe-body with elegantly simple lines the effect was, to her
private dismay, hopelessly provocative.

She deflected five to ten passes a day from yammering
horndogs with refusals that were polite, firm, even humorous
but never cutting. Too voluptuous for modeling, unwilling to
make quick money table dancing at one of the better clubs,
Philippa aspired to class. A decade ago in the Bridgeport projects while her few girlfriends got aurally stroked by Luther
Vandross she listened to diction tapes and studied fashion

design.

Two years after her mother went to work for UPS she married her supervisor – a bifocaled Steady Eddie who wore white shirts with lots of ballpoints and never raised his voice. Twin boys – Jerry and Andy Jr. – were born when Philippa was five. Although the family tried to include her, she grew up not relating to them, constantly wondering about her real father. Her mother, normally easy going, refused to give her any information except to say he was someone her daughter shouldn't know. Sometimes, during her wild and headstrong teen years, she caught her mother looking at her with a pained expression and imagined she was seeing Philippa's father, intuiting the mysterious "badness" she felt inside herself.

She waitressed the last half of her senior year and that summer took a bartending course in New Haven. Newly graduated her first gig was at some 18th century tavern turned rock club. The mixed hip-hop techno house band supposedly had a demo under serious consideration at Warner's but also a buffed blond blue-eyed singer with a slow sexy smile. Intense looks from the bandstand, heartfelt conversations after sets, a first torrid kiss in his dressing room, led to a week of fucking. Philippa, half in love with him, half in love with where he might take her, believed she was on her way up.

That year his group went down to SXSW in Austin where, she later discovered, her devoted boyfriend had hooked up, quite literally, with a hot New York lady publicist. Almost immediately they became the new house band at a hip venue in Hoboken and Philippa's rock n' roll romance went down the toilet with over a grand in loans. She was determined to get it back with interest from somebody soon as she got out of bad luck New Haven but first she had to pick a new city.

Not lowly Bridgeport - home to the P.T. Barnum Museum, Remington electric shavers and not much else. New York, at least for now, was too big and scary. Boston was a possibility but smaller Providence seemed less threatening. Her ex had once mentioned the Villa Tuscano and she'd remembered the name. A black barmaid in an alta cucina joint was a rarity but when they heard the polished syllables that went with the rest of the package she was hired.

Good thing too. She'd just been turned down for a fashion design scholarship at RISD and so needed to come up with a semester's tuition. But no matter how generous the tips from dazzled male customers, she'd never have enough to swing it for next spring unless she hitched herself to a fat wallet - the owner of which would most likely be a total lame. Then, unable to con herself into believing she was in love, she'd be forced to see herself as a high-priced fuck. Self-hatred and God knew what else would follow. As much as she wished to latch onto some big score, she had little prospect of doing so. It would take luck, something in which Philippa didn't have much belief.

When Joey showed up for work that Friday everything slid sideways. Half the time the little mook was on his cell trying to chisel some fish on a record deal so Kevin had to redo his sloppy jobs. The owners saw it going down but, not wanting to trouble Bonnano with cheap problems, only gave out mild warnings. Cocooned in music, eyes straight ahead, Kevin still couldn't shut out his body's reaction working next to the yammering little shit. He imagined shoving the Weasel's cell down his throat, drowning him in a sink full of soapy water, braining him permanently with a cast iron skillet. He took to dosing himself with herbal tension reducing drops. Each time he fixed in the restaurant's parking lot, he was reminded of how badly he missed Marlene. She had hipped him to the concoction as well as many other little things he had up to now taken for granted.

By the second day Joey was predictably putting the moves on Philippa who froze him from the jump. When they ate at the stainless steel kitchen table Joey couldn't take his eyes off her. "Hey bartender, you can serve me anytime."

"Only thing I'd want to serve you with," she enunciated clearly, "is a subpoena."

"What's the charge?"

"Impersonating an asshole."

"You're right. This is just an act to hide how sensitive I am."

Philippa didn't laugh. "You're about as sensitive as an unplugged dildo."

"You oughta know. Seriously though, I'd really like to put some cream in your coffee."

"Charming but I doubt if I'd even notice. You'd be better off relieving yourself with a magnifying glass and tweezers."

"That one's older than your mother."

"You don't know anything about my mother, fleaboy."

This re-bop became a nightly feature, Philippa usually getting the last word delivered with typically perfect diction. Kevin looked forward to her slams. One night at dinner she asked if anyone knew how to make a Sazerac. She'd gotten an order for one and had drawn a blank. Kevin answered without thinking "Two and a half ounces of rye, one demerara sugar cube, two dashes Angostura Bitters, three dashes Peychaud

Bitters served in a chilled, small lead bottomed glass rinsed with Absinthe or Pernod, edge rubbed with lemon. There're variations but that's the traditional recipe."

Philippa stared at him."Hey. You've done this, right?"

"Yep."

"So what're you washing dishes for?"

"It's quieter."

She raised her eyebrows. "I hear that."

Kevin glanced over at Joey expecting a crack but the Weasel just smirked as he cut into his Steak Fiorentina.

One late November night, Kevin came out the side door to the parking lot thankful to see that Joey had already left in his silver Hummer spaccone-mobile. Above the surrounding rooftops was a clear black sky with tiny white stars. Philippa was pacing up and down in a long fur collared coat. "Somebody stand you up?" His breath was visible in the cold.

She looked down the quiet street. "My car's in the shop and I don't know what's happened to my girlfriend."

"Where do you live?"

"East Providence, right over the India Point Bridge."

"That's not far from me. I'll drive you."

She hesitated, smiled. "Okay. Thanks."

While they waited for the Mustang to heat up she said "These vintage cars are pretty but not that comfortable."

"The eternal choice," he said putting it in gear, "style or comfort."

"I like both. Did you choose the color too?" She saw his expression and laughed. One of his radio show tapes was in the deck. The Mello-Harps on Tin Pan Alley started harmonizing. "How old are you?"

"You don't like 50's vocal groups?" He went to turn it off. She put her gloved hand on his wrist.

"It's not too bad." They listened for a while. "You'd get along with my great Uncle Ben. Earliest I listen to is Motown. So, tell me: how do you make a Ramos Gin Fizz?"

For the rest of the way they chatted about the work staff. She directed him to pull up in front of what looked like a redone brick apartment building, "The Torrington Arms" spelled out in black curling script on a white sign. "You don't like Joey a whole lot do you?'

"Who does?"

"Did you know him before?"

"It's a long story."

She opened the door, "Look, do me a big favor? Don't tell him you gave me a ride."

"Why should I? But then why shouldn't I?"

"Just a feeling I have."

"Okay. You want me to pick you up tomorrow?"

"That's sweet. But I wouldn't want to impose."

"Philippa, it's literally ten minutes out of my way."

"Only if you're sure we can get there before, uh..."

"Absolutely."

She laughed. "Come by at six?" He nodded and she was out of the car.

Driving back to the apartment in the quiet cold, Kevin examined his motives. Nothing wrong in being a Good Samaritan. Anybody who had to put up with Joey was deserving. Well, sure there was a sex thing. How would there not be with anyone who looked like that? Plus he'd been a long time celibate with only that one night with Marlene.

Seriously horny for the first time in weeks, he reminded

himself that, evidence to the contrary, he was an adult. Recognizing the attraction didn't mean he had to act on it. Besides a chick that desirable probably had a boyfriend. Even if she didn't why should she want him? 'Cause he was white with okay features? Dream on.

Next evening, freshly shaved and showered, he drove up, reached over and opened the passenger door. She slid in. "Okay, tell me about you and Joey." He looked at her, smelling the perfume, taking her all in. It felt like a date. Last night he'd whacked off thinking about her, promising himself that was as far as it was going to get.

"Oh. Yeah. Sure." He tentatively began, giving an abbreviated version, getting into it, picking up speed, adding detail. Several times she called Joey a "little bastard" and once softly yet clearly enunciated "motherfucker" but for the rest of the time listened without comment. He had gotten as far as his ride to the Bonnano house when he turned into the Villa Toscano lot and braked. She stared at him. "Are you making all this up? You know just to – entertain me?"

He raised his right hand, "As God is my judge." They each got out. He went through the restaurants side door, she went through the front.

Halfway through his shift, he was called into the owner's office. Giorgio in a tailored dark blue suit with muted, almost invisible red stripes, handed him an expensive cell phone. Kevin spoke into the mouthpiece. "Hello?"

"How'd you like to be out of there a little faster?" Bonnano's voice. Kevin strolled to the other end of the office.

"Sure. Who do I have to kill?"

"How about starting with your sense of humor? Italian-American Social Club on the Hill, twelve noon tomorrow."
The line went dead.

Giorgio's head was down, checking orders as if he hadn't heard. Before leaving Kevin put the phone down on the desk. "Thanks." Still counting, Giorgio nodded.

After work, Kevin strode out into the chilly parking lot, hands jammed into the pockets of his black leather coat, wondering what Bonnano could want from him. He started as Philippa stepped from the shadows. She giggled. "Sorry. I didn't want our little friend to see me."

When he turned onto the street she looked over at him. "Okay, part two." Kevin wound up the story in less than five minutes. "You can't be the only one he's ripped off."

"No kidding. It's a miracle he's still breathing, connected or not."

"At least you got some payback."

"Not nearly enough."

They made the connection to 195 in silence. After a minute she turned to him. "Listen, you know my uncle, the one I said you'd like? He's here in East Providence and he's got a lot of old records. He used to be a deejay in Mississippi."

"Really? What was his name?"

"Ben Akers. On radio he called himself The King Bee. His show was – are you ready for this?" She rolled her eyes, "The Jive Hive."

"Never heard of him. What town and station?"

"Greenville, maybe Greenwood, I can't remember the station. Anyway all his records have been in storage since he came here. That was the late 1970's. You think they could be worth something?"

"Possibly."

"If they were could you get a good price?"

"For all of it? Sure. But if it's really good it'd be better to sell it by the piece."

"So we'd work out some kind of three way split?"

"Yeah, but does your uncle want to sell?"

"He has to. They're tearing down the building he's in. He has to move in a few weeks."

He pulled to the curb in front of her building. "Okay, but don't say anything to Joey. Don't even hint at it."

She smiled sweetly. "I wouldn't piss down that little slime's throat if his guts were on fire. Talk to you later." He watched her walk away, the sexiness not totally blotting out the curious image she'd just laid on him.

Philippa unlocked the outer door, then her mail flap in the vestibule removing an envelope of Valu-Pak discounts and her maxed-out credit card bill. She stuffed them in her handbag, entered her apartment and flicked on the wall light. The white Ikea couch jumped out from the other nondescript furnishings. Above it was her framed Seurat print – the pointillist confetti style enhancing the holiday mood of moneyed fin-de-siècle picnickers. She stared at it hungrily feeling both a slight lift and subtle pang.. They were there and she was here.

She removed her pink and white air-cushioned running shoes, turned on the "James Newton in Venice" CD with a remote. The solo flute trembled and swooped, dove pure notes under the basilica of San Lazzaro Degli Armeni where it had been recorded.

Villa Toscano had sold her a second-hand espresso machine. In the small white kitchen she steamed milk before pouring it into a mug with a shot of Fra Angelica. On the couch she flicked enviously through Harpers, reminded that her tits and ass were too pronounced for the severe lines of costly haute couture. Tossing the rag aside she drained off the elegant soporific.

The small bathroom was light pink with muted blue accents – the walls, shower curtain of embossed fish, a framed print of Watteau's gauzy dreamlike "Embarkation to Cytherea". Only the 80 watts in the sea scallop light fixture above the medicine cabinet mirror was harsh.

Philippa washed her hands with antibacterial liquid soap and pinched out her soft contact lenses. Her green eyes were now yellow agate – tigerish and feral. She avoided looking into them as she applied a wet green clay mask. The sinuous flute music played on. She shucked off her dress, peeled off her stockings, unhooked her filigreed white bra, stepped out of her sheer white panties (both on sale at Victoria's Secret) and slipped into a silken pale yellow robe. She sat on the padded toilet seat and examined her toenails, scarlet polish complementing her dark bronze skin. Her face was now stiff from the clay. She carefully brushed her teeth with an ortho-pik and flossed. When she had rinsed off the mask and patted herself dry she applied a moisturizing cream. She clicked off the music, went into her white bedroom and slipped between the clean peach-colored silken sheets before hitting the TV remote. Conan O'Brien was listening to some young good looking black actor wearing a tan gabardine suit. As he spoke about the martial arts discipline that had changed his life she fell asleep.

The Italian-American Social Club, a former private

home, was a white Victorian on a side street off Atwells. The matching front doors with white curtained windows displayed a Christmas wreath with red velvet bow. Kevin gave the young maitre d' his name. In the main room on his right, a buzz of voices came from the middle-aged and elderly diners. He'd been here only once before, the food a few cuts above Chef Boy-Ar-Dee.

He was ushered up the curving stairs. Halfway down a narrow carpeted hallway, Charley Tuna in navy blue suit, dark red and blue plaid shirt buttoned at the neck leaned against the wallpaper. He nodded to Kevin and opened a door. In a small room Bonnano sat at a table drinking San Pellegrino, chewing on a bread stick. He wore a double breasted grey suit the color of a liquid lead pencil, a medium blue shirt of soft cotton open at the collar. He nodded towards the empty chair. Kevin hung his old black leather car coat on the old fashioned wooden wall rack next to Bonnano's cashmere overcoat and sat down. He had on a pink tee shirt under a 50's black sport jacket with pink flecks.

"Food better up here?"

"Definitely." Bonnano pointed half a bread stick at him, "You gettin' on okay?" Kevin pushed out his lips, slightly raised his right shoulder and opened his hand. Bonnano gave a short barking laugh. "What's this? You been aroun' guineas so much you startin' to act like one?"

"Well, I have to hear your nephew run his mouth all the time."

"I hear they got a black girl in there can shut him up."

"She's not bad."

"It's not smart to get involved with women outside your background. Hard enough dealin' with the ones you're familiar with."

To Bonnano's left a window, framed by dotted Swiss curtains, looked out on a few white upper stories under tarpaper roofs. Above them the neutral sky was divided by a power line. For no good reason Kevin remembered his father telling him of going to dancing school with the Protestants. A place in Pittsfield called Trescott Hall, his father's parents paying the money so their son could advance himself socially. The boys wore white gloves, navy blue suits, white shirts, maroon ties and black shoes. Girls wore pastel crinolines, white anklets and Mary Jane shoes. "We did the friggin' box step for three years while one old lady played the piano and the other hit two pieces of wood together. Claves. 'Step, step slide young people.'" Up through the 1950's they had allowed Irish, some Italians but no Jews. In the mid 1960's the place became, with thudding irony, a B'nai B'rith.

A waiter with black eyebrows and perfectly barbered white hair entered setting a small green salad in front of Bonnano who regarded it unhappily. The man turned to Kevin, handed him a small typed menu. Out of his right nostril a single white hair curved back towards his nose like the tusk of a wild boar.

"This doesn't look like the downstairs menu."

Bonnano nodded. "It isn't."

From the limited selection Kevin ordered the calamari appetizer with hot cherry peppers and then the osso buco.

The waiter stopped writing on his pad. He shook his head. "Unh unh."

"Unh unh?"

"That's right."

"You're out of it?"

The man glanced at Bonnano, back at Kevin. "You don't want it."

"So what do I want?"

"Swordfish pizziaola."

Kevin handed back the menu. "Okay, and a glass of prosecco." The waiter left.

Bonnano took another breadstick. He bit off a third, chewed, took a sip of the San Pellegrino, swallowed.

"You must be on a tough diet."

He grunted. "Doctors. You a gambler?"

"Literally or do I like to take risks?"

"I already know about the risks."

"I can play poker and blackjack okay."

"You're not a counter?"

"Like a real mechanic? Not even close. Someone say I was?"

"No, but I was told you were just a bartender and you come into my home with a recording like some hotshot Fed." He took a swallow of water. "Okay. So you're maybe a little better than average but nothing special Ever had a problem with it?"

"Nope. I've seen enough of those losers." Bonnano was silent. "When I was a kid my old man took me to Atlantic City and gave me ten bucks in chips. I went over to the craps table and bet with the house. I won and cashed in. Figured I was ahead."

"Suppose you'd lost?"

"Goodbye ten dollars."

"That's it?"

As Kevin shrugged, the waiter entered with the calamari and a flute of prosecco. Kevin took a bite, sipped the crisp slightly carbonated wine.

Bonnano was regarding him fixedly, "Good, huh?" Kevin, still chewing, nodded. "Okay, here's what this is about. Every Tuesday and Sunday at five o'clock you drive to Foxwoods Casino with a hundred dollars which you get from me. You lose it no big deal. You keep anything you win. Spend maybe an hour making little tweety pie bets, come back to the restaurant. First time you go take two extra keys to your trunk. Leave the first one on top of the front driver's side tire when you get down there. Second one same place when you get back to the Toscano. If it works out, after two weeks you quit dishwashing."

Kevin shifted in his seat, "This about drugs?"

"No. But even if it was you don't know anything. You're in no way attached to me."

"Suppose I was seen comin' up here?"

Bonnano smiled thinly. "Then we wouldn't be talking. Yes or no?"

Kevin took another swallow of prosecco. He felt like he'd lost his balance, was teetering on the rim of a cliff. He imagined a lady newscaster on TV, his photo in back of her with MULE FOR THE MOB underneath it. He opened his mouth to refuse and heard himself agree. Bonnano counted out four hundred dollar bills onto the table cloth. Kevin picked them up. If he lived through all this it'd make a good story to tell his future son or daughter.

In the backseat of the Lexus, seated on a folded blanket, Brandy, the Golden Retriever, looked longingly out the window hoping the car was headed to Roger Williams Park where Charley often took him to chase squirrels.

Bonnano leaned back, stuck another tasteless stick of gum in his mouth, and shook his head. "First Irish gourmet I ever met - must have some Frenchie in 'im." He looked over at Charley. "Sorry." Charley's mom had been French Canadian.

"He gonna work out?"

Vincenzo shrugged. "You try someone. If they don't screw up you give him a little more responsibility. Keep moving 'em up. Not so fast other people get pissed, but fast enough so they don't start feeling resentful. Good business management."

Going south on 95, he saw the giant blue exterminator's bug on the right was wearing a Santa Claus cap. He'd been looking at that bug – a Providence landmark - since he was a little boy in his parent's car. At Easter it had bunny ears, Halloween, a pointy witch hat, Fourth of July, a white goatee and striped Uncle Sam topper. Most things change but a few don't. You just have to be able to spot what they are.

"Hey there, it's Philippa. My uncle took me to his storage space. There's over a thousand 45's – maybe fifteen hundred – all in boxes. I convinced him to meet you tomorrow afternoon. Give me a call as soon as you can." Kevin rewound the cassette and played the message again, stomach tightening with excitement. He'd found the odd rarity junking or buried in somebody's list for cheap but no undiscovered mother lode. By now the whole country had been pretty well strip-mined. All the really big hits - the Ace warehouse in Jackson, Krupp's in El Paso, Sammy Torrito's in Gretna, Ratner's in San Diego and many others - had passed into misty legend, their fabled riches still able to animate old timers and mesmerize envious newbies: "It was so hot in there the sweat was dripping off my nose. I pick up this box of broken records and there are five copies of all the red wax Flamingos on Chance in mint condition!"

"Wow."

"Yeah, and I only took the stuff I knew!"

Kevin had never been more than an audience for these sagas. Now maybe he'd be the one telling the story. He saw himself casually handing Marlene the baby's college fund as well as... Whoa! Hold up. Only the tiniest percentage of leads ever panned out. The old man's records could be junk, or thrashed, or stolen or –. He steeled himself to keep the persistent gut thrill under control, stop his brain from throwing up shimmering dream castles.

On Saturday he picked up Philippa. Smiling radiantly, open camelhair coat and silk paisley scarf over an off white sweater and tight jeans, she immediately warmed up the grey day. She held up her hand, gloved fingers crossed. He did the same. As they drove on the 10 to where Cranston meets Providence she warned him. "He's very eccentric, might be getting Alzheimer's. Whatever crazy stuff he says, don't argue or he'll get stubborn. Just agree and he'll take off on something else."

"You can't remember anything you saw?"

"They just looked old."

"Banged up or in pretty good shape?"

"Oh they weren't scratched or anything." She smiled. "He took better care of them than he did my aunt," pronouncing it "ont".

At the bottom of a dead end street a row of frame houses weathered from age appeared near collapse. She had Kevin him park across from a charred structure whose open upper floor windows were covered by tarpaper. "That's his place. Some boat people firebombed a family up there; killed the mother, father and two little girls. "

"Why?"

"Who knows?" She looked stonily out the windshield. "These people are rough. A few months ago a black gang was messing with some of their teenagers. Next day the kid's relatives flew in from Chicago with automatic weapons. Shot 'em all after school on the outside steps. Killed most every one and a young kid that just happened to be there." She shivered, turned to him putting on her smile. "Shall we go?

Kevin followed her across cracked pavement up steps into the door-less building. It was dark inside, smelling predictably of urine and damp. They mounted the wooden staircase. Wallpaper hung in mildewed strips. Somewhere a radio played contemporary jazz - Joshua Redman or maybe James Blake. Philippa knocked on the door at the top. No answer. "You try." Kevin banged three times. There was a curse from within. In another few seconds locks were unfastened and the door was opened.

Before them was a little hunched figure wearing several overcoats, sunglasses, woolen gloves, scarf and pulled down wool knit cap. The jazz tenor blared behind him, overloading a cheap radio's speaker.

"Who're you?" The voice was hoarse, whispery, barely audible in the din from the radio.

"IT'S PHILIPPA! YOUR NIECE! I BROUGHT THE FRIEND I TOLD YOU ABOUT! KEVIN, THIS IS BEN AKERS!"

The small man made a guttural sound and moved to one side. Kevin followed Philippa into the apartment. The walls were still blackened from the firebomb blast. In the room's center was a greasy bottom sprung couch and ripped over-stuffed chair. A big wooden telephone line spool served as a table. Amongst the clutter on its stained top was a peeled back can of sardines, an open box of saltine crackers and an open half pint of Hiram Walker's Peppermint Schnapps. A large screen TV against the opposite wall with the color messed up showed a soundless porno video. The copulating figures had lime green flesh. It took Kevin a few seconds to realize it wasn't sci-fi.

Uncle Ben broke off staring at Kevin, made a question-ing sound at Philippa. She walked over to a small rickety ta-ble, turned down the radio's volume. "This is my friend who wants to see your records. Remember? We talked about him coming to see you?" The little man looked from her to Kevin and back again.

"Philippa tells me you were a deejay down south." Uncle Ben grunted. "You meet any blues singers? Howlin' Wolf? Son-ny Boy Williamson?" Uncle Ben nodded vigorously. "You met 'em both?" Another nod. "What were they like?"

There was a brief pause. "Goddamn assholes!"

Philippa turned away to hide a smile. Kevin tried again. "You got a good record collection, huh?"

"Mm-hm!" Like Richard Pryor's Mudbone character he smacked his lips for emphasis.

"Do you have any here?" Uncle Ben nodded. "Can I see them?"

"Unh-unh."

Philippa gestured Kevin to step back. She led her un-cle over to the couch and sat down with him speaking slowly and quietly. Occasionally the old man would break into her pleadings with a short protest. She kept on soothing him. After some minutes he began to nod his head. He got up and with a quick glance at Kevin shuffled pigeon-toed out of the room. Philippa looked at Kevin and rolled her eyes. What'd I tell you?

Ben shuffled back into the room holding a small torn cardboard box with sleeved 45's. He put it down on the spool table. Kevin came over. "Okay if I look at these?" Ben nodded. Kevin began to flick through them. They looked Vg+ or better. Lil Greenwood and the 4 Jacks "My Last Hour" on gold top Federal maybe a Vg+ about $300, a Joe Houston's sax instro "Atom Bomb" on blue script Imperial Vg++ maybe $60, Sonny Boy Williamson's "Boppin' With Sonny" on yellow Ace M- another $60, and The Master-Tones" Tell Me" on Bruce the first with the push marks and publishing on the left side Vg++ maybe $1,000. Kevin looked at it for a beat longer than the others. "These are nice records," He was trying to sound casual. "You want to sell them?"

"No."

Philippa smiled at him. "You don't want to but you will, right Uncle Ben?"

He shrugged, held up his hand and rubbed his fingers together.

"Philippa tells me you've got about fifteen hundred 45's. How's fifteen hundred dollars?"

"Hmpf!" He jumped to his feet. "Get your cheatin' ass outta my house!" He opened his mouth to add something and began to cough. He jackknifed over, tumbled back onto the couch, jerking about, wracking spasms shaking his body. Wildly he reached out, knocking a bottle of pills off the spool table. Philippa darted in, snatched up the bottle popping the lid. Uncle Ben, arms wrapped around his chest as if it would crack open, held up two shaky gloved fingers. Philippa shook out two pills, dropped them into his gloved palm. He threw them into his mouth, washed them down with a slug of the Schnapps. His coughing began to subside. She whispered to Kevin to go out and wait in the car. Fifteen minutes later, looking worried she got in shaking her head.

"What?"

"I'll tell you. Let's get out of here before I get more depressed than I already am."

They were back headed towards Providence when he turned to her. She was looking out the passenger window, "So?" he prompted.

She was silent a few seconds. "You shouldn't have offered him a dollar a record."

Kevin slammed his hand down on the steering wheel. "What the hell does he expect when I haven't seen all the stuff? What he showed me may be the only decent things in the whole load!"

"Take it easy. That's what I said." It was the same tone she had used on her uncle. "But he's not all there and you have to remember what these records mean to him. Anyway he won't go below thirty thousand. Maybe twenty five if you gave him cash. So I don't know. This whole thing was probably just a waste of time."

"It all depends, but since he wants to see the money first it's a catch 22."

"He just wants to know you can afford it."

"Well I can't. Not right now."

"No savings, no parents, no –"

"My father hardly has enough for himself. My wife definitely won't."

Frustrated, she bit the tip of a manicured thumbnail. "He's liable to change his mind any moment."

"Couldn't you go in there, read stuff off to me on a cell phone?"

"Hmm, maybe."

"'Cause otherwise it's not gonna work."

CHAPTER TEN

Tommy Rivers was 36 years old, 6' 2" and solid as the Providence Biltmore. Eighteen years ago he graduated from Mystic High in Connecticut with a football scholarship to Colgate. That summer he was blasting down through Noank, CT on a friend's rice rocket, totally tanked on 'Gansett when he hit a pothole and slammed into a telephone pole, shattering both his right kneecap and his football career. Four years later he became a patrolman for the Mystic Police until 1991 when he got bounced for juicing. Harold Shank, his Pequot cousin and a counter at The Foxwoods Casino and Resort helped get him hired as security guard. He'd been there ever since.

He saw himself as a heavy duty poker player, but because Foxwoods employees weren't allowed to gamble in public places, had to drive up to private games in Providence. One of the oldest was held weekly at the Florida Hotel off Eddy Street, pink and green exterior complete with fake palms. Late one Saturday night after losing a hand, he started bitching about his shit salary. Since the Japanese had recently acquired rights to Foxwoods, Tommy accused the tribal owners of selling out their own people. One of these days he'd rip the place off and disappear. How would he do it? Never mind. He had "a golden window of opportunity". Bonnano heard about the boast before the game was over. On his instructions one of the players suggested that Tommy could possibly improve his salary without leaving town. They'd be in touch.

Tommy figured his stoop shouldered, sad sack cousin Harold might take a risk if the pot was big enough. Six days a week for four years Harold had sat on his middle-aged butt, counting out vast sums of money when his salary didn't allow him to do much more than support a fat wife and make bullshit mortgage payments on his dumpy house in Richmond. His one pleasure, 'Wave Breaker", an eighteen footer, had been unseaworthy for almost two years ever since a bad late summer storm had crashed it down on a piling. The bank wouldn't allow him a second mortgage. He'd never been able to afford the five grand to fix its stove-in hull.

One slow Sunday afternoon in September, at Tommy's invitation, they'd sat in a back booth at Eddie's High Life, a dingy Warwick corner bar. In the front Eddie and a handful of customers watched college basketball. Tommy had started feeling Harold out, mildly bitching about his own life to get the droopy closemouthed bozo to open up. When he did – a trickle of complaints that became a droning flood - Tommy had steered him back to The Foxwoods and why someone hadn't taken it down big time. "Security's too tight," said Harold morosely, hands folded in front of him. "You oughta know that."

Tommy swallowed off his Sam Adams draft. "Aw, it's just no one's thought of how to do it yet."

The Foxwoods Resort and Casino in Connecticut was a sweet deal for the Pequot Tribal Nation. Immediately south of the Rhode Island state line, surrounded by woods in the middle of fuck all, tourist buses constantly in and out, it generated about a billion dollars a year. Smack on the New England Cosa Nostra's doorstep and no way for them to cut themselves a decent slice out of all those daily millions. A few lone wiseguys had made decent coin capping at Blackjack – a practice wherein a player is surreptitiously given, or takes, extra chips from the dealer after a winning hand. But the multitudes of those eyes in the sky - the evenly spaced "decorator" black balls hanging from the high ceiling, each with a vid cam, two trained on every table - had caught the rest. Besides, individual stings of 20 to 30 K were too small for an organized mob effort. They needed the promise of a far bigger score. Now they had it.

Paul Lemongello, thinning black hair, drawn ascetic features, was a devoted family man in his late 50's living in Pawtucket. A very fine engraver and printer, he did wedding invitations, brochures and ads for local businesses. He also had created a set of plates in the mid-90's that made near-perfect counterfeit bills which he was too nervous to try and pass. When word leaked to Bonnano that the plates were for sale, he'd had some of the queer paper examined by a local expert. The verdict was impressive. Lemongello was told to keep his handiwork safe until an opportunity presented itself.

As soon as the tall bald man with glasses walked into the shop, the printer didn't have to ask the reason. He went in the back and returned with a brown paper package wrapped in twine. He handed it over.

Charley Tuna nodded. "We'll be in touch."

At the Foxwoods Casino, bills were counted, put in

stacks by denomination and fitted with paper collars before being transferred to metal eyelet canvas bags. The amount of each, written on a form, was put inside, the bag's neck secured and padlocked with a combination lock. Stenciled on the bag and applied to the lock were matching ID numbers. Twice a week, a Foxwoods truck with two guards took ten to twelve million to the bank; approximately a half million per bag. Because of his DUI record, Tommy was never allowed to drive, always riding in the back with the money. When Bonnano heard that last bit everything came together nice and tight - like the separate parts of a machine reassembling when a film is run backwards.

Early in the week Tommy was to call in the amount of one bag. Bonnano would have a double layered brown plastic bag – the same kind the casino used for trash - driven down in the trunk of a car. It would contain a matching amount in counterfeit bills, the larger ones marked as if by a cashier. Tommy would stow the bag of counterfeits inside a metal half-full firearms chest kept in the far back corner of the casino's armored truck. When he wheeled out the canvas bags he would, courtesy of his cousin, know the combination to one which had the identical amount as the trash bag. Once locked inside the truck, he simply switched the fake cash for the real. On the ride back he rode in the passenger seat. Later, during a break that night, he'd transfer the trash bag of legit bills from the firearms chest to a specific car trunk and walk away clean.

Bonnano figured to do this for a few weeks, quit for a month and do it again. Eventually the bank would catch on and the Casino would instigate tighter security. Until then Bonnano and company would make millions. Whoever drove the trash bag of real bills out of the lot would be at Foxwoods twice a week. A known crime family member might raise suspicions. Kevin seemed ideal.

Even though Tommy was taking the risks, the split would be 60-40 in Bonnano's favor. Out of their shares Bonnano would pay Lemongello and Tommy would take care of his cousin – so far the only missing piece.

Harold looked morosely at his glass of untouched lager. "That's it?"

Tommy nodded. "After we make each bank deposit you call my cell that night from any pay phone and tell me the amount, combination and number of any bag you've packed. Every time you do this you get ten grand. Not bad for a fifteen second phone call."

Harold shivered in the heated air of the bar. "How do I get paid?"

"Your choice. These guys'll make a drop in cash, wire it into an account, whatever you want."

"S'pose something goes wrong? I could be a witness against them."

"Against who? You've never met them. They've never met you. Besides, no one can prove you made a phone call."

"The casino could have someone follow me."

"But first they gotta discover something. By then you'll have made enough to be living quietly and nicely wherever you want."

"You'll quit at the same time?"

Tommy smiled smugly. "Don't have to. Since I got a drunk collar I'll just get tanked on the job. They'll fire me and I'll do a big boo hoo hoo. They'll never suspect."

Harold sat motionless for a few seconds before reaching for his beer, taking a cautious sip. He put the glass down and wiped his mouth with a plain paper napkin, "Just a short phone call?"

"Twenty seconds tops."

Kevin didn't like gambling. Losing his money – or anyone else's – was at best unpleasant. True, he gambled every time he bought a record to trade or sell, but that was tied to what he loved. Pure gambling was too raw. It made him nervous.

The slots were moronic and blackjack too much of a headache. Tuesday night under the Foxwoods high ceilings, he played roulette and craps, generally losing most of his hundred, fantasizing hooking into a hot streak and buying Uncle Ben's collection. On Sunday he walked out with $275 but was down to $26 by Sunday. At least the money wasn't his and for the time being – thank you, Jesus – he was free of Joey. However, the time margin to buy the records was shrinking.

When he got in Marlene had called. He dialed the Dedham number.

"Kevin, Lucy Meisner told me she saw you at the Foxwoods Casino. Have you been gambling?"

Fuck. "Well, uh- yeah but not with my money. See this guy gives me a hundred to go down there twice a week and gamble for him. He's an old bar customer but he's confined to his bed and he pays me to –"

"What's wrong with him?"

"Cancer. He hasn't very long. Anyway he called the bar, they gave him the number here."

"And he trusts you to bring back what you win?"

"That's the good part. I keep what I win. I just have to tell him as I'm doing it on the cell."

"But he doesn't want anyone to know his name?"

"That's right."

"Kevin?"

"Yeah?"

"You're fulla shit." She hung up on him.

Kevin put down the phone. If he called her back with the real story she'd never believe anything he ever said again. The way Lucy Meisner was always bragging about where she'd been, her fat ass should've shown up in some ritzed-out place like Monte Carlo - not the Foxwoods. Because of her, Marlene thought he was running amok, blowing coin everywhere and lying about it. Probably never come back to him. Now, more than ever he needed to make that buy.

Next night at the restaurant Kevin's cell rang. Philippa was calling from the lady's room. "Go to the men's. I'll call you back."

"What is it?"

"Just go."

Seconds after he'd come through the door his cell rang again. "My uncle told me he's decided to sell on eBay."

"He's got a computer?"

"He says he'll pay me or somebody else to do it."

"How much?"

"Not enough. Besides it'd take forever. If he sees actual cash he'll forget all about eBay."

"But he's a paranoid loony tune. He'd actually let you spend time in his storage unit?"

"Oh, sure. I'm family. Once I'm there I'll call and tell you what he's got. Only I don't know anything about value and conditions."

"I'd have to school you."

"Better make it fast. Tomorrow afternoon?"

Kevin picked up a six pack of Dogfish 60 minutes IPA and a medium pizza at Casserta's and drove over to her apartment. She met him at the door in a shiny teal green blouse with scooped neckline, tight black velveteen slacks and open toed green sandals. Like Philippa herself, the gooey colorful pie when plopped down amidst all the minimalist white looked impossibly voluptuous - like a stripper in a Quaker meeting-house. She had a good appetite, matching him slice for slice and knocking back two ales. Then, with the aid of price guides and 45's in differing conditions, he gave her a crash course in grading. After twenty minutes he began quizzing her. She did surprisingly well.

"So," she asked when he told her she was ready, "what do you want to do now? Wait with me until he calls?" Seated next to each other on the white couch, she looked brightly into his eyes, their knees almost touching.

The familiar undertow of mutual attraction was suddenly in the room. The beers had relaxed his vigilance, made him want to surrender. He stared at her full lips, high thrusting tits, warm curvy body, but held back. Was it loyalty to Marlene or something about the woman herself? "No, uh, that's okay. I've got things to do at home."

"If that's what you want." A little put out, her lips curving in a half smile. Scaredy cat.

He gathered up his guides and records, "I think it'd be

best for now." Keeping the door open for another time unsure if it was gallantry, lechery or both.

"Well...maybe you're right." Amused green eyes looking right at him, telling him she knew what they were really talking about.

Headed back to the apartment Kevin blew out a lungful of relief. He'd side-stepped big trouble - Brer Rabbit refusing to get stuck in the tar baby. Huh? The image shocked him before he reminded himself that everybody was part racist. Hell, maybe she thought white guys' dicks looked like uncooked chicken legs or something.

Suppose he'd fucked her and she'd fallen in love with him? Okay, it was unlikely, not to mention egotistical, but you never knew. Sex with no strings was as rare as "Stormy Weather" by the Five Sharps. Or suppose he flipped out over her, blowing what was left of his marriage. She was obviously high maintenance. Would probably dump him for anyone halfway presentable with more money. He expelled another big breath. Jesus, she was sexy. Too bad that "doing the right thing" almost always translated into "denying yourself major pleasure".

When her call came in Kevin was reading an old paperback of "The Wench Is Dead" by Frederic Brown and relating to the grad student character living a skid row life for sociological research. He picked up the receiver, adjusted his pad and pen. "Yeah?"

"I'm here looking through the first box."

"Did you choose it or did he?"

"I did. You want me to start?"

Kevin heard some exclamation from Uncle Ben in the background. "Sure. Just tell me artist and label. Oh, how's the condition overall?"

"Good. Most of them are shiny with no scratches – maybe a little scuffing. Okay. Leroy Washington on Excello, McKinley Mitchell on Boxer, Rudy Green on Chance, Moroccos on United, Flamingos on –"

"Which Moroccos?"

"Uh – 'Hex Me' and –"

"Red or black?"

"Maroon."

"No, I mean the wax."

"Oh, wait a second...red."

"Good. What label for The Flamingos?"

After twenty minutes Kevin knew that this was the score of a lifetime. All were early 1950's to mid 1960's blues, r&b and vocal groups from thirty to two thousand dollars. He did some quick calculations, figured he could make his cost back in days with say, fifteen to twenty single sales to major collectors. Already he was tempted to hold back a few heavies but no, to be an ice cold dealer he had to sell 'em all.

"Tell him I can only raise twenty five thousand cash for everything."

There was a muffled conversation, during which Kevin heard a few outraged yelps. Philippa got back on the line. "I had to tell him that before he could go somewhere else he'd be evicted and that you were honest and wouldn't try to short change him."

"And?"

"He agreed as long as you can come up with it in a week."

"I'm on it right now."

Kevin hung up, forehead covered by a fine film of perspiration. Good thing he hadn't told her about the casino runs. She might have urged him to clip some of the bills at the start of the week, buy the load and sell enough to replace the money before it was counted on Sunday. Or was he making her into a ventriloquist dummy so he wouldn't have to cop to his own idea? The thought caused his skin to prickle.

Via telephone he started trying to pre-sell some of the heavier pieces to collectors across the country.

"Ralph? Kevin...Good, How're you?...Hey, I got a couple of group things you might need...Okay, The Dolls on Teenage mint...I know...Fifteen hundred...Okay, good...Willows on Allen Vg++. The hard one...That's right...two grand...and get this: Fatman Matthews and the Four Kittens Vg++ for five... Thing is, to secure this load I gotta be paid right away...Postal money orders or cashier's checks only."

"Dan, Kevin Dougherty...Not bad...Got some killer blues...How about Willie Nix on black Herald stone mint....a thousand...I can't. Not in this shape. Hey! You're the first person I called." He hustled effortlessly, without prior thought or preparation. Having listened to the same pitches when the roles were reversed he could do them in his sleep.

At the end of four days he was trying to think if he'd missed anybody when Philippa rang. "He's called me twice today already. 'Where's that boy's money? Is he gonna pay me or not?' "

"He said in a week."

"I reminded him but his sense of time is a little shaky."

"Can't you cool him out?"

"I have – for the moment. How're you coming?"

"Fifteen grand."

"And the rest?"

"You'll know soon as I have it."

He clicked off, sat looking at the black cordless like it was a poisonous insect. Could he tap Bonnano for a loan? Maybe, but he'd have to pay some huge vig and if instead Kevin asked him to invest he'd want at least half, probably more. Waste of time.

By Monday he should have $13, 500 from the collectors. He had a little over $1,500 in the checking account. If he did skim $10,000 from his Foxwoods collection on Tuesday he could buy the load on Wednesday. Since Bonnano's guys only picked up the bags from Villa Toscano's safe on Sunday nights he'd need to replace what he took by Sunday before driving back from the casino. Of course there'd be more cash in one bag and less in the other than there should be but it'd total out correctly. After being puzzled they'd most likely shrug it off without reporting to Bonnano. Better yet if they didn't count the bags separately there wouldn't even be a question.

Kevin's nerves twanged like rubber bands. He'd seen enough films noirs to know how this shit turned out. Somewhere out there a seemingly unrelated incident was poised to intersect his path causing failure and doom. Like "Quicksand" (1950). Grease monkey Mickey Rooney has a hard on for a blonde tramp but not enough jack for a date. He swipes a twenty from his boss' car dealership cash register, then almost gets killed trying to pay it back. Shit. For ten large the Mick probably would've been disintegrated.

Kevin continued to screen his own movie. Suppose he dipped into the till and couldn't make the 10K back in time? Someone could be late or renege. Bonnano might change the pickup schedule. They could be scoping him out, see him cop the money. A demonic little Porky Pig head popped up before his eyes. "Eh-eh-eh, th-th-that's all folks!" Kevin shivered, seeing his dead body thrown in an acid vat, covered in a quicklime pit, dumped in a backwater marsh.

Suppose he didn't take the money, didn't buy the collection, worked off the "debt" to Bonnano and just schlepped his way along? He was an average Donald Duck not a lucky Gladstone Gander. No big greenbacks would ever blow into his hand. Without taking some risks nothing good was ever gonna happen.

Marlene and her mother went to a matinee at the local Cineplex, posters outside of grimly determined male stars brandishing firearms. Inside color and lights, a concession stand, candy machines, noisy arcade games all on busy patterned carpeting. They sat in the middle of a mostly empty theatre awaiting a movie based on some famous novel about how women were mistreated in the 19th century. The screen showed a slide.

QUESTION: IN WHAT FILM DID BRAD PITT PLAY A VAMPIRE?

Joanne turned to her daughter. "Heard from Kevin?" Marlene nodded. "And?"

"He said he's working on something that'll make us a lot of money." Joanne covered up the bottom half of her face with her left hand, made a gun out of her right and pointed it at her daughter. Marlene slapped it away. Joanne shrugged. Marlene started smiling, then giggled. So did her mother.

ANSWER: "INTERVIEW WITH THE VAMPIRE"

They were trying to muffle their laughter as the lights went down.

CHAPTER ELEVEN

The Providence Athenaeum founded in the mid-18th century was one of the oldest libraries in the US. Its hexagonal sides were ringed round by balconied walkways on three levels connected by corkscrew staircases. Kevin, a longtime member, had to sign for Philippa and her uncle.

She stood in the doorway of one of the top reading cubicles which broke up the encircling shelves of books. Inside, Kevin seated with a gym bag at his feet, counted out money under the green metal shade of a reading lamp. Uncle Ben, nearly buried in wraparounds, woolen cap and scarf stood motionless halfway behind his niece. His lips moved in silent repetition as the bills were stacked up in piles. An occasional far off cough or scraping of a chair echoed in the building's stillness.

When an even thirty thousand was on the table Kevin looked at Ben. He nodded. Kevin scooped up the piles and put them back in his bag. Ben coughed, whipped out a handkerchief and buried his face in it. Philippa took a step towards him. He waved her away. After a few more hacks he gained control of himself, put the handkerchief back in his overcoat pocket. The three went down to the first floor and out the front door, the old lady librarian at the checkout counter peering over her half-moon glasses at the odd trio.

Outside snow flurries fell out of an off white late afternoon sky, flakes meltingly cold on their faces. Philippa and Ben got into her honey-colored Toyota. Kevin followed them in the Mustang through narrow downtown streets towards North Providence. While he drove he tapped his wedding ring finger on the steering wheel, thought of playing a tape, decided not to.

The storage building had an electronic gate. Through the Toyota's rear view window he saw Uncle Ben tell Philippa the code and watched her punch it in with a slim tan gloved hand. The gate slid back jerkily. They each bumped over the bottom runner before parking side by side next to the main entrance – a metal door with a single bulb above it. Out of the cars, standing under the falling snow, they watched Uncle Ben press the buzzer. "Yes?"

"Morganfield 307."

Kevin frowned. Philippa leaned in to him, whispered, "He gave them another name for 'security' reasons." The buzzer sounded. Uncle Ben with an effort pulled the door open. A cinderblock interior lit by white fluorescents. Floor and bottom half of the walls gray, top half and ceiling white. Steps echoing faintly, they got in the elevator without talking. Ben hit #3, the car rose, stopped and let them off. They walked down an identical corridor to 307. Ben took out a ring of keys, unlocked the door, turned on the overhead single light bulb. In the dim wattage Kevin made out about eight open boxes of 45's mostly in paper sleeves. Wondering how Philippa had been able to grade anything in such poor light he walked in, sat down on the one chair, put the gym bag down and bent forward to look in the nearest box.

All at once beside him Uncle Ben began coughing, the small body convulsing, head jerking down to his knees as he fought to control the spasm. Kevin looked at him, then at Philippa who had been going through a box in the far corner.

"Get some water!" Philippa ordered him. And then to Kevin, "Look at these I think they're rare!" Kevin went over to see, the coughing not as loud coming from outside in the corridor.

The box Philippa showed him had a Specialty 45 on top – Little Sonny, a New Orleans r&b singer. Kevin knelt down, pulled it out. Red wax. He tried to see the condition but the light was poor. He ran his fingers over the surface, felt deep scratches. "It's trashed."

"This looks good." She pulled out a Hickory 45 of the Varieteers "I've Got a Woman's Love" and gave it to him. He peered at it, began sliding it out of its sleeve and stopped - it was almost cracked in two. She handed him a gold top Federal Little Esther. It looked M- but felt too thin. He stood under the light angling the record so he could read what was etched in the dead wax of the run out grooves: "Issued 1974". A bootleg.

Kevin became aware that the coughing had stopped. He looked up. No noise came from the corridor. His gym bag was missing. He ran out of the room. The corridor was empty. He heard Philippa call out behind him as he sprinted to the stairway door, flung it open and took the steps three at a time. No one on the main floor. He was about to run outside when he saw a metal trolley, wheeled it over and, opening the front door, jammed it in behind him. It was dusk, the snow heavier now, swirling around in the street lights. Kevin ran out to the fence, went through the pedestrian opening and looked up and down. No one on the street or sidewalks.

He turned, ran back to the building. Philippa was at the entrance behind the wedged in trolley. Before she could ask he told her Ben had left with the gym bag. Philippa stared at him, mouth open. "He stole it? He must be on foot. We'll catch him."

"Okay. No! Wait!" Kevin was pacing about wildly. If he didn't move he felt he'd explode in pieces - an over wound watch. He stopped and held up his hand. Flakes swarmed around the outside bulb like bugs. "We'll take the records first."

"Why?"

"We find him without the money, he says he never took it and I've got nothing. Pulling something like this he had to have a car stashed. He's gone back home or he hasn't. What I'm saying is I need some insurance." They re-entered the building, Kevin grabbing the trolley ahead of Philippa who, wide eyed, was shaking her head in shock.

"I cannot believe he did this!"

"Maybe he figured I wouldn't buy them. When you checked 'em out did he let you pick?" They entered the elevator, pushed the button.

"Yes, like I told you. Only..."

"What?"

"That box I went through? It was in the middle of the floor by itself - the only one open."

"Sure. So you'd look at it. Probably had the best stuff. Was it that dark when you were here?"

"No, much brighter."

"He switched the bulbs." They went inside the open unit, "How about the other boxes?"

"He pulled records out and showed them to me."

"So the only one you actually picked yourself was the first one?"

"Yes. I'm sorry. I didn't think my own uncle –"

"Hey! Not your fault." They began loading the trolley.

After two trips all the boxes were packed in the two cars. Kevin drove up to the gate. It didn't open. He stared at the electronic exit box on a pole, about to lose it.

Behind him Philippa rolled down her window and called to him. Kevin rolled down his window, turned to face her. "I think I remember what he pressed going in. Uh, star-six-eight-two." Kevin entered the numbers - nothing. She was calling out to him again,"Oh wait! Try pound sign–six-eight-two." He did so. There was a whirring and the gate started sliding open.

"Thank God for small favors," he muttered meaninglessly. His mother's phrase. He rolled out into the street, following her as soon as she pulled ahead.

Surrounded by darkness, peering through the whirl of dime size flakes, and an occasional oncoming pair of headlights, Kevin tried to control a rising panic, freezing his imagination, jamming his mental projector so he wouldn't see pictures. It was a losing battle. Finally he braked behind her on Uncle Ben's street. They got out, bent themselves into the snow-laden wind, walked down the sidewalk to the building's entrance and gingerly walked up the creaking stairs in total darkness. Ben's apartment door was open. The wall switch didn't work. Kevin went back to the Mustang, returned with a pen flash, playing it over the interior. Everything was as he remembered. Only the TV was missing.

"Were you in here today?"

"No. He was waiting for me out front."

"Well he's gone now. And I can't call the cops on him either."

"Why not?"

"I just can't. Let's get the stuff over to my place."

She unloaded the boxed records as he hauled them up-stairs. He spot checked each one feeling the nausea rise. They were in a word – junk. 1970's hits, 1950's pop, 1960's drek. Stuff from two to ten dollars. Anything halfway good was hammered, cracked, warped to hell. It'd take years of nickel and dimeing to make over five hundred on the whole load. He was absolutely and truly fucked.

"Philippa," Kevin said as she was leaving, "you hear from him or anything about where the money is call me right away no matter what time it is, okay?"

"Promise," she said softly and slipped out the door leaving him in the empty lit up apartment with boxes of valueless plastic.

Marlene was supremely pissed off. She'd just been treated to a pre-Christmas gift massage at Joanne's health club, lying on her back in a towel. Was it imagination or was she starting to show? Would she eventually be gazing down at what was once her carefully maintained flat stomach grown into a great mound so distended and bloated she wouldn't be able to get up without assistance? She shut her eyes, willed herself to relax and think positively.

Kevin had either become a compulsive gambler or was trying to win the lottery or had some dumbbell Ralph Kram-den-like scheme "Alice we're gonna be rich! Shoe polish that glows in the dark!" Here she was in self-exile with her mom and that pipe-smoking stick Phil who never spoke, while her so-called husband, free as a goddamn bird, enjoyed the apart-ment and didn't have to wait on her one bit. All the stupid movies she'd seen featuring solicitous young hubbies were turning out to be a total crock. She'd figured they were exaggerated but believed they had to have had at least a germ of truth. Hah!

So it was coming down to the crunch. Cut him loose and go it as a single mom or try and squeeze him for as much support/help she could get - pretty bleak either way, definitely no birdies or valentines. He wasn't evil or stupid, just way the fuck off her current wave length and likely to remain so when she needed him most. Gee, life wasn't fair. What a big surprise.

Bonnano, also prone, lay, post-colonoscopy, on a gurney in a white open back hospital robe covered by a sheet. Still hazy from the anesthetic, he blinked in the light, squinting up at the doctor's clean, smooth antiseptic face - pale eyes behind steel-frame glasses, rubber gloves being pulled off clean, smooth hands. Somewhere a phone was ringing. He shut his eyes; opened them. A woman was speaking nearby. He drifted off again, back to the time he was twelve years old in the hospital after an appendectomy on that long ago early summer. The sun shone on his face. A cooling breeze came through the partly opened window bringing the far off cries of children. He envied them. He also felt comforted by and superior to them too. Now, as he again broke the surface of consciousness he felt somehow the same.

Joey the Weasel was totally grooved. His Uncle Ben costume of tattered overcoat, scarf and knit cap lay in a jumble on his folks' old fashioned stuffed sofa, emptied red nylon gym bag on the floor. The low blond coffee table held two neat stacks of fifteen grand apiece and a chilled bottle of

Cristal with two cocktail glasses. A Frank Sinatra Christmas CD played "Silent Night". Set, game and fuckin' match! As he wiped the last of the Max Factor off his face with cold cream the doorbell chimed the first eight notes of the Platters' "My Prayer". He tossed the Kleenex, checked himself in the hall mirror, wiped off a remaining line of brown makeup under his hairline and went to the door. "Philippa, that you?"

"Yes. Open up."

With a lordly gesture he ushered her down the short hallway to the living room. "How'd it go? You two went back to the shithole, right?"

She nodded, brushing the snow off her coat. "And then I had to help him take the records to his place."

"He's welcome to 'em. Fuck with me, huh? Well we cleaned his clock but good and here is our ree-ward." He gestured to the two piles of bills. Unnecessarily, since Philippa had eyeballed her future RISD tuition upon entering. They'd actually pulled it off. As the tension relaxed in her neck and shoulders, she kept wishing it was she and Kevin who'd taken Joey, but you couldn't have everything. "So – how'd he seem? All set to track down old Uncle Ben? Only place he's gonna find him is on a fucking box of rice!"

Philippa sighed. "Oh, he'll be looking alright." Joey's crowing pride in what they'd done irritated her. She just wanted to forget it.

"Great! That'll cost him more money. Hey! Maybe you should go too. Get him to pay your expenses as you investigate hot leads."

"Just give me my share so I can go home."

"C'mon'! We gotta at least have a drink of champagne to celebrate!"

"No thanks. Those are the wrong glasses anyway."

"Whattya mean? They're champagne glasses."

"Old style. Today people drink it from a tulip glass or flute so the bubbles last longer."

"Huh. Well don't you at least want to count it?"

"Why?"

"Because I coulda made a mistake. I doubt it but on the off chance I did I don't want you thinkin' I shorted you intentionally."

She gave him a look, went over to the sofa, sat down and hesitated for a second before realizing it made no difference which stack she chose. She took the one closest to her and started counting hundred dollar bills. He picked up a box of Camel filter tips, fired one up watching her. She had just passed four thousand when Joey made a strange noise. She looked up.

A man in a woolen ski mask dressed in black had materialized in front of the living room's drawn curtains. He moved forward to face her across the table, a large automatic in his black gloved hand. Open mouthed Joey raised his hands.

"You!" He pointed the gun at Philippa. "Take the bag off the floor and put the money in it." She didn't move.

"Chrissakes do as he says!"

The fear in Joey's voice cut through her paralysis. Unfeelingly, she lifted up the empty gym bag, placed the money inside. "Now zip it up and toss it to me." She did. He caught it with his free hand. "I'm leaving. You run after me I'll shoot you." Facing them he moved swiftly out of the living room, down the hallway and out the front door.

Joey and Philippa looked at each other, ran over, parted the drapes to see out the living room window. A light snow still fell on the houses, sidewalk and street. Somewhere close by a car started up and drove away. Philippa ran toward the phone. "Call the police!"

Joey stepped in front of her. "What? Tell cops somebody just stole thirty grand in a freakin' gym bag? That'll sound real legit. Then it gets around, Dougherty finds out and no, no, no were not gonna do that."

"So we just let him run off?"

"Hey! I guarantee you. That little punk is history. My mom's maiden name is Bonnano, right? I'll call my uncle right now. No, it'd piss him off this late. Okay, first thing in the morning."

Philippa became aware that she was trembling, hands shaking. Joey went over and took her elbow. "Here, siddown. Take a few deep breaths. You'll feel better."

She sank down onto the couch, heart fluttering, sick to her stomach. "I think I could use a drink of that champagne." Joey grabbed the bottle, tore off the covering. She frowned faintly. "Where'd he come from? He just appeared!"

Joey twisted the wire loose, popped the cork. "Probably through the basement window. That's the third shithead to break in here. I gotta get myself an alarm system. The big question is how'd he know when to hit us. He sound black to you?" She shook her head. "Me either. You tell anybody about this?" He poured two glasses, his hand dead steady.

She shook her head. "You seem pretty cool."

He smiled. "'Cause I know we're gonna get it back. There's an old wop saying: 'Revenge is a dish best eaten cold.'" He clinked his glass against hers.

"How're you so sure you're going to eat it at all?"

"I'll show you how fuckin' sure I am." He took out his

wallet. "Little brain dead jerkoff didn't even think about how much I might have on me." He counted out ten hundreds onto the coffee table. "Take it. That's an advance against the recovery of our money." Philippa looked at him. "I mean it. When this kinda shit goes down in my neighborhood those responsible always pay – unless maybe it was done by a master criminal which this moron is definitely not!"

Philippa drained her glass, picked up the money before he changed his mind. Joey gave her a refill and topped off his own glass. "How do you think he knew we had that money?"

"Maybe he got onto Kevin. Maybe he overheard us in the goddamn library and tailed us - doesn't matter. I'll get it back. I promise."

Afterwards she couldn't remember all the details. She'd drank several glasses trying to wash away the coldness inside, Joey constantly assuring her he was going to recover the money. She'd been grateful for the thousand, thinking maybe she'd misjudged him, maybe he was halfway decent under his asshole exterior. He kept comforting her. She kept drinking pushing down the persistent fear and, somewhere in there her memory got hazy, but it had happened - a weasel fuck.

She woke up naked on the couch under a blanket with a dull throbbing headache. The lights were on, Sinatra still singing, "Oh by gosh by golly, it's time for mistletoe and holly". Night showed through a side window. The small elegant Patek Philippe copy on her wrist read 12:45. She got up, began retrieving her clothes, concentrating through the pain in her temples. Her purse was next to the empty champagne bottle, the thousand still there. For services rendered. She imagined Joey crashed out in whatever was his bedroom, a victorious smirk on his face, saw herself lifting up the empty champagne bottle and smashing his head in with it. No, she needed him alive to get back that money. Her head hurt. She finished getting dressed.

Outside an icy wind blew wet snowflakes into her face. The headache became piercing. Her Toyota was still parked behind his wish-I-had-a-big-dick Hummer. She got in and fired it up, letting the engine run for a few minutes before putting it in gear. She was almost to the end of the block when a big acidic bubble burst in the back of her throat. She swerved over to the curb, braked, pushed open the door and vomited the champagne and most of her dinner onto the street. Depleted, shaking, she shut the door against the awful cold, turned off the headlights, turned on the heat and, after wiping her mouth with a Kleenex, slumped down in her seat, teeth chattering.

Half an hour later, she was still there, a little warmer, not wanting to be anything but still, when she heard what sounded like a car navigating slowly towards her. A light colored panel appeared through the swirling flakes, rumbling past in the opposite direction. She stretched to get rid of the stiffness and was about to put the Toyota in gear when she glanced in the rearview. What she saw made her pause. The truck had parked across from Joey's house. The driver, a young guy all in black got out, ran across the street up to the front door carrying a red nylon gym bag.

Kevin, shoes off otherwise fully dressed on his bed, was just going under behind a few shots of Maker's Mark when the doorbell rang. He went to the window. A coating of snow lay unbroken on sidewalk and street, Philippa waving up through the dancing flakes. He went down the rubber carpeted stairs and let her in.

Ten minutes later, sitting rigid on the couch, he'd finished her confession, telling him everything but the couch fuck. "If you saw Lino go into the house with my bag why didn't you confront Joey right then?" He was pushing past the grogginess, on full red alert, suspicious of another setup. "Demand your share or you'd run it all down to me like you just did?"

Sunk in a butterfly chair, she shook her lowered head. "He would have only denied it and then he'd have been on his guard. This way you might get it back."

"So what's your interest? If I do, I'm not giving you a cut. I can't give you one."

Philippa nodded. "That's okay. If I can't get half why should he get it all?"

A pause. "Why should you have gotten half in the first place?"

"We had a deal."

"Yeah, right. We had one too."

She looked at her hands. "I didn't know you. I needed my tuition money. I still do."

"You would've done this even if you did know me."

She looked up. "I wouldn't have liked it though."

"That's nice. So what was that come on at your place about, just a little fling with the mark? Curious to see if it'd make any difference once you'd robbed me?"

"No, it was just...well, I liked you and I haven't been with anyone for a while." She smiled tightly. "I doubted if I'd have much of a chance later."

"Oh yeah, I forgot. Style and comfort - have your cake

and eat it too." He gestured to the boxes of records. "Know where these came from?"

"Um, he said he bought them for two hundred from some guy who answered that ad he's got."

"When?"

"Last weekend?"

"So he hasn't really checked them out?"

"No, he said it wasn't worth it. They were junk. Why?"

Kevin thought a moment. "Okay then. You want to help me get my money? Here's what you do. First thing in the morning you call and tell him I phoned you all excited because I found a Vg++ copy in here of uh, Jerry Butler and The Impressions on Vee-Jay. Remember the label – Vee-Jay."

"What song?"

"For Your Precious Love."

She frowned. "Wasn't that a hit?"

"Huge – on Abner - but it was first released on Vee-Jay and recalled. Only a few exist - none in mint condition."

"What would one be worth?"

"Five, six grand easy. He'll be more than interested. Then tell him I called you from the car and I'm driving down to New York to sell it and when I get back I'm gonna go through to see if I can find anything else. Tell him maybe he oughta check out the boxes before I get back."

"Why?"

"It's already Sunday. There're no banks, no access to safety deposits. I'm gonna drive down now and park in front of his place so he can't slip away from me. He comes to search here I go right back and search his place for my money - earlier the better."

"You're sure he'll come?"

"If you do like I told you."

"Suppose he gives up and comes back?"

"He won't. Soon as you see him go inside here you're gonna call the cops. A suspicious-looking man just broke into 223 Wolcott who's now banging around inside the upstairs apartment. They ask who you are, you say you don't want to get involved and hang up. That way I don't take him apart and then his uncle doesn't have to have me taken apart. Capeesh?"

Philippa thought for a moment, smiled wryly. "Molto bene."

During the early morning the snowfall had gotten heavier. Kevin, layered in warm clothes under the black leather car coat, red woolen scarf wrapped around his head, covered by a thermal blanket, opened his eyes to the sound of a passing engine. The Mustang's windows were snow crusted, entombing him. He stretched, breath making frosty puffs, and with a gloved hand rolled down the window. The whole world was pillowed in bright white. Curbside cars nearly buried, the trees looking like sharply etched lace patterns. A fresh path furrowed the middle of the street. The plow had probably woken him. His watch read 9:06 AM. Shivering, he rolled up the window, clearing it, did the same with the one on the passenger's side. He started the engine and hit the wiper button but the snow was too heavy. He jumped out, wiping it off with his forearm before doing the same to the back window. Inside again he hugged himself, twisting the stiffness out of his neck, waiting for the engine to warm up so he could turn on the heater.

Philippa was feeling better. Once home she had rehearsed her lines in a hot bath, washing Joey off before calling him. His "Yeah" had been guarded. She had continued playing into his charade, asking if there was any news yet from his uncle, pretending to be only mildly put out with him over the couch incident, dropping hints so the little needledick would think he'd sent her over the moon before she set the hook. That part had been easy.

The Mustang's interior was just beginning to get cozy when Kevin's cell rang. He blew on his hands again, fished it out from an inside pocket. "Yeah?"

"I think he was impressed but he said it was too risky." She sounded put out.

Kevin opened his mouth wide, stretching his stiff face muscles and concentrated. "Bullshit. He's already gotten in and out of there with my entire collection."

"He meant too risky for taking a chance that he'd find another copy."

"Come on. He'd hardly tell you he was gonna do it if he was gonna do it. First it'd be admitting intent to commit a burglary. Second, if he found anything good in that crap he wouldn't want you to know, right? Hey, his report cards probably read 'Doesn't share well with others.' I think you should be ready to get over to my place." Kevin had been watching Joey's front door the whole time. Now, as if on cue, it opened. Enter The Weasel. "It's him." He killed the ignition so the exhaust wouldn't draw attention, grateful for the covering snow. "Shit! He's carrying the bag!"

"What do I do?"

"Stay on the line." He tossed the cell onto the passenger seat.

Joey walked down the snow covered steps and through the drifts to his Hummer. He wiped off the side mirrors and windows before getting inside. Dimly silhouetted, he started the engine. Kevin did likewise counting on the other's noise to cover it. The Hummer pulled away from the curb, trundled down the street, came to the corner and turned left, Kevin following. *The Weasel smells the bait.*

Snow was falling again by the time the Hummer turned down Kevin's street. Five car lengths behind, the Mustang made the turn pulling immediately into the curb. Kevin cut the ignition. Through the drifting flakes, he saw Joey get out holding onto the red gym bag.

"SonfaBITCH!" Kevin hit the steering wheel inadvertently sounding the horn. He froze. Joey stopped halfway across the street, looked up and down a few times, saw nothing coming and continued on up the snow buried steps to the apartment building. Kevin peered over the steering wheel, watched him unlock the front and disappear inside. *He must also have a key to my apartment.*

Kevin and Philippa had kept talking while he'd tailed Joey. He picked up the cell. "Still there?"

"Yes."

"He took the bag into the apartment."

"Do I call the police?"

"No, I can't prove that money is mine and I need it right away."

"Be careful. His cousin had a gun last night."

"I'm going up there. Wait exactly ten minutes and call my apartment. As soon as the machine comes on say it's you and ask for someone to pick up. When Joey answers, and he will because he'll be curious, keep him talking for as long as you can, what does it look like, has he found anything, does he want you to help him – like that. Okay?"

"What're you going to do?"

"I'll call you afterwards if it works."

He turned off the cell, put it back in his inside pocket. Outside the melting flakes stung his face. He crossed the packed street and into the alleyway, cutting behind the building. As he entered the small backyard shared with Francine, his legs plunged into thick drifts wetting his Levis and Nike tops. Quickly, holding himself tense, he mounted the back wooden stairs and peered through his kitchen window. An indistinct shape filled the entrance to the living room. He dropped down in a crouch. Above him, snowflakes whirligigged against the power lines.

The muffled ring of a telephone. He rose up, looked again into the now deserted kitchen. Noiselessly he unlocked the backdoor and slipped inside, breathing through his mouth. One last ring, then his familiar spoken message over a slow surf guitar. There was a beep. Philippa identified herself. Footsteps, a button being pressed, Joey's ready-to-be-irritated voice "It's me, whatsup?...Yeah, well I thought about it an' decided to check 'em out... I'm gonna go through 'em now but don't hold your breath."

Shoulders hunched, Kevin crossed over the kitchen's black and white linoleum squares to the living room entrance. Joey, phone at his ear, still in his overcoat, sat on the couch, boxes of junk 45's at his feet. The gym bag was on the floor between the back of the couch back and the front door. Kevin looked around the kitchen, spotted the broom standing in a corner.

"No, stay where you are...Because you won't know what

to look for. Also it'll be twice as risky if he comes back...Who said?"

Crouching, holding on to the bottom of the broom he slid a few steps into the living room, extending the handle towards the bag, slid another step and hooked its tip through the carrying loops. He lifted it an inch off the floor and moved backwards, pulling it into the kitchen.

"Of course...Look, I'm gonna hang up. I'll call if anything happens."

Joey put the phone down. Kevin backed into the kitchen. As he was slipping out the back, the phone rang again. He locked the door behind him, hurried down the wooden steps. The snow was slowing down, fat flakes spiraling lazily. Gaining the sidewalk he stuffed the bag inside his car coat, walked swiftly within existing footprints and got back into the Mustang. Hidden from view, he unzipped the bag and counted, expecting Joey to have pocketed some of the thirty grand. Miraculously he hadn't. Halle-fuckin'-lujah! He let his head fall back, breathing deeply, loosening chest tension. Soon as he turned his cell back on it began ringing and vibrating.

"Hi. I got –"

"Where the hell are you?" Marlene!

"I'm, uh, right in front of the apartment."

"Oh – I thought you'd forgotten. Francine just called."

His brain began scrambling. "Francine?"

"She thought she heard you in the apartment just now but no one answered the phone. You didn't forget did you? You know what this means to him."

Shit. Wiley's sleepover. "Oh yeah, absolutely. "

"Good. Listen, I made an appointment with Howard. I'd like you to come too. We could talk to him together."

"When?" Not that it would do any good but for her it was symbolic of wanting to fix their marriage.

"Tomorrow at one. You'll be back with Wiley in the late morning."

"Yeah, okay. One o'clock tomorrow. Will you do me a favor? Call Francine and have her send Wiley out to the car. I've been having some trouble starting it up right after I turn it off."

"You think it's serious?"

"No, no. Probably on account of the cold. I'll get the gas station to check it."

"Oh – okay then."

Another close call. At this point any number of straws with Marlene could be the last. He clicked off, got out, pushed a new layer of snow off the front and rear windows, expecting to look up and see Joey racing out of the building gun in hand. Back behind the wheel he dialed Philippa.

"I got it while you were talking. He's still up there. Now call the cops. Tell him a man came out of a silver Hummer and broke into the apartment building."

"What are you going to do?"

Kevin laughed. "Take the neighbor's kid to a cub scout sleepover on a battleship."

"Practicing being a dad?"

"Exactly. I'll talk to you later."

He pressed END. Minutes later, Wiley, bundled up in a red parka, striped knit cap and earmuffs, burst out the front door carrying a rolled up blue sleeping bag. Francine stepped out in sweatshirt and jeans. She yelled her son's name. Still running he looked back and returned her wave.

Wiley yanked open the passenger door, flung the bag

in back and jumped in. He pulled the door shut, held up his wrist. "Look what I got!" Partially obscured by a blue woolen glove was a yellow, red and green watch. "It's the official Power Ranger Watch. It has an alarm."

Distracted, Kevin almost said "cool" but stopped himself, remembering how many bored parents automatically use both it and "awesome" as unthinking approval. He shot a last look up at his apartment window before driving off, wishing he could stick around for the last act. Pop goes the weasel. At the building's front door, Francine was biting her cuticle.

Wiley's blue eyes shone with excitement. Kevin marveled at how little it took to make a kid happy. He used to be like that - extracting every shred of enjoyment from a movie, a comic book, even a jawbreaker. Ha! Were those days ever dead and gone. Now, after scoring a sought after 45, he oftentimes wouldn't even hear it all the way through. Wiley was waiting patiently for his reaction. He refocused, "Fasten your seat belt. So uh, you can tell time now?"

"12:17. See?" He held up his wrist grinning.

Kevin nodded approvingly. "Any of your friends going?"

"Yep, they are."

"Who?"

"I think Peter Zigler and uh, Russell Chang. I think."

"They good friends?"

"Pretty good. I have play dates with Peter. We've been to each other's house for sleepovers."

"Good, you can hang with him and his dad while I leave for a few hours."

Wiley's mouth started to crumple. "I have to spend the night alone?"

"No, no, no. I'll be back well before bedtime. You got a

schedule?"

Wiley ripped open a Velcro'd pocket flap and extracted a folded fax. Kevin shook it out with one hand. "Hey! They got a lot more goin' on since I was there in the 60's! Documentary about the ship hosted by an original crew member, two Hollywood movies, Morse Code class." He punched Wiley on the arm. "Not bad!"

The woman's answering machine message coming in after Philippa's call had made the Weasel jumpy. Unless you were Speed Racer how could you drive all the way to New York and be back in time for this kiddie sleep over thing? Aww, the dipshit probably forgot all about it when he saw that Vee-Jay. Joey began sifting through one of the swill boxes, then hearing a car door slam outside, stopped. He jumped up, went to the window. A pale blue snow topped car was driving down the street - a Mustang. It turned the far corner and vanished, Joey still picturing it after it had gone. Same as the one Kevin had driven to the storage unit. So that'd been him.

Smelling a rat, he wheeled around to grab the bag, saw it was missing. Frantically he looked around the room. Car doors slammed outside. He ran back to the window, looked down. Two cop cars parked in front. No lights, no sirens.

Joey ran into the kitchen almost tripping over the broom lying on the floor. He unlocked the back door, noticing snowy foot prints on the small porch. He did a swift calculation, swung over the stairway dropping into a deep snow bank. He pulled handfuls down on top of him and rolled into a ball.

Seconds later the crunch of footsteps came around the building. As they mounted the steps he heard the crackle of a walkie-talkie. He counted slowly to thirty then carefully pushed up through the freezing covering. No cop at the back door steps. Snow matting his hair, face and coat, he ploughed through heavy drifts to the alley, flattened himself against the brick wall and inched forward peering around the corner. Across the street, a tall cop stood by the Hummer, stamping his feet in the street, breath vaporizing in the cold air. Joey inched back to the end of the building, walked in the opposite direction, a cyclone fence on his left. He came out on a parallel street, wiping his face and hair, whacking snow off his overcoat, stepping gingerly along the sidewalk, trying not to let any more cold wetness into his shoes.

So, somehow Philippa had found out she'd been conned and joined up with Kevin. Well it wasn't over yet. That fruity Mustang would be easy to spot. As for the Hummer, he'd cover his ass by reporting it stolen. Let the fuckin' cops find it for him. Too recognizable for a good tail job anyway.

Joey kept walking on half frozen feet until he reached Hope Street. A restaurant on the corner had an OPEN sign in the window - blue gingham curtains and tablecloths, sturdy blonde furniture, blackboard with different breakfast specials. Entering the warm interior he chose a corner table. A big brunette waitress bustled over with menus and a place setting. She frowned, "Looks like you took a tumble."

Joey smiled. "Yeah. It's real slippery out there."

"Coffee?"

"Sure, and a Florentine Omelet with whole wheat." She started to take the menu. "I'll hold onto it, might get something else."

"Our cinnamon rolls are real good." Joey thanked her. He took out his cell and dialed Lino.

CHAPTER TWELVE

Battleship Cove, directly under the Bragga Bridge on the Fall River side, began business as a tourist attraction sometime after the 1950's. Four major dry-docked fighting vessels were open to the public year round.

A curved exit ramp off the bridge led Kevin onto a city street. He made a left, another at the first light and then under the overpass down a double dip hill to the Cove's parking lot.

A blustery chilly wind had come up along the harbor, sparse wet flakes blowing about. Kevin wrapped the scarf tighter around his neck, tucked it inside the front of his black coat. Tied sleeping bag under one arm, gym bag full of money under the other, he and Wiley followed a few scouts and their dads into the gift shop and ticket office. Among the usual postcards, historical booklets, pennants, placemats, pencils, pens and key rings were blank ID tags. Each had a four line capacity for name, phone number, rank or title - whatever you wanted. Fifteen characters/spaces per line. For five bucks apiece, they could be customized and delivered that night on board. Kevin and Wiley filled out forms in pencil keeping their choices secret. They went out the exit through a large wooden structure housing a few grey PT boats, up a series of metal gangplanks which led first onto a submarine, then a landing craft, then all the way to the broad cream colored deck of the SS Massachusetts – one of the biggest WWII battle ships.

Boy scouts, girl scouts, cub scouts and brownies swarmed the iron stairways, clambered on anti-aircraft turrets, disappeared through small elevated entrances into pillboxes. In front of them a cub scout was talking to his mom on a cell phone, dad standing by. Wiley's crew cut scout leader wore a white tee under a halfway open quilted parka, whistle dangling from a neck chain. He nodded at Wiley and Kevin, checking them off on a clipboard. Serious and military, he told them to stow their gear, pointing with the ballpoint at a hatchway on the left.

They descended steep metal steps into the warm belly of the ship. To their right was a glassed in mess kitchen, mannequin cook with toque mixing something in a metal bowl. Above out of a small speaker The Andrews Sisters sang "Don't Sit Under The Apple Tree". On the floor a painted yellow stripe led them along shiny twisty dark red passageways to interconnecting sleeping sections. Bunks, in tiers of four, were fastened to the walls by chains, sleeping bags both rolled and unrolled atop crisscrossing canvas straps.

Their small section along the passageway was separated at both ends by hanging clear plastic strips. They were quartered in the one remaining stack of unoccupied bunks. Kevin wanted the top one but with a smile, gave in to Wiley, just as his father had given into him years ago.

Wiley hoisted himself up, reached inside the unrolled royal blue sleeping bag and scrambled down holding an Olympus camera. "Mom wants you to take pictures." He looked at the red nylon bag in Kevin's hand. "You're supposed to put your stuff on the bunk so no one else will claim it."

"I'll hold onto it for now. Spread out your pajamas on that bottom one. That oughta do it."

Topside again, Kevin called his answering machine. Next to an anti-aircraft gun was a framed WWII photo of the ship's rotund commander. A plaque said he had just ordered that the entrance to his quarters be enlarged.

Kevin heard Francine's message. Then: "Mr. Dougherty. This is Sergeant Diaz of the Providence police. Someone reported a possible burglary in your apartment. We investigated and found your back door unlocked. We secured the door but if you find anythin' missing you can report it to –"

He disconnected and called Philippa, told her that Joey had gotten away. "He's gotta know you crossed him. Maybe even thinks you somehow got the money. Be careful."

Wiley was zigzagging about, exploring. Kevin heard him shout "Hey, Peter!" He ran to show a dark haired boy his watch. Kevin rang off, walked over and introduced himself to the father. Larry Ziegler was smooth-faced, average height, wearing a stone-colored parka. He told Kevin how much they'd enjoyed Wiley's visits, how polite he was and how skillful at video games, especially PlayStation 2. Clueless, Kevin smiled. The two groups took pictures of each other standing under the ships big guns, Kevin holding the gym bag.

They descended to the submarine deck and went inside, following single file through the narrow space. Wiley raced ahead to sit astride a shiny black torpedo and peer through the periscope. Kevin, crouched over, head bowed, threaded his way along the confines, passing the cramped quarters, noticing the officer's elegant sliver of a dining space with silver cutlery and glass goblets.

They re-emerged into winter dusk. It had become colder. Above the black water the Bragga was silhouetted against the darkening sky, headlights passing back and forth. Kevin's cell rang. Francine. Wiley got on, told her they were having fun. As he spoke Kevin realized he really was having fun. Maybe one day he'd do this with his own son.

The cops called Joey with good news. They'd found his Hummer. A thief or thieves may have intended to use it in a burglary but when they'd staked it out probably decided to abandon it. There was no damage. Joey thanked them, was told where he could pick it up and had Lino drive him over.

Back home, he went on the computer, continuing his Google search for every scout webpage in Rhode Island. Finding nothing he switched to Massachusetts. In minutes he'd clicked on a Fall River calendar. "Scout Sleepover on the SS Massachusetts, Battleship Cove." Twenty minutes later he and Lino were on their way.

Kevin and Wiley stood holding trays in the chow line for lukewarm creamed corn and pasty-looking fried chicken. Kevin got two cokes from the vending machine, handed one to Wiley. They sat down across from them the two Zieglers. When Kevin said he had a small emergency to attend to, Larry assured him there was no problem; Wiley was welcome to stay with them.

Kevin passed on the food, swallowed off his coke. The bag between his legs, 10K of it's contents mob money, alienated him from the whole scene. He got up to leave. Wiley looked up anxiously. "When are you coming back?"

Kevin knelt down, tried to sound casually reassuring.

"Couple of hours, maybe a little more. Tell me about the movies. Okay?" He rummaged in his coat pocket, found a service station receipt. "Here" he said, writing down his cell number on the back. "Borrow a cell phone and call me if you want but I'll see you before bedtime." He mussed Wiley's hair, stood up and made his way through adults and children to the door leading onto the deck. When he looked back to wave, Wiley, hair sticking up, was gripping the receipt watching him go.

As the panel truck came over the first dip before the parking area the powder blue Mustang shot past it going the other way. Joey yelled at Lino who swung the truck around and back up the hill. Seeing the Mustang take the on ramp to I95 West, they kept a few cars back, thinking Kevin would get off in Providence, slightly surprised when he turned onto 95 heading south. Surprised but not really worried. Joey knew they were following the money.

The Mustang exited off the interstate onto the Foxwoods Casino road. Joey and Lino wound around behind it all the way into the huge casino lot, watched Kevin park and get out, red nylon bag in his hand. Joey groaned. "Jesus! What's he gonna do? Blow it at the tables?"

"We gonna take it when he comes out?"

"No, too much security. We wait and see what happens."

Inside the casino, bag clutched between his knees, Kevin thoughtlessly played craps, pushing his stack of chips back and forth from win to pass, hoping and praying that after he'd replaced the money there'd be no questions.

Preoccupied, he lost track of time before noticing he was up over two grand. Winning big was so unfamiliar he kept staring down at the green baize as if it were a Ouija board. Two more passes. He was up almost six thousand. His watch read 7:10. It'd been over an hour. He had to leave to get back to Wiley before the ship closed. Cursing under his breath, he pushed some chips into pass. The player threw a six, then a nine, a five, a three and – made his point. Down to fifteen hundred! One more play. He started pushing his remaining chips towards the pass line and stopped. Minus the hundred he had fourteen hundred dollars more than when he came in. If he didn't go back to Wiley now he might lose it all.

Lino and Joey were still watching the Mustang when some big guy in a shiny FOXWOODS CASINO SECURITY jacket came out between cars holding what looked like a trash bag. He looked around, unlocked Kevin's trunk, set the bag inside, locked the lid and walked away.

Lino turned to Joey. "What was all that about?"

The Weasel couldn't put it together, "How the hell should I know?"

"So are we gonna do anythin' at all?"

"Yeah. We're gonna be patient. Not like those gook punks you knew in school."

Lino snorted. "Those guys! Look at 'em wrong, they'd just take out a gun, shoot you right there."

"Good way to get busted."

"You'd think, but people were too scared to say anythin'. I know. One of the leaders was a friend of mine."

"Unh huh."

"Seriously. This guy Minh Lee? He told me I ever wanted anyone killed he'd do it for a real good price."

"Discount shopping."

"I'm not lyin'. Swear to God."

Joey lit a filter tip Camel. He was thinking about what they'd just seen when Kevin appeared making his way between the parked cars towards the Mustang.

"He's got the bag," Lino said.

"I can see that. Does he look happy or sad?"

8:26 pm. "Ghost Train" a ferocious and expensive guitar instrumental by The Swanks on Charm pounded through his speakers while Kevin sped up I-95. Above him skinny clouds like skeleton fingers raked across a full wafer moon. Bedtime on the ship was before 10 PM. If he did the restaurant drop he'd never make it. Joe and Sally could do the pick up tonight if they wanted to drive to Fall River. Bonnano wouldn't exactly like it but he probably wouldn't be too pissed off either.

Past Exeter R.I., a little before Green Airport, he pulled into a semi-circular rest stop and jumped out. An icy wind numbed his face. He unlocked the trunk, put his gym bag inside, stuffed his gloves in his pockets and blew on his stiff cold hands preparing to unfasten the trash bag's heavy twist tie and put in the 10K he'd borrowed.

A vehicle swerved off the highway. Glaring headlights shone on his back. He slammed the trunk lid, pivoted around temporarily blinded. Doors opened. A snatch of techno hip hop cut off by two slams. Lino and Joey came around either side of the truck. Joey bareheaded in his dark wiseguy overcoat, Lino in gold quilted parka, knitted watch cap, an automatic in his gloved fist. Out on the highway two cars wooshed by in succession.

Joey was just starting to speak when a dark gleaming Lincoln slid into the rest area, braking hard alongside the truck. Joey and Lino turned, shielding their eyes against the double set of lights. A tall man with dark rimmed glasses and fur hat got out holding a gun. Two sharp explosions overlapped in the frosty air. For seconds Kevin was paralyzed, ears ringing. Then he turned, jumped into the Mustang, jamming the keys into the ignition. He gunned the motor, whipped around the semicircle and shot out onto 95 past screeching brakes and honking. His instrumental cassette played loudly while he wordlessly boppity-bopped along, cascading reverbed surf notes blanketing thought.

Lino ran a few steps towards the road, stopped and trudged back to where Joey was standing. On the other side of the Lincoln's open door the bald man sprawled motionless on the ground. Black camelhair overcoat, grey scarf, blue eyes in the large fleshy face staring sightlessly through heavy black rimmed glasses.

"Congratulations, asshole. You just did Charley Tuna." Lino looked at him blankly. Joey viciously kicked at the fallen fur hat. "Jesus Goddamn Christ! We're dead!"

"Why? He's the one threatened us with a firearm. Justifiable homicide, right?"

Joey laughed bitterly. "I'm not talking about cops."

Heart thudding, body tingling with adrenaline, gunshots still echoing in his head, Kevin mashed down on the accelerator and sped towards Providence. Was anyone wounded, dead? Did a bullet hit the car?

When his breathing had slowed, he struggled to get to his cell then stopped. He didn't know any of Bonnano's numbers. Instead he called the Villa Toscano, told Carlo he had to leave a message with the owner for Mister Bonnano. He waited, gripping the cell phone tightly, other hand on the steering wheel, looking out at the dark highway. "Pronto?"

"Hi Giorgio. This is your dishwasher. Tell Mr. Bonnano there was some trouble but everything's fine. I won't be able to deliver this evening so he should leave a phone number on my machine or with you."

Giorgio sounded unsure, like he was stalling, trying to think if he ought to get more information. Kevin rang off before he thought of a question. Now, no matter what was said later, at least he was on record.

Bonnano in black v-neck cashmere sweater and taupe slacks stood in the dark looking out the glassed-in porch. Moonlit snow was piled on his exercycle and rowing machine, the snow covered dock above black water. He jingled his keys and pocket change, an irritating habit of his father's that he had first objected to before unconsciously copying.

His thoughts, always tinged with melancholy, turned morbid when alone at night. The power that he'd held, nurturing all his adult life would die with him. There was no one to pass it on to – no heir, no close friend, no one with the smarts and balls to maintain it. Christ! He himself could hardly keep hold of it. Way things were going, in a few years he might only be holding air. At least Laura would be secure. Barring some kind of unforeseen improbability she'd probably outlive him. Even with her disease, stabilized as anything could be, she was strong as a goddamn block of cement.

It'd been over two years since they'd cut the cancer out but she remained terrified it might return, kill him and leave her penniless. No way. Fat Danny knew if he tried to siphon anything at all evidence would fuck him with both the D.A. and the family. That's why Laura was safe. Better to do business with a smart man than a dumb one. Dumb ones are unpredictable. They get agitated, shoot a hole in the boat, sink you with them. Like it or not everything was business and that meant being objective. Mushy thinking was why, when you got old, they wanted you out.

Hiring that kid was a perfect example, temporary lapse of judgment, probably because he and the old man used to like those 1930's movies with Jimmy Cagney and Pat O'Brien. Now it looked like the idiot had ripped him off for a short score. He shook his head, disgusted. Seventy-five percent of all Irish were not only dumb but fuckin' crazy. This is what happened when you ignored what you knew. Exasperated, he sank down on the couch. bright summery floral design throwing his aloneness into relief.

Almost immediately he pushed himself up, wandered into the little den off the vestibule. "The Caruso Room" was done in a rich somber 1920's style – wine deep velvet window sashes, windup phonograph with gleaming red and gilt horn, fine luxuriant dark patterned oriental rugs, maroon and green silk striped settee. He had conceived it as a kind of joke – a stage set from an old gangster movie – but soon realized that it was a temple where, surrounded by yellowing photographs of deceased family, he could feel less alone. Seated in the nighttime quiet, he let his thoughts drift about, bumping up against each other in murky waters.

The antique phone was ringing. He unhooked the black earpiece. Giorgio relayed Kevin's message. Before he could respond there was a beep on his cell phone. He told the manager he'd be right back and hit the cell's TALK button. Suddenly his

little cacarone nephew was saying something about a shooting. Bonnano had him hold on, told Giorgio he'd call back and
then made Joey repeat his story .

9:10 pm. In below zero weather Kevin rolled into the
lot under the bridge, hauled both trash bag and gym bag out
of the trunk and raced over to the gift shop to get through to
the ship. It was closed. He swore, hustled around to the side,
tossed the bags over a cyclone gate before hoisting himself up
and dropping down on the other side.

Nearby, behind the steering wheel of his two year old
gold Caddy, Sally Lipstick snorted, "C'mon', a woman can't
sweat inside her own pussy. You sweat inside your mouth?"
  "I mean like around it, "said Joe Low. "It hadda been a
hundred degrees, she's wearing these really tight black – "
  "Fuck!" Sally Lipstick spilled coffee on his crotch.
  "What?"
  Sally blotted himself with paper napkins. "He just ran
by and went over the fence there." Joe Low opened the passenger door. "Hold on. I don't get this dry I'll freeze my nuts
off." He kept blotting with more napkins, opened the door and
tossed them all out into the night. "Okay."

Bonnano, holding his disconnected cell phone, sat very
still breathing softly though his mouth. Laura was calling
from upstairs. Mechanically, he made the trek to her room.
  "Is Charles back yet?"
  "Not yet."
  She was put out. "How long does it take to get shots for
a dog?"

"That's tomorrow."

"Veterinarians aren't open Sunday."

"Petco is"

"Well, whatever. I wanted him to fix me some soup."

"I'll do it."

"The carrot ginger if we have any left."

Grateful for the distraction, he slowly went downstairs. Tomorrow he'd tell her Charley had gone to Italy for a visit - a family thing. From there he could string it out until she didn't ask anymore. The real problem was he couldn't promote Sally over Joe or vice versa. Besides, being around either one for too long would drive him nuts. Charley had been perfect and now all at once he was dead. It was beyond stupid.

He turned on the kitchen light. Joey, followed by his little pal, was driving in Charley's Lincoln with Charley's body folded in the trunk. If they got to the Villa Toscano parking lot without fucking up he'd handle the rest. Charley would have to disappear. Otherwise there'd be cops, warrants, no end of shit. Poor sweet guy never complained or asked for anything. Just did his job. If anyone deserved a nice funeral it was him and now he couldn't have one.

Maybe he'd heat up some of that soup for himself, might calm him down. He opened the refrigerator, couldn't find the soup - didn't even know where Charley bought it. Fury boiled up inside him. Holding tightly to the refrigerator door handle he took deep, even breaths. Something made him look up. Brandy, the golden retriever, was in the doorway, muddy brown eyes fixed on him.

On board the ship, Kevin slipped inside the darkened cabin. A whirring 16mm projector was showing the old Technicolor naval comedy "Operation Petticoat". Silhouetted heads watched Cary Grant look pained at Tony Curtis' bullshit. Bags held aloft, he moved alongside the wall until he saw Wiley slumped in a metal folding chair beside the Zieglers. He sat down on the other side mouthing a "Thanks" across to Larry who made a dismissive gesture with his hands. Wiley straightened up.

"Here's your tags," he whispered handing Kevin two cheap shiny metal ovals on a chain.

Kevin held them up in the projector's light. "Kevin Dougherty/ Record Freak/ Mixologist/ 454-478-9985"

"What's a mixologist?"

Kevin told him. Wiley showed his: "Wiley Rogers/ Power Ranger/ Soldier of Fortune/ 454-478-8665"

Kevin pointed at 'Soldier of Fortune'. "You know what that is?"

Wiley shrugged. "It just sounds cool."

"It is - in the movies." Somebody in back made a shushing noise.

"Can we go?" whispered Wiley.

"You don't want to see the end?"

He made a face. "It's too old. Besides I want to show you something."

They stood and went out into a round charcoal carpeted space, lists of Massachusetts WW II casualties wrapped around the huge central shaft. Narrow metal stairs led below deck. Stenciled nickel and dime prices for candy and cigarettes were still above the canteen. Below decks the wartime hits continued to play, "I'll Be Seeing You", "Boogie Woogie Bugle Boy", "We'll Meet Again". Kevin followed Wiley towards the sleeping quarters. "Me and Peter explored all over. We went down really far and I found the – what's that place that's like a jail?"

"The brig?"

"Yeah, the brig. And this place where they operated –"

"I want to hear about it but I have to go back upstairs to the men's room."

"There's one down here. Come on." Wiley led him through the tiers of bunks, full of scouts and dads, to an open space. Glass cases held guns, bayonets, uniforms, bombs, flags, photos. Mortar shells and mines stood in corners. "It's around there." Wiley pointed to the central shaft, "Inside the first room. But you better hurry. They're going to close the bottom part off soon."

Kevin followed the shaft around, crossed through another large bunk area and up one step to the cream colored head.

"It's all this fuckin' coffee!" Back turned to him, Sally Lipstick stood at the one urinal, cell phone wedged between left shoulder and ear. "So? All you gotta do if he comes off the ship is call me." He began shaking before zipping up.

Kevin about faced and sprinted back to Wiley. "Come on." he whispered.

"That's not –"

"I have to get something." Wiley ran to catch up. They reached their quarters. Kevin scooped up Wiley's pajamas on the lower bunk, jammed them back into the rolled sleeping bag on the top bunk. He handed him his red parka. "Put this on. There's a guy out there I don't want to see. What gets closed off?"

Wiley shrugged into the lined coat. "Everything underneath us."

"When?"

"I don't know. Soon." Wiley unstuck the Velcro flap, and handed over the Xeroxed sheet. Kevin unfolded it, read "9:30 P.M. all levels below sleeping quarters closed. 10:00 P.M. all entrances to decks closed." His watch read 9:18.

"Good." He handed it back to Wiley. "The brig have bunks?" Wiley nodded. "Alright then we're goin' on a little adventure." He bent down, face level with Wiley. "You trust me?" Wiley nodded solemnly. "Okay. You walk ahead. If you see a tall dark haired guy in a black overcoat, don't stare at him. Just turn and come right back, casually, you know, like you forgot something. Can you do that?"

"Sure." Kevin handed him the rolled sleeping bag. Wiley strode determinedly ahead through the crowded noisy bunk rooms, Kevin holding the bags full of money, keeping a good distance behind, ready to turn and run if he saw Sally. He paused before going into the main shafts open space. Wiley ran back. "There's no one. Come on! The stairs are right here."

Kevin followed into the large space. Wiley turned right and disappeared down a steep stairwell. Kevin took a few steps, looked into the small opening, dropped both bags onto a catwalk grid and descended. Banks of pressure gauges and other heavy machinery were intersected by metal walkways. Only a few were sealed off.

Wiley looked over his shoulder. "What's in that other bag?"

"Papers I have to deliver."

"Newspapers?"

"Special papers."

Wiley gave up trying to understand. "How come you don't want to see this guy? Is he bad?"

"Not really. I just owe him money."

They took corkscrew steps further below ships to a space with shiny cream colored floors. Evenly spaced doors were individually labeled DISPENSARY, OPERATING ROOM, and QUARANTINE. Opposite, behind a heavy glassed wall, a doctor mannequin was posed to operate on a mannequin patient. Wiley ran up two steps and turned right into the brig area. One of the three cells was open. It had two bunks.

"Can I have the top one?"

Kevin grinned in spite of himself. He heaved Wiley's sleeping bag on top of the metal strips, dropped his two bags on the bottom ones.

"Kevin?"

"Yeah?"

"Are we going to get in trouble?"

"Hell no. No one'll ever know were here. Even if you told Peter he probably wouldn't believe you."

"Sure he will. He'll see we're not in the other bunks."

"ATTENTION!" blatted a loudspeaker from somewhere above decks. "ALL ENTRANCES BELOW THE SLEEPING AREAS WILL BE CLOSED IN THE NEXT FIVE MINUTES. THEY WILL REMAIN CLOSED UNTIL NINE A.M. TOMORROW MORNING."

Some of the tension left Kevin's back and shoulders. Did Bonnano want him because of the money, the shooting or both? Sally Lipstick would keep searching above decks until all entrances were about to be locked. Come morning they'd be outside waiting. What was he going to do then? Jump overboard with Wiley on his back?

"Guess how many people have been killed on this ship?"

"A lot?"

"None. While you were gone they showed a movie."

His cell rang. Could Bonnano have gotten the number? He fumbled it out of his pocket, pressed the button, very carefully said "Hello?" Through crackling static Francine asked if everything was okay.

He told her yes and handed it over to Wiley who covered the mouthpiece and grinned at him, "Don't worry. I won't freak her out." But when he got on, he had to keep repeating himself. At last he shouted, "I'M FINE MOM! G'NIGHT!" Kevin resignedly took the phone back. He had been thinking about calling Bonnano. Not now. A garbled call would be riskier than none at all.

Wiley was looking at Kevin's bags. "Aren't you going to get your stuff out?"

"Naw, I'll just sleep in my clothes and use these as pillows."

"Can I sleep in mine?"

"Your mother wouldn't like it."

"How she gonna find out?"

"Women always know. Believe me."

"Okay. Can you tell me a story while I change?"

"Sure."

Kevin untied Wiley's bright blue sleeping bag. Pinkachu – the big-eyed yellow Pokémon character – covered the front flap. Wiley saw Kevin looking at it. "That's something I had when I was little. What's the story?"

"Get in your pajamas." Kevin helped him get out of the parka. Wiley scrambled up to the top bunk. "Well, uh, hmmm. Okay. Once there was this worm crawling around looking for food. He came upon a big red apple that'd just fallen off a tree, so he crawled up onto it and started eating his way in, even though it made him a little nervous."

"How come?" Wiley stripped off a green sweater and white jersey.

"Because a bird could just yank him out before he'd gotten completely inside. It took him two whole days to tunnel in so he couldn't feel the cold air on his butt. But the more he ate the bigger he got so he couldn't wriggle backwards because the hole was now too small behind him. He had to keep making it bigger in front."

"But if he was working really hard wouldn't he lose weight?" He pulled off his sneakers, shucked off his little boy jeans.

"Some, but he was eating more than he was losing. Anyway in about three more days he hit the core of the apple and started to go around it but it was so dark he lost all sense of direction."

Wiley pulled on his Batman logo pajama top. "Was he scared?"

"Not really. He knew eventually he'd push through the outer skin – which is what he did. Only soon as he got his head out in the air, a young robin who'd seen the movement on the apple's surface, grabbed the poor worm's head with his beak. He tugged and tugged trying to gulp him down. He tugged so hard that the worm came out with a POP! right down the robin's throat."

"Is that the end?"

"Nope. Fortunately for the worm he'd gotten too fat for the robin to swallow. The bird gagged and spit him out. He was going to pick him up with his claws and fly away but something happened."

"The worm ran away?" Wiley pulled on his bottoms.

"Worms can't run. Two other robins saw the commotion and flew down to eat him and while all three were fighting, the desperate little fat worm managed to crawl back inside the apple far enough to be safe, even though he could feel the birds trying to poke into his hiding place."

"Then what?"

"They finally gave up and flew away. Then the worm had to decide. Was he going to risk coming out again or stay where it was safe until the apple turned rotten. In the dark he might not know when that happened and if he ate it he'd be poisoned. But if he came out too soon he could be eaten by a robin."

"So what'd he do?"

"I dunno. That's where the story ends."

"C'mon!"

"Seriously. When I find out I'll let you know."

Kevin threw back the sleeping bag cover. Inside, Wiley was zipping himself up when the lights went out.

CHAPTER THIRTEEN

Alone in the dark with her mother's blinking Christmas tree, Marlene was freaking out. Joanne and Phil had gone to a movie. Kevin hadn't called to confirm the marriage counselor meeting. She'd left another message on his machine and then, a few minutes ago when she tried calling his cell, it rang and went dead. Maybe he never would call. She'd have the baby alone. What was his problem? She wasn't asking him to change 90 degrees. Just be more responsible and get a decent paying job. He was such a child! Ever since they'd married she'd seen it more and more. Loving him wouldn't change it. Joanne had told her that. Depressing how she was usually right.

Well, half right. For Joanne it was always Kevin's fault. Yet how secure could he feel with her running back to mommy every time they had problems? Okay. They were both babies but at least she was trying to be an adult whereas his level of commitment was just about zero. What the hell was she gonna do? Didn't he have any feeling for her at all? On the coffee table was the elaborately wrapped present she'd gotten him – a really beautiful vintage Hawaiian shirt that'd set her back almost $400. Her vision went red. Bastard! She grabbed it, jumped up, hurled it against the wall and then smiled in spite of herself. Good thing it wasn't a record.

Soon as the lights went out Wiley remembered he hadn't

brushed his teeth. He clicked on his small flashlight and got out of bed. There was a bathroom here but it wasn't operable. Francine had put a quart of bottled water inside the sleeping bag. Kevin shone the weak light on him while he brushed, rinsed his mouth and spit in the tiny steel sink. Predictably he needed to urinate. He and Kevin chug-a-lugged the water and then laughing, held the light for each other and took turns pissing down the sinkhole.

In the total blackness, Kevin lay awake on the lower bunk, car coat buttoned up, head on the gym bag, feet propped up on the trash bag. Above him Wiley's slight sighing breaths were barely audible between the constantly pinging, clanging pipes. Kevin couldn't sleep. Maybe this was what death would be – a conscious brain suspended in darkness for eternity.

Wiley shifted making the metal cross strips creak, Kevin was grateful for the small, warm presence distracting him briefly from the image of his weighted corpse being dumped into the freezing waters of Narragansett Bay. His watch glowed 12:45. In the narrow bunk he extended his arms and touched thumb to second finger on both hands in the classic yoga position. He breathed deeply, slowly, trying to quiet his brain and sink into sleep.

Eventually he had a dream inside a dream. A privately mailed record auction with incredible bargains was ending in less than an hour. He couldn't find it anywhere. Obsessively he re-sifted through stacks of paper, combed through junk mail in the wastepaper baskets, pulled out desk drawers, searched under tables, couch and bed. He cried out in frustration, began calling other collectors to fax him a copy. No one had the list or knew of the person who sent it. He paced about, kicking doors and cursing when, dreaming still, it struck him that he might have imagined the list, that the desirable and elusive records were a false memory, a wishful fantasy. That somehow he'd stumbled upon a metaphor for his entire life.

Fiery light needled his eyelids, he screwed them shut, bombarded by a constant yammer of overlapping questions. His inquisitors yelled, shoved him around, pushing hot lights at his eyes. He awoke in the lit up brig, Wiley dressed and eager, shaking him, wanting to go to breakfast.

Kevin half-crawled, half-rolled out of the bunk blinking against the electric glare of the cream colored walls, rubbing his sandpaper chin. A bag in each hand, he followed Wiley through the tangled innards of the ship above decks to the chow line. He was hungry, stomach growling, but the sight and smell of greasy sausage and dried out eggs sickened him. He called his answering machine for messages. There was only one - a man's voice. It was urgent he call a particular number. Kevin played it back, writing the seven digits on a napkin. He dialed it. Sally Lipstick answered. Mr. Bonnano wanted to speak with him right away. He gave his cell number and rang off, turning away from the sight of the many scouts and dads shoveling in breakfasts. The phone rang. His heart leapt like a fist trying to break through his ribcage but it was only Francine wanting an update, He assured her they'd be leaving soon, privately hoping it was true.

Next to him, Wiley, back from the head, was intent on eating his breakfast. Kevin stared at the back of the small blond head and neck. How would Marlene and Francine explain it to him if he Kevin, suddenly disappeared? He shivered briefly inside his car coat. The cell rang. Bonnano. He got up, walked over to the soft drink vending machine in the corner.

"You still have it?"

"Yeah," speaking low but distinctly, "I'm aboard the ship here with the neighbor's kid. Soon as I take him back to his mother I'll come to you. Is that okay?"

"When're you leaving?"

"Ten, fifteen minutes."

"You've made some very stupid mistakes. Don't make another." The line went dead.

Wiley and Kevin went out into the drizzle of a cold grey morning. The ship's wet deck was mostly empty. Kevin wrapped his scarf around his head, shoved his hands in pockets. They stood at the railing. Down on the pier around the gift shop piles of dirty slush resembled coffee sherbet. Wiley, gnome-like with his parka hood up, ran to a pillbox at the bow. He called for Kevin who followed him up into the semi-darkness. They sat across from each other on chilly metal seats underneath two large anti-aircraft guns. Wiley wanted to tell his mom about sleeping in the brig. Kevin nodded. "Just say we did it for fun."

Wiley stayed close to him on the walk from the ship out to the car. As Kevin put both bags in the trunk, he saw Sally Lipstick watching from inside a gold Cadillac on the other side of the lot. He pulled out, looping underneath the bridge to get on 195 back to Providence. In the rearview the Cad followed them. Wiley was quiet, seemingly content looking out at the rainy windblown highway.

When Kevin pulled up, Wiley opened the door with an effort. "Thanks for taking me. I had a really good time."

"Hey, thanks for letting me come. I had a really good time too."

Wiley hauled his sleeping bag out of the back and trudged up the snow-cleared steps. Looking very small, he turned around and watched as Kevin waited for the Cadillac to pass. Kevin waved to him before following it out of sight down the snowplowed slushy street.

The Cadillac paused at Bonnano's electric gate for a moment and was ushered through, Kevin close behind. It drove into the garage. Kevin parked the Mustang off to the side alongside Joey's silver Hummer. He got out and retrieved both bags before silently following Sally Lipstick to the front door. Bonnano opened up immediately. He wore a camel hair sport jacket, maroon shirt, grey slacks and cordovan loafers. When Kevin had last seen him upstairs at the restaurant he'd looked frailer, slightly shrunken in his clothes. Now he had a subtle aura of energy.

They filed down the hallway to the glassed in porch. Baroque music played at low volume. Joey and Lino sat side by side on white wicker chairs, Lino looking at the floor. Kevin caught a hint of a familiar perfume but couldn't identify it. Bonnano dismissed Sally with a jerk of his head. He turned a knob on the Bose radio in the bookshelf. The precise cerebral music got louder. He sat down on the couch. Everyone looked at Kevin. Bonnano said, "Charley Tuna's dead."

"That was him in the other car?" Kevin still standing, heard Joey snort derisively.

Bonnano's eyes were locked on his. "Yes."

Kevin sat down. "I'm sorry. I saw it happen but I didn't do it."

"These two say you did."

"They're lying." He was trying to keep his voice even. "I don't own a gun. I never have."

"Neither do Joey or Lino. Or so they say." He turned to them, "Right?" They both nodded.

"Hey, I pulled off 1-95 to put back the money I'd borrowed –" Joey started to laugh. Bonnano shot him a look and he stopped, "- from the casino delivery." Kevin held up the red nylon bag. "It's all here." He set it back on the rug next to the full trash bag.

Bonnano ignored it. "Start at the beginning."

Nervously Kevin explained Joey's con, words tumbling out before he had a chance to order them. Bonnano raised his hand. "You "borrowed" money from me and you didn't think I'd notice?"

"I was gonna put the difference back last night."

Bonnano regarded him coldly. "Hey genius, I get a count soon as it comes into the restaurant. I knew we were ten light Wednesday morning. If you had grasped that simple fact, Charley wouldn't have had to follow you and he'd still be fuckin' alive!" He sat motionless, mouth a thin line, breathing heavily. "Go on."

Kevin ran it all down without interruption, all the way to the shooting. "He must've seen two guys trying to take me off," he finished. "That's why he got out holding the gun."

"What a load o' shit," said Joey. "After he pops Charley an' drives away of course he leaves a message sayin' he's gonna bring in the money. What choice did he have?"

Bonnano's black obsidian eyes remained fixed on Kevin. "In this message, why didn't you say anything about Charley?"

"I didn't know who the guy was. It was dark. Everything happened real fast. Soon as Lino started shooting I was outta there."

Bonnano called out towards the kitchen. "Miss Roberts! Would you please come in?"

Philippa entered from the pantry wearing a simple beige sweater and pleated skirt, string of pearls at her throat. She stood there, elegantly composed, waiting. Joey stared at her. She didn't even glance his way. He badly wanted to announce he'd gotten a drunken fuck off her only hours ago, but decided it probably wouldn't help his case.

Bonnano looked over at her appreciatively. He jerked his head at Kevin. "You ever know this idiot to have a gun?"

"No."

"How about these two?"

Philippa recounted the staged robbery, Joey goggling at her, mouth half open about to speak. Lino didn't raise his eyes. When she got to the part of being held up, Joey jumped out of his chair. "Yeah I ripped off her share and that's why she'd say anything to get back at me!"

Finally she turned to face him. "You're right Joey. I would but in this case I don't really have to."

"That was a fuckin' cap pistol Lino had – a toy."

"I know what a real gun looks like."

Joey turned to his uncle for exoneration. Bonnano raised his hand. "What we got here is a criminal case but we have to treat it like a civil case. See, to convict in a criminal case you have to find the defendant guilty beyond a shadow of a doubt. But to convict in a civil case you only need to find him probably guilty - fifty-one percent or more."

He paused and looked at Joey and Lino. "I may never be a hundred percent clear exactly how Charley died but I'm way over fifty-one percent thinking you two are to blame." Joey started to speak. "Shut up. If I thought this was intentional the both of you and maybe you," he looked at Kevin, "would be fucking dead. But I believe it was an accident because it was just too goddamn stupid a thing to plan!" He took a deep breath. "That's why Joey, you and this defective with you, soon as you walk out this house are going to leave this part of the country. Not a week from now or even tomorrow but right now. Fly, drive, take a train – whatever. Go home. Pack a bag. You can send for the rest and sell your house later. I don't care where you go but once you're gone you stay gone. If either of you ever come back to New England while I'm alive you will disappear for good. Is that one hundred percent clear?" Joey swallowed, nodded jerkily. Bonnano shouted for Sally Lipstick. He came into the room. "These two are leaving." Joey opened his mouth. Bonnano pointed to the door. "Now."

Joey and Lino got up, walked from the room, Sally following them. Bonnano waited until the front door opened and closed then adjusted his shoulders. "This lady," he said indicating Philippa who still stood in the pantry entranceway, "thinks you're okay. Your wife's having a baby, right?" Kevin nodded. "You brought me bad luck but maybe you brought me good luck too. The interest on that ten thousand you took is five thousand. Open that bag and count out fifteen."

Kevin began to count. He'd gotten to just under twelve when they heard the front door open. Brandy came in, Joe Low holding his leash.

"Everything, okay?" The dog had gotten distemper shots.

"Yeah, 'cept he's always looking for Charley. Keeps wantin' to go up those stairs next to the garage." Brandy pulled towards the kitchen.

"Probably hungry. Go in and feed him. One can. They're

on the shelf right of the sink. Pour out some of that dry stuff into the other bowl."

Joe unsnapped the leash, followed Brandy into the kitchen. Kevin finished counting.

"Maybe you think I'm a prick but maybe now you learn every action you do has a consequence. Lemme ask you something. You're a man. What's all this with records?"

"It's something I know."

"Hey, when I was a kid I knew comic books. I don't play with 'em."

"What ones?"

"Eh, Bat Man, Plastic Man."

"The originals are worth a lot of money; much more than records."

"I know that. 'If only my mother didn't throw 'em out', right? So how much can you make from records?"

"All depends. You got to work to find the good ones and have the knowledge to know when you do." He couldn't understand why Bonnano was interested.

"You need a store to sell 'em?"

"If you did you'd have to have a partner. Someone has to always be out looking."

"Why not just sell 'em on the internet?"

"You'd do that too but with a store people can come in off the street with valuable stuff. Also the guy in the store processes and lists what the other guy brings back."

"Anybody around here know as much about records as you?"

"He just left."

"Besides him."

"Not in this town."

"So get a partner, school 'im and set up. You got respon-sibilities. You can't just be floating around free as a fuckin' bee. Now go on home to your wife and stay out of trouble."

He suddenly got it. Bonnano was showing off to Philip-pa. Being a good Don, gruff yet fair, dispensing hard won ad-vice.

As he stood up with the lightened gym bag the sliding glass door slid noiselessly open and a thin Asian boy in black jeans and hooded sweatshirt stepped inside raising a gun. Kevin yelled once dropping to the carpet. Bonnano rolled off the couch banging his knee against the coffee table as the si-lencer-equipped pistol pointed at him made a phfft! sound. Brandy bounded in from the kitchen. The Asian boy wheeled, shot the dog once in the shoulder, once in the throat, knock-ing him sideways.

Joe Low and Sally Lipstick stumbled into the room pulling guns from their shoulder holsters. The boy pivoted to-wards them as Bonnano rose up from the carpet and shot him with a snub-nosed 38 automatic. The impact smacked into the gunman's chest, throwing him back against the open glass door. He slid down onto the carpet, sitting up, eyes and mouth open, gun still in his hand. Dead, he looked about fifteen. Half of his right eyebrow was shaved off or missing. His splayed out snowy white running shoes were still spotless. The glass behind him, smeared with blood, had a small cracked hole where the 38 slug had lodged after exiting.

Kevin smelt the cordite, felt the chill air wooshing in from outside. The baroque music continued to play. He rubbed his hands to get them warm. Joe and Sally were pointing their guns down at the lifeless body seemingly unaware he was no longer a threat. Bonnano got up and knelt by the bleeding, twitching dog. From upstairs Laura Bonnano called her husband's name. Bonnano went over, took the gun from the shooter's dead hand, knelt again by the dog, put the tip under the left front foreleg and shot him in the heart. The dog lay still. Bonnano's face was white and rigid. He slid the glass door shut, locking it before he left the room. They heard him shout something upstairs about the television being on. He returned, went through the dead boy's pockets. He took out a cell phone placing it on the coffee table, extracted a wallet, counting the bills inside.

He held up five hundred dollar bills looking at his two employees. "This is all I'm worth?"

"Nah," said Sally soothingly. "That's probably just all some stiff was willing to pay."

"Yeah," said Joe Low. "This kid was an amateur."

"Lucky for me, seeing how speedy the both of you were."

Sally asked, "Want us to find his car?"

"What car? There're no keys here."

Joe Low frowned. "He walked?"

Bonnano shook his head, gestured, "Look outside." A dinghy was tied up to the far end of the dock. "He fucking rowed here. Then very conveniently found the door unlocked."

"I didn't –" Joe Low began.

"I know that. Go into the kitchen. Electrician's tape and twine in the top drawer to the right of the sink. Glass cleaner's in the cabinet below. There's folded up tarps in the broom closet."

Philippa who had been standing soundlessly next to the pantry entranceway, stepped to the side, moved to a rattan chair and sat down. Bonnano regarded her.

"You okay?"

"Second attack in three days - I'm getting used to it." She tried to speak lightly but her voice was strained. Kevin's cell was ringing, vibrating in his pocket. He ignored it. Bonnano went into the pantry and came back with a bottle of homemade grappa and a tumbler. He poured it a third full and handed it to her. She forced a smile, gulped down half and shuddered.

Joe and Sally returned, shook out an olive green tarp on the carpet, slid it under the corpse's leg. They pulled the body by the feet until it was fully extended. Sally looked over at Bonnano. "Want us to put the dog in here too?"

"That dog saved my life. He gets buried in the yard with a goddamn headstone."

Kevin, momentarily forgotten, sat down breathing evenly, watching Joe and Sally wrap the small body, wind the twine around the shroud and tie it. Repeating the procedure for the dog, they cleaned off the blood on the glass door and taped over the crack. Bonnano picked up the dead kid's cell phone. He hit MENU and CALLS to check the last dialed number.

Fat Danny Silvestriani lay hugely naked, face down on a wide linen-backed rubber changing mat. Dee Dee stood by the king size bed wearing only a white satin thong with scalloped edges and a white nurse's cap. Her small well-formed breasts jiggled as she dusted him with Johnson & Johnson Baby Talcum. The container was nearly empty. He looked like a hairy sugared Bundt cake. The phone rang interrupting his pleasurable grunts.

After three rings the answering machine picked up, a generic voice asking the caller to leave a message, then "Hey

Danny, Sally Lipstick. If you're there call Vincent on the cell phone right now."

Without being asked, Dee Dee handed him his cell. He hit the speed dial. Bonnano answered right away. "Danny?"

"Speaking."

"If you were to hire some street gook to kill me for a lousy 500 dollars would you be stupid enough to leave your number on his cell phone?"

There was a long pause. "No," said Danny carefully, "I would not."

"You would not. That's what I thought."

"What's going on?"

"Nothing. Academic question. Anything you wanna tell me?"

"The Indian's nervous. He thinks they may have noticed the money's not right."

"He say why?"

"Naw, nothin' definite. You know, he's an Indian."

"All right, why push our luck? Let's hold off for now. We can always try again later."

Bonnano turned to Kevin. "Well, whattya think?"

"About what? I didn't see anything."

Bonnano held his gaze, "Then I guess we've got nothing to discuss. Take your bag and go home."

Kevin walked towards the hallway. "Hold it." He turned. Bonnano nodded at the money lying on the coffee table. "You can have that five grand back. Just be sure you don't remember anything later. I'll be in touch about the other thing."

"Thanks." Godfather.

Bonnano shrugged magnanimously. "If you hadn'a

yelled we might've all been killed."

Kevin unzipped the gym bag, scooped up the money and put it inside. He walked away from the loud classical music, down the hallway, outside into the wintry sunlight. Seated inside the Mustang he realized he was shaking, his mind a runaway horse galloping off in one direction then twisting in mid stride and tearing off in another. With an effort he roped it in, steadied it down. Felt both grateful and lucky to be alive, stupid to have been almost dead. He flexed his trembling hands, cracked the knuckles, turned on the ignition imagining movie-like the car blowing up.

The gates opened. He drove out onto the street suddenly incredibly hungry.

Bonnano was thinking. He was sure that before he was told to sit Joey had his back against the glass doors. And who else would use a Laotian or Cambodian punk for a hit against a capo? Little motherfucker had zero respect for anything. If he was responsible Joe and Sally would find out. Meanwhile he'd have them stake out his house, be sure he left. The bodies were in the cellar freezer. Brandy would stay there until spring. Charlie Chan and his boat would be disposed of tonight.

He looked over at Philippa, her face starting to thaw a little. A classy black version of Sophia Loren. For the first time in over a year he felt warmth in his groin. As he mentally undressed her he imagined setting her up, taking her around. It'd shock a few people, get back to the families but they'd know he wasn't some doddering old vecchio to be replaced. That he was still a man.

Eh, why try and impress them? The organization was

going to hell. Russians probably be moving in sooner or later. Everyone else was. He ought to retire. Take off to Florida. Live outside the country even – Bermuda, Mexico - wherever the dollar was still worth something. Laura would bitch but she only talked to her friends on the phone anyway. Soon as he took care of this Joey thing he'd do it.

He watched Philippa finish off the Sambucco imagining her waiting for him in a little beach cottage. "You know," she said casually, "there's an awful lot you could do with this room."

"Oh, yeah? You a decorator?"

She smiled softly. "That's my ambition."

"Ambition's a good thing. You got any more?"

"Anymore what? Ambitions or good things?"

"The former, I can see the latter from here." Smart too. Outspoken but ladylike.

Philippa faked a blush then realized it was real. She was actually flirting with a mobster, part of her watching the other part feel shocked. Maybe the last couple of days had made her vulnerable. What was zapping between them scared and excited her.

Bonnano got up aware of a semi-hardon. "Come on. I'll drive you home."

As they rolled out of the driveway in his Lexus, he was too busy impressing her to notice the dark blue van with smoked glass windows parked across the street. As soon as the bank had discovered counterfeit bills from the Casino they called in the Feds. Every employee who handled The Fox-woods money was under surveillance as well as any local who might have the resources to pass queer paper.

Driving to the gas station pay phone Joey had had to tell Lino to shut up three times. Fuck Uncle Fish. No more begging for a little break or a scrap of goodwill from the old wop. He'd had his chance and he'd blown it. Siding with Kevin and that high-assed moolie whore (at least he nailed her even if it was like screwing wood). Well, if that's all family meant to him why should it mean jackshit to Joey? And who knew if the sly bastard was only setting him up? That's how it worked, right? Put the mark through some shit so he doesn't get suspicious and then, when he thinks he's safe on the other side, clip him. Smart to have had everything in place so he could act before they put the word out on him. Double smart not to let Lino in on it.

That thing about setbacks being opportunities in disguise - maybe it was time to move on. He'd outsmarted too many people around here who wouldn't deal with him. He'd get a place in Vegas. That's where he really belonged anyway. If he ever wanted to come back – well, Uncle Fish wouldn't be around to stop him and no one else would care. He grinned. Dee Dee might be looking to relocate soon herself. Actually, he ought to be grateful to Kevin. Except for getting him in that accident the fuckwad'd been a real help.

Joey came out of the bank, got into the driver's seat of the Hummer imagining how people would dig it in Vegas. He spoke to Lino, "You got anything at home you wanna take with? Clothes, stuff like that?"

No response.

"Good. We'll go by my place. I'll pack and we'll blow this cheap shit town."

Lino stared straight ahead, rubbing his hands together

between his legs - a whipped dog. He'd caved in, totally dependent on Joey. That was good and bad. Bad because it got on Joey's nerves, good because he'd already been useful and would be again.

Sitting in bed, Laura Bonnano took a swallow of Canada Dry ginger ale over ice. She set the glass down on the tray, put the cap back on the Elmer's Glue-All, dropped the pile of unused clippings from Martha Stewart's Living into the wastepaper basket and closed up another scrapbook. In front of her on the TV, the Discovery channel was running a repeat episode about Australian crocodile hunters.

She hadn't believed Vincent's explanation of that gunshot just as she hadn't believed him when he'd told her Charles had gone to Italy. Charles was dead and someone had just been shot downstairs. Things were beginning to unravel. Not that she understood all the politics and shifting alliances. You didn't need to know the actual details to feel the growing desperation. Television, newspapers, parts of overheard phone conversations told her that he and his organization was losing. Vincent would try and look out for her but if something should happen, if he was killed or financially ruined or both she hadn't nearly enough of her own savings to make it through more than a year. What she did have was a fifty count bottle of 100mg Darvan. She could put an end to herself any time she chose. Thinking about it lightened her depression.

She picked up the remote, increased the volume. The hunter was trying to lure the croc into a box trap alongside a riverbank. Laura liked hearing the man's funny Australian accent but, although she knew otherwise, was somehow hoping the animal would get away.

CHAPTER FOURTEEN

Off Thayer a car pulled out of a parking space. Kevin backed in. The sun shone on curbside snow speckled with dirt. Close to Brown University, Thayer Street's narrow sidewalks were thronged with young winter-clad students visiting restaurants, crystal shops, book stores and used CD shops. Red gym bag in hand, Kevin went into a narrow, noisy place whose logo was a big cartoon Bull Dog. He ordered a coke, fries and three dogs with different toppings, took his tray over to a thick bright red table on a stand.

Across from him a male student wearing yellow tinted sunglasses, smoking a clove cigarette spoke to a girl and two other boys about the influences of the post-symbolists on Bob Dylan. At another table a dark haired girl told another how she couldn't wait to get to Aruba. Kevin, whose chin stubble made him blend in with the clientele, ate with unhurried concentration, enjoying each mouthful, hoping the killings would eventually fade away turning into scenes from an old movie. Maybe one day he'd be able to listen to baroque classical music without remembering, not that he'd ever particularly liked Vivaldi and those guys anyway.

Wiley in jeans and an old Tasmanian Devil jersey sat on the floor watching a Christmas movie he'd seen twice already. In it a kid who lives with his mom and new husband, loves his real father who left him to become Santa Claus. He liked that other one too where the dad is killed and comes back as a snowman. "Hey mom! You think he's home?"

Francine wearing a baggy navy blue Roger Williams University sweat shirt was seated at the kitchen table paying bills. "I don't know, honey. You already left him a message. I'm sure he'll call when he gets it."

She stared at her son feeling her heart open to him. Poor little guy wanted a dad. But from what she could see Kevin was going to be a pretty iffy father to his own baby. Realizing she was picking at the cuticle on her thumb, she stopped herself and pushed a loose strand of hair over her ear with the offending hand.

Her first New Year's resolution was to stop making up bullshit "seminars" as an excuse for Marlene to babysit. Now that she'd finally accepted her true sexuality, Wiley was never going to have a stepfather. Trudy wanted them both to move in with her. She'd said so a few times. It was a major temptation, big house and no more struggling to pay the bills. Trudy and Wiley hadn't even met. The whole thing needed to be done gradually. Wiley was always asking for a pet. Trudy's sheepdog would help him get over Kevin. If you lost what you loved you found a substitute. That's how the world worked.

Kevin let himself inside the empty apartment, sinking down onto the couch, gym bag beside him. Back to square one. The light was flashing on his answering machine. Probably Marlene pissed at him for missing their meeting. He didn't want to hear it.

He picked up the remote, turned on the television - holiday specials at Home Depot. Mechanically he opened up a set sale record list from Donnie Lawler that'd been waiting in the downstairs mailbox. Probably be the last one until after the holidays. His eyes started combing down through the listed columns when he saw it.

"Blue Jays   White Cliffs Of Dover   Checker 782 Vg++ $4950   ultra rare!"

That wasn't the only four digit item either. Suddenly it came to him. Henry Krasna, the guy those New Yorkers said got popped for embezzling, must've been the one beat him out of Gil Coates' copy, then consigned his collection to Lawler to make restitution. He checked the envelope date. Mailed yesterday. Lawler was in central Mass. Kevin was probably one of the first to get the list. One good thing about Donnie: on the big pieces, it was okay to pay him off gradually.

He reached for the phone, then stopped, puzzled.. The desire was still there but it wasn't like before. He smiled, slightly puzzled. Nothing like almost being killed to help cure an obsession. I should stage near-death scenarios for other addicts. Go ahead, he told himself. If you don't grab it somebody else will. So what if they do?

The door opened. Marlene came in wearing a navy parka and yellow scarf . She pulled off her gloves, folded her arms, regarding him levelly. "I'm not going to yell. I just want to know why you weren't there."

"I don't think you'd believe me."

"Try me."

"Okay. The Mafia was deciding if they were going to kill me."

It threw her for a few seconds. "Is that the truth?"

"Yes."

"And just how did this happen?"

"I can't talk about it. I shouldn't have said anything."

"Are you trying to scare me?"

"No, it's over. One day I'll tell you the whole thing. For now you just have to trust me."

Her mouth twisted to the side. "The most important part of a marriage."

"So they say."

She looked at him a while longer, sighed and sat down a few feet away on the couch. The TV babbled on. For a while neither spoke. Marlene noticed the stapled pages on the coffee table. "New list? Anything good?"

He smiled. "Blue Jays on Checker."

"Cheap?"

"Almost five grand."

"You buy it?"

"No."

"Why not?"

"Couldn't go anywhere with it." She didn't understand. "From now on I'm only going to be buying to sell." He indicated the gym bag. "There's almost four thousand in there that's mine. You better put two of it in the baby's account."

"You mean before you change your mind?"

"If I did would you run home to your mother?"

She met his look. "I don't know."

The television was tuned to a local station. The newscasters, a well groomed man and woman, wore Santa Claus hats and bright smiles. Two men had just been found shot to death in a silver Hummer which had been used earlier in an attempted burglary. Kevin didn't hear the victims' names. He and Marlene sat side by side trying to find a way back.